Also by Ruth Francisco

Confessions of a Deathmaiden

Good Morning, Darkness

GOOD MORNING, DARKNESS

RUTH FRANCISCO

New York Boston

This book is a work of fiction. Names, characters, places, and incidents are the product of the author's imagination or are used fictitiously. Any resemblance to actual events, locales, or persons, living or dead, is coincidental.

Mysterious Press
Warner Books

Time Warner Book Group
1271 Avenue of the Americas, New York, NY 10020
Visit our Web site at www.twbookmark.com.

Printed in the United States of America

First Printing: September 2004

10 9 8 7 6 5 4 3 2 1

Library of Congress Cataloging-in-Publication Data

Francisco, Ruth.
Good Morning, Darkness / Ruth Francisco.
p. cm.
ISBN 0-89296-807-9
1. Venice (Los Angeles, Calif.)—Fiction. 2. Police—California—Los Angeles—Fiction. 3. Young women—Crimes against—Fiction. 4. Mexican Americans—Fiction. 5. Missing persons—Fiction. 6. Fishers—Fiction. I. Title.
PS3606.R366V46 2004
813'.6—dc22 2003025205

For John Houghton,

who wanted to hear the rest of the story

Not only is our light full of darkness,
the darkness grows with the light.
"The Lord is light and no darkness can find any place in him,"
yet his unapprochable light itself produces our darkness.

—Isaac of Stella

Twelfth-century Cistercian

PART ONE

VIGILS

I found the first arm. The second one washed up on Malibu Beach, seven miles north of here. The rest of the body must've gotten eaten by sharks.

The newspapers gave credit to a jogger who came by later, and that's okay by me. I'm legal and everything. I was born here. But that doesn't mean I want to talk to cops.

Two or three times a week, I get up at four-thirty and take my beat-up Toyota truck down Washington Boulevard to the beach. I go to fish. They say the fish are too polluted to eat, but it tastes better than what you can buy at the store, and it's free. In the two hours before work, I catch enough bonito, bass, or barracuda to feed my family and my neighbors for a few days. When I snag a halibut, I give some to Consuello Rosa, my landlady, and she lets the rent slide awhile.

Usually I fish off the jetty in Marina del Rey, at the end of the channel, because it's quiet and beautiful. That's the real reason I fish. My younger kids prefer to eat hot dogs, and the fourteen-year-old won't eat nothing her mother cooks, period. So I fish for myself.

The marina fills me with a peace that I used to feel at church before I found out you can't live your life by their rules and survive in this world. I guess you could call the feeling I get joy.

Every time I go fish, I'm amazed that a Mexican like me can wake up in a stucco dump in Culver City and after a five-minute drive be walking past the most beautiful million-dollar mansions in the world. They're not hidden behind high walls covered in concertina, like in Mexico. You can see into their living rooms. Not that I'd want that life. I feel lucky. The people who own those mansions have to take care of them. They have to hire maids and gardeners, make mortgage payments, buy insurance, worry about earthquakes and property taxes. I get to enjoy their gardens and their beautiful views and don't have to worry about nothing. Late at night, when I fall to sleep on the sofa so I won't wake the little ones who've crawled in bed with the wife, I close my eyes and I imagine I'm looking out a picture window at the marina, the moonlight reflecting on the sailboats and the rippling water. I fall asleep with a smile on my face.

On the morning I found the arm, I'd decided to go fishing on Venice Pier for a change. That's about a mile north of the marina. I woke around four on the sofa with a toy truck in the middle of my back. When I got down to the beach, it was still dark. The moon was setting over the ocean, cutting a white path to the horizon. I threaded leftover chorizo on my fishing lines for bait. I like to think that it's like home cooking for the fish who got spawned down in Baja. I don't want them to forget where they come from. I threw in three lines, then unscrewed my thermos and poured myself some coffee. I was leaning on my elbows, not thinking about much, watching the black night fade to gray and the low mist pulling back from the shore like a puddle drying up on hot asphalt.

Then I saw the arm.

It lay on the sand about twenty feet from the water, where the beach is hard and smooth. The tide must've brought it in and left it.

At first I thought it was a piece of rain gutter like I bought from Home Depot the other day for a job. Then I saw it was an arm. I climbed down from the pier to take a closer look, hoping it was from a mannequin but knowing deep inside it wasn't. I didn't have to get close to know it was too bloated to be plastic. It was a left arm. It didn't smell like the seals I've found on the beach or the whale from a few years back. That you could smell for a mile. But then the morning was still cool. I could tell it was a woman's arm, white with fine hair. The fingernails had chipped pearl and clear nail polish, which, 'cause I have a fourteen-year-old daughter, I knew was called a French manicure. There was a pretty ring on her third finger.

I probably would've taken the ring if her fingers hadn't been so swollen. I looked to make sure no one else was around, then squatted by the arm. There was a small scar on her elbow and bites on the inside of her triceps, where fish had nibbled. I touched the skin; it didn't bounce back. It felt like a mushroom—fragile and a little slippery. I wasn't repulsed, but maybe a little sad, like when you stop to move roadkill to the side of the highway and realize it's an animal you don't see much anymore, like a silver fox or a bobcat.

As I stood up, the waves pushed a white rose onto the beach. Most of its petals were gone, and it had a long stem, like the expensive kind people buy to throw off their sailboats along with someone's ashes.

The sun was beginning to come up, and it was going to be one of those hot spring mornings that acts like summer's in a hurry. I knew someone else would come by, so I went back to my fishing poles and kept an eye on the arm. In a half hour a jogger found it, a white man in his forties running on the beach. He was working at it like his lower back hurt, and I bet he was glad when he saw the arm and had an excuse to stop. He touched the arm with the toe of his sneaker like he thought it might still be alive. That made me laugh. He reached into his pocket and whipped out a cell phone.

From then on, it was his arm.

A lady with a couple of dogs walked toward him, and he yelled at her to put them on a leash. She looked pissed until she saw what he was fussing about. By the time the cops showed up, there was a ring of people and dogs around the arm. For some reason, the dog people weren't afraid of getting tickets for having their dogs on the beach. Maybe they were too excited to care. They all stood there, dogs barking away, until the police told everyone to go home.

Plainclothes detectives and the coroner showed up twenty minutes later. They spent an hour poking at it, taking its temperature, snapping photos. I even saw one of the detectives bend down and sniff it. Finally, they put the arm in a blue plastic bag and drove off with it.

It wasn't until that evening, after I told the kids and the wife about it, and the neighbors on both sides, and my cousin Paco who dropped by just in time for dinner, after the house finally got quiet and I was drinking a glass of tequila behind the garage on the brick patio I'll finish one of these days, that I thought about the woman the arm belonged to, of what she must've looked like.

That was when I realized I knew who she was.

Laura Finnegan woke with a start, her heart pounding, her white tank top sweaty and clinging to her breasts, the sheets twisted around her ankles. She let her head fall back on the pillow and exhaled with a bleating sound. She could feel the blood throbbing in her neck, and she imagined her heart and its network of veins and arteries as an octopus caught in a trap, convulsing, thrashing its arms. A dull headache began above her eyebrows. She wiped the sweat from under her arms with the bottom of her shirt.

What a horrible dream.

As soon as she was awake enough to command her muscles, she propped herself up on her elbows and turned her head.

Scott lay sleeping beside her, soundless, oblivious. He never seemed to wake up gradually to morning sounds—birds, traffic, garbage trucks—but slept deeply until the alarm went off, like a child dead to the world. The top sheet, white with blue cornflowers, curtained over his shoulder and tucked under his chin. She found it odd that it had never before occurred to her that sheets with flower prints were meant to give you the impression of sleeping in a field of blossoms. She squinted, blurring her focus, and imagined a boy napping on the hindquarter of his dog in a meadow of wildflowers. He looked so sweet, so harmless.

She shuddered, remembering him in the dream. Her terror lingered, leaving her drained, her stomach raw and nauseated.

Slowly, she pulled the sheet off his body, admiring his shoulders, his chest, his muscular thighs and calves.

He slept on his right side, facing her, his right arm draped over the pillow, his left thigh at a forty-five-degree angle, as if he were climbing. He had a long face with a squared-off chin, tanned skin, and a mop of straight blond hair. She noticed faint wrinkles on his neck and at the corners of his eyes, which were set a little too close. He was a perfect L.A. boy-man.

As if pricked, she jerked her hand back to touch her neck. Never had she been so frightened by a dream. Never had a dream felt so real. She seldom remembered her dreams, but this one she could still smell—the stench of red tide at dawn, decaying fish, rancid seaweed. Even with her eyes open, faint images, black, white, and red, flashed like danger signs over her irises. She could still see the coldness in his eyes and an odd twist to his mouth, like when he was close to coming.

Yet here he was nuzzling the pillow, innocent as a toddler.

Scott was a generous man, an enthusiastic though not a particularly adventurous lover. He claimed to adore her. He was handsome, athletic, attentive, and funny. He acted like she was the first and only girl he'd ever loved. Her girlfriends told her that when he asked—for there was no doubt in anyone's mind that he would ask—she should agree to marry him. When they said this, they invariably looked wistful yet happy for her, as if she'd won the lottery, as if having a guy like Scott being nuts about you happened only to the lucky few.

But in her dream he'd stood glaring at her with red in his eyes and black in his heart, an image far more vivid than that of the man who lay beside her.

Was it true that every character in your dreams was an aspect of yourself? She had long accepted the dark side of her personality, but she knew without a doubt there was nothing in her subconscious that could produce images that terrifying.

Was her subconscious telling her that Scott was dangerous? Warning her? She tried to think of anything about Scott that had ever frightened her. He was a little jealous, she admitted. He acted proud when other men looked at her, but bristled if they looked too long. She avoided talking about her male colleagues, hating the way his face froze and his eyes stabbed hard into hers until she explained that Ralph, Harry, or Tom was gay or sixty.

But most men were like that, weren't they? A little insecure? Scott couldn't hide his emotions. He complained obsessively about imagined slights, his face turning beet red, his voice rising, usually out of proportion to the transgression. But he'd never directed his anger at her. He'd never raised a hand to her, never yelled at her. Never.

Nothing she could think of explained the dream. With her arms and legs still fluttering with adrenaline and a fuzzy skunk-like taste souring her mouth, it didn't feel like a dream at all.

It felt like a premonition.

Scott Goodsell was in love. He was sure of it. He felt like dancing in the middle of the day, in the middle of the bank parking lot, like some crazy homeless person on Venice Beach. He was in love with the most beautiful woman in the world. She was a goddess.

Scott thought of himself as a sensitive man, a post–women's-liberation man who respected women and treated them as equals yet appreciated their oddities. He'd grown up with three sisters and had listened when they wept about their boyfriends. On occasion, he'd even flipped through women's magazines, astonished by their tales of sexual abuse, even more astonished by all the products women could buy to make themselves more appealing to men, stuff men don't even like—perfume, makeup, shit like that. He couldn't understand guys who shouted obscenities at beautiful women walking by. Did they really think women found that sexy? Or did it give them pleasure to torment women they could never possibly have?

Scott felt he'd tried to be honest in his relationships—at least during the last few years—and when he broke up with a woman, he did it in person, gently, reassuring her that she was incredibly desirable, but it was all him, a problem with commitment he was working on. He was almost always able to remain on good terms with them, usually to the extent where they'd welcome a call if he got stuck alone on a Saturday night without a date.

He even had women friends. True, he'd slept with most of them at one time or another, but now they were friends, and he was surprised that sometimes he felt closer to these women than to his male buddies.

Of course he would never *call* himself a sensitive man, a description he found emasculating. He liked to think of himself as a man from whom other men could get explanations for the maddening behavior of their wives and girlfriends, as well as a man to whom women could ask probing questions about the male species.

Yet, even though he'd had his share of women, and despite what he considered to be his special understanding of them, he'd never before been in love.

Laura had changed all that. Her beauty took his breath away. She was thin and delicate, with long fingers, a long neck, and long thighs. Her dark brown hair fell perfectly straight down to the middle of her back, and when he turned her to him, pushing back her hair to reveal her piercing blue eyes, he lost himself.

She was a Modigliani come to life. She possessed a sad, mysterious quality, her body relaxed but alert, her head angled slightly to one side as if she were trying to catch the words to a distant song. And if he stood quietly beside her, it seemed that he, too, could hear the music.

He loved her efficiency and that she never complained. To his relief, she never talked about her job. All the other women he'd dated yapped on about their careers, office politics, job deadlines, chauvinism from superiors, both real and imagined. Not exactly what a guy wants to hear after a long day. Nor did Laura jabber about her periods or her mother or her ex-boyfriends. In fact, she didn't talk much at all.

Laura talked with her body. To Scott, her movements were enchanting. Even something as simple as picking up a book or walking across the room seemed choreographed—graceful, fluid, pregnant with meaning. Starting with her lips, her smile spread down her shoulders, up her lifted arms, then to the tips of her fingers. It was like watching a flower unfold in time-lapse photography.

She'd been a dancer all through high school and college. He asked her once why she hadn't become a professional, and she said she didn't like the endless counting of beats to match the music, to hit your mark. She simply wanted to dance.

She earned her living as an accountant. Go figure. He liked that, the way women contradicted themselves, as if simultaneously speaking two languages that revealed separate planes of consciousness.

He liked to play a game. He'd watch Laura while she did something simple, like peel an orange, then try to guess what she was thinking. Then he'd ask her. He loved her all the more when he guessed right. And when they made love, he forgot about himself, completely enchanted by the undulations of her body.

This must be why he loved her, he thought. No matter how anxious he was about his work or family, when he saw her, he forgot everything, seduced like a pyromaniac gazing into a fire.

So this is it, he decided as he sat in his white BMW convertible, queued up to make a left turn from a backed-up Westwood Boulevard. What was he waiting for?

He stepped on the gas and swerved into the right lane, accelerating through a yellow light. Two blocks down, he pulled up to the red zone in front of a flower shop. He dashed in and bought a dozen long-stemmed red roses. Before the florist had finished wrapping them in silver paper, he impulsively asked her to add one white rose. He didn't know why, it just seemed right.

He jumped back in his car and raced toward the beach. He swerved into a parking lot next to a liquor store.

It was the grungy kind of store that made most of its money

from junk food, beer, and lottery tickets, but in a refrigerator hidden in the back, Scott found a dozen excellent champagnes to choose from. Overpriced, of course, but what did he care? This was a once-in-a-lifetime event. He selected a bottle of Dom Pérignon.

He stood in line behind a construction worker who wanted cigarettes, and a woman wearing too many clothes who smelled like urine, but Scott barely noticed them. He rocked back and forth on the balls of his feet, eyes darting around the store. What else did he need? Dinner. He needed to make reservations, then call Laura for a date. Where? It had to be just right. Ambience was more important than food. Geoffrey's in Malibu, right on the water, small and intimate. On his cell phone, he dialed directory assistance, got connected, and made reservations for seven o'clock. Laura liked to eat early. God, this was fun.

Then he rang up Laura at work. She answered with that sleepy voice of hers. "Good afternoon, this is Laura."

"How 'bout dinner?" Scott tried to sound sexy.

She hesitated before answering, but he didn't make anything of it. She was probably preparing for a client. Then she said, "I would like that."

"I'll pick you up around six-thirty." He couldn't wait to see her.

The clerk, impatient, glared at Scott in a way that said he hated cell phones and hated the people who used them even more. Scott slipped the phone into his pocket, then paid for the champagne in cash, something he rarely did. He was jazzed.

He started up the car. What else? A ring. He was prepared for that one. He knew she'd love it. His grandmother had given it to him before she died. He was only sixteen at the time, but by some miracle, he still had it in his sock drawer, fourteen years later, in a cracked leather box embossed with gold. It had a great history, something about his grandparents fleeing the Nazis to Switzerland and stopping at a jewelry shop in some mountain town in France. Grenoble, he thought. Before he picked up Laura, he'd call his mother to get it straight. Laura loved stories.

He had twenty minutes before he had to show a house in Brentwood. He dashed home to put the roses in water, cutting the ends at an angle like he'd seen his older sister, Martha, do.

He stopped. His heart was pounding. He hadn't felt this stoked since surfing the Banzai Pipeline in Oahu. That was awesome, but how many years ago was that—two? three?—way too long between mega rushes. What had he been doing with his life?

His eyes drifted slowly around his apartment, a beige affair with Berber carpets and motel furniture left over from a fraternity brother who'd moved out. His surfboard leaned against one wall. He'd never gotten around to hanging pictures, not wanting to put up posters like a teenager but also not wanting to take the time to figure out what else to hang.

He'd have to give all this up. He laughed at himself. Grow up, Scott! But was he doing the right thing? Was she the right girl?

Yes. The answer was clearer to him than anything in his entire life. Yes, he would ask her to marry him.

I'm not a pervert. I don't go sneaking around peeking into people's windows. But if someone leaves their blinds open after dark, or if they get up early in the morning and open the sliding glass doors to let out the dog, I look. It's impossible not to.

So about eight months ago, I noticed a young woman who got up as early as I do. She lived at the end of the Marina

Peninsula in an older two-story Craftsman that was covered with bougainvillea like a pink cloud. She lived in the rental unit over the garage. It was pretty nice. She had huge windows that looked out over the channel and a deck with planters of white roses and lavender.

The morning I first noticed her, she was in her kitchen making coffee in a white tank top. She was in her late twenties and very pretty, with long dark hair parted in the middle. She looked like a princess. But she seemed lonely. She had that look I see in women her age. Doesn't matter if they're rich or poor, single or married, they all get it. Like life has disappointed them.

Her light was the only one on at the end of the peninsula, so naturally my eyes were drawn to her. There was something about the way she moved—graceful, like she was still sleeping. I set my fishing rod down on the toe of my boot and stood mesmerized. While she waited for the water to boil, she fed a mourning dove that perched on the bougainvillea outside her window. The bird took the food right out of her hand. She left the kitchen, then came back with a hairbrush. She stood brushing her hair, looking out at the ocean. It seemed to give her pleasure. If she'd turned in my direction, she would've seen me, but she didn't. She looked off toward Catalina as if waiting for the mist to clear so she could see her homeland.

From then on, when I came down to the jetty I looked for her, and there she was. Her routine was always the same. Coffee, bird, brush. On warm mornings she'd pull back her hair and pile it on top of her head, arching her long neck, stretching her arms and her shoulders. She smiled and closed her eyes as if imagining someone kissing her neck. Not that *I* thought about kissing her neck. It wasn't like that. I just enjoyed watching her—like watching the egrets in Grand Canal wading in the mud at low tide.

My friends call me a philosopher. I like to look at things and think about them. That's the way it was with her—she made me think about stuff.

Sometimes I worried about her living all alone and looking so sad. It's never made sense to me the way white people want to live alone. Even though I have to watch where I step when I walk through the house, and most nights I have to sleep on the sofa, I can't imagine coming home and not having people around, my kids and the neighbors' kids, my wife, her sister, my two cousins, and whoever else has showed up for dinner. It makes me nervous, thinking about these lonely ladies, like when we begin to have a lot of small earthquakes. I wonder how they've been so hurt that they'd rather be alone than risk their hearts and bodies. Maybe they like it. I like to fish by myself. Maybe it's the same, but somchow I doubt it.

After I found the arm, I didn't see her no more. I tried to pretend that she'd moved in with that handsome man I saw sometimes, the one who drank his coffee with one hand while feeling her breasts with the other.

I was afraid to admit what I knew was true. The girl and her arms had been separated.

When Scott called Laura, she heard the excitement in his voice. She figured he'd gotten a job promotion, a new motorcycle or some other toy, maybe one of the vacation bonuses that his office doled out to motivate their salespeople. She didn't ask. She wasn't even curious. She knew he liked to tell her such things in person, drawing out the telling like a ringmaster holding the spotlight while the house lights go down.

She liked Scott. She liked his boyish energy. She liked being treated so well. Perhaps she even loved him.

She put on a short black dress with spaghetti straps. She had small breasts so she knew she could get away with it. Funny, she thought, the unwritten rules: Large breasts had to be strapped in; small breasts could breathe under thin chiffon and no one would think twice.

This dress made her feel like she was wearing nothing at all—empowered yet exposed—and that's exactly how she wanted to feel when she told him. She wanted to be vulnerable and strong. She wanted to feel his hurt, and she wanted to appear her most beautiful when she hurt him.

It was a small revenge for what he did to her in her dream.

As he entered the restaurant, Scott overtipped the valet, the doorman, and the maître d'. He wanted everything to be perfect. He got a table on the terrace and ordered a fancy wine.

She was so beautiful in that black dress that resembled a slip, her hair loosely piled on top of her head, her eyes blue as tropical water, her mouth red, her bony shoulders fragile and seductive, her only jewelry a single black pearl he'd brought her from Tahiti, its pear shape falling in the crevice between her breasts.

He wanted to give her the ring so he could watch it on her long, graceful hand as she lifted her wine goblet and ate dinner, but he knew you were supposed to wait until after the meal, down on one knee before the waiter brings coffee and dessert, before you order champagne to celebrate.

They ate in silence. She ordered Chilean sea bass in mango sauce, he the rack of lamb.

As the waiter took away their plates, Scott felt his heart beating rapidly and sweat gathering inside his shirt collar. But he didn't take off his sport coat. He didn't quite know where to start. He'd prepared a short speech, something about coming of age, taking his place in the community, sharing his life with the perfect woman, but now it seemed so clichéd. He wanted words that were more genuine, that told her how happy she made him.

Then she said, "Scott, I have something to tell you. Perhaps it isn't the right time, but I don't suppose it will ever feel like the right time."

"Go on," he said, after his initial surprise. It occurred to him that maybe Laura was pregnant. A bit of a shock, but what could be better? They'd start a family right away. That sure would make his mother happy. Or maybe she was going to propose to him. He loved how she continued to surprise him, her secrets, her little revelations. He waited as she paused, searching as she always did for the right words.

"You know how much I think of you—"

"No, tell me," Scott said, his smile crooked, a smile he'd perfected in front of the mirror as a teenager to pick up girls, a smile that had become part of him, that he now used to sell houses. "You know I can never hear enough about me." That got her to smile back, which flooded his body with warmth.

"You're wonderful," she said. "You're generous and kind and handsome—"

"And a sexual athlete."

"That, too. You're the greatest guy I've ever met."

"Gee, thanks," he said, not used to blushing, his body tingling all over. He felt a flash of heat in his groin and wanted to leap over the table and take her right there.

"But I don't think we should see each other anymore."

It was like someone had slammed a two-by-four in his face, his ears suddenly pounding, his dinner burning in his chest, threatening to erupt. He was speechless.

"It's not that I don't care for you. I do. But I don't feel comfortable anymore. I think we should stop before things get out of hand."

"Out of hand?" he nearly shouted. "How can things get out of hand? I want to marry you."

It was her turn to be surprised, but she shook her head and said, "No, it's too late for that."

"Too late? What are you talking about? You've been fucking someone else?" Several diners looked over with raised eyebrows.

"No, nothing like that. Calm down, Scott. There's no one else."

"Then what? I don't understand. Tell me." A shiver went through him; he felt he might lose control, as if he were driving on ice.

"I had a dream."

Scott paused, then laughed too loudly. Everything would be all right after all. "So . . . you had a dream?"

"Not just a dream. It was horrible. Last time you slept over."

A nastiness crept over him, something akin to jealousy. He pushed it aside. She was obviously upset. He should listen. "What was your dream about?"

"I dreamed you killed me."

Scott paused, then laughed warmly, confidently. How he loved her, her face so serious, her neck taut and defenseless. He wanted to reach over and kiss the spot that drove her crazy, where her neck joined her shoulders. "It's a metaphor, don't you see? It's so obvious. You're afraid if we marry, you'll lose something of yourself, that some part of you will be killed off." He took her hand. "That won't happen. I promise you."

Laura slowly slipped away her hand. "In my dream, you became obsessed with me, stalked me, then brutally murdered me."

The word *murder* stung him, took his breath. "I can't believe it," he sputtered. "You're more afraid of commitment than I am, and I'm the playboy of L.A. I'm the guy Hefner publishes for."

The corners of her mouth turned down in a slight frown. "When I look at you, even now, I see your face just as you were about to kill me, your eyes filled with loathing. I don't want you ever to hate me that much. I couldn't bear it."

He saw her lips tremble as she folded her forearms across her chest, her hands cupping each shoulder. Her fear stabbed deep into his heart. "Laura, darling. I love you. I could never hate you. It was just a dream."

"It wasn't just a dream. It felt real."

"Forget about it, sweetheart."

"I can't forget about it. Besides, it doesn't matter if it was just a dream. I'll never feel comfortable around you again. Not really. I'll always wonder when you'll start hating me . . . when you'll hate me enough to murder me."

Again that word. He suppressed a small ulcer of anger blooming beneath his ribs. He had to make her believe him. "Laura, I'm here in the flesh and blood." He paced his words deliberately. "All I can think about is how much I love you. I want to marry you. I want to have children with you. I want to live with you until we're old and ugly and our dentures clack together when we kiss. I was going to ask you tonight. I even have the ring in my pocket."

He reached into his sport coat, pulled out the cracked leather ring box, and opened it. An antique diamond ring, simple and exquisite. He set it in the middle of the table for her to look at, then reached over and gently caressed her left hand.

Her fingers were shaking, cold as ice. He looked deep into her eyes. "Who are you going to believe? A dream or me?"

I got caught once. The guy who lives in front is a famous sculptor from Belgium or someplace. A heavyset guy with crazy white hair and a white handlebar mustache. He owns the place. I don't know what he was doing up so early that morning.

Maybe he woke from a dream all inspired and wanted to start work.

He uses the sandy lot beside his house as his studio, which is always covered with logs and half-finished pieces, heavy chunks of wood bolted on top of one another. Over on one side of the lot is a cheap shed filled with his tools.

As usual, I was standing by the Japanese boxwood hedge watching the girl, the pink dawn reflecting in the kitchen windows. It made her face look like it was floating in the clouds. Like a goddess brushing her hair, smiling down on a poor Mexican fisherman.

Then the sculptor saw me. He was barefoot and wore cutoff gray sweatpants. His naked chest was matted with gray and white hair, and his shaggy eyebrows were pinched together over his eyes. He saw that I was watching her. He picked up an ax resting by the shed, gripped the handle with both hands, raised it high over his head, and slammed it into a log. His body quivered. He looked up and glared at me.

I backed up and ran.

Later, I wanted to go explain myself, to tell the guy I wasn't a Peeping Tom, that I didn't touch myself while I watched the girl, or even later, when I thought about her. I wanted to tell him it wasn't like that, that she was like the morning to me, sacred and beautiful. He might understand. He was an artist. But then he might not, and he was a scary fucker.

I stayed away for about a week, fishing a mile north by the Venice Pier. But then I started feeling like I was depriving myself of something. I was acting like I was guilty, and I didn't do nothing. That made me mad, like when people look at us Mexicans like we don't have a right to live here, like we're rats or something. I figured the worst he could do was call the police, and I'd blend in with the other fishermen and they'd never know who it was.

So I went back to fishing off the marina jetty and to my predawn walk past the million-dollar homes, past the egrets in Grand Canal, past the girl brushing her hair. I didn't stay as long watching her, just long enough to get that feeling like when you watch an eclipse or a meteor shower, a feeling like awe, like there's something out there that's both beautiful and unknowable.

I never saw the sculptor again. Not in the morning, anyhow. I suppose he thought he scared me off, or maybe he knew I was harmless, not worth waking up so early for.

A few weeks later I found the arm.

"Just because you don't believe her dream doesn't mean *she* doesn't believe it. Sounds to me like she's really scared."

"There wasn't any fuckin' dream. She just wanted to break up with me and came up with this lame excuse."

Scott wasn't much of a drinker, but it seemed like the thing you were supposed to do when you got dumped—go to a bar with a friend and get blasted, maybe go home with someone who wouldn't rip your heart out. He called Peter Flynn, a loan officer at Bank of America whom he'd befriended a few years ago, a dull, pasty-faced fellow, but really nice, the kind of guy you don't mind spilling your guts to, who'll watch you get drunk and not make you feel like an asshole, and who won't remind you of it for years afterward. They went to an Irish pub on Lincoln Boulevard called Brennigan's, the kind of place that opened its back door at six A.M. for the real drinkers, the ones who wake at five in the morning dry-mouthed, hearts fluttering, dressed in the clothes they've had on for two days, who stumble out of bed to find a drink to dull the pain. It was the kind of place where the drinkers all looked sixty, leaning on their elbows, sitting on their bar stools like pigeons in the rain. It was the kind of place that felt like you'd stepped into an abandoned subway station, grimy and dark, like it was the home of every bad thought and feeling you'd ever had.

Peter's eyes got big when they entered the bar, but when Scott headed for a booth in the corner, he shrugged and followed. That was the type of easygoing guy he was.

Neither of them seemed to have the stomach for drinking. Scott was too keyed up, and Peter didn't even like the stuff. They sipped their Dos Equis, letting the tequila sit, waiting for a moment of courage.

"I just want to know *why* she broke up with me," Scott whined. "Is that so much to ask? When you send a sweater back to J. Crew, don't they ask why you're returning it? Don't you owe them an explanation? Don't I deserve an explanation?"

"She isn't a sweater, Scott. She's a woman. She has her own reasons. If she doesn't want to tell you why, that's her business. Accept it. You're not going to change her mind."

"I'll accept it, but I want to know why first." Even as he said this, Scott knew it wasn't true. If she told him, he could change, and then she'd take him back. Hadn't she even told him that she wished for a more romantic era, when men won the hearts of women through gallantry and brave deeds? He wasn't going to accept it: He was going to fight for her.

"You're gonna make yourself crazy." Peter started tearing his napkin as if Scott was making *him* crazy.

"I think she's testing me."

"Testing you? How?"

"She wants me to prove how much I love her."

"By annoying her?"

"Goddammit!" Scott slapped his hands hard against the table, his voice outraged, his body tense, ready to spring. "I'm not annoying her. I love her. Why are you taking her side?"

The bartender looked at them, slipping his hand under the bar.

Peter sighed. He never knew what to do when Scott got like this. He waited for the vein on Scott's neck to stop pulsing and for him to slump back in his seat. "Scott, if she doesn't want to be with you, why in hell do you want to be with her? It's over."

Scott chugged his tequila, wadded up his napkin, and threw it across the table. It wasn't over, not by a long shot. He had to know the real reason she'd dumped him. It was like a pimple; he had to squeeze out the pus, even if everyone told him to leave it alone. He needed the satisfaction of the pain, the ugly truth, the thing she saw in him that made him detestable.

He had to know.

It was all he could think about.

Laura's boss, Mr. Johnson, called her into his office. Was there a problem? Something he could help her with? he asked, his doughy face squeezed into a lecherous smirk. Her personal telephone calls were distracting the other employees. As were the flowers she refused or threw in the trash. The receptionist was upset, threatening to quit. The poor girl had to call security once last week when Laura's friend showed up demanding to see her. As floor supervisor, Mr. Johnson didn't want to lose Laura, but her work was suffering. Did she want to take some time off? Or perhaps she should talk to someone in human resources who could refer her to an agency? There were laws in California now, stalker laws. She could get legal protection.

Laura thanked her boss for his concern but assured him she could handle it. She got the feeling he enjoyed watching her squirm. He obviously got a prurient thrill out of asking personal questions. He gave her the creeps.

As she walked back to her desk, she avoided the curious glances of her fellow workers, who now fell silent when she joined them in the lunchroom, as if she were suspected of stealing office supplies or worse.

How long could it go on? Surely Scott would give up sooner or later. Find another girl. Go away on a vacation and forget about her.

It had started with nonstop phone calls, followed by flowers and presents. When she didn't return his calls and refused his gifts, he showed up at her house or at work, each time a little more desperate. She didn't think Scott would hurt her, but there was something wild in his eyes. A craziness. When he grabbed her wrist in the parking lot at PowerHouse Gym, she felt afraid. Her knees weakened, her arms went limp. She knew that was the wrong response.

"Is it because I didn't ask you to marry me earlier? That's it, isn't it? But I was going to, don't you see? The very day you dumped me."

"We've been over this, Scott. It's not that at all."

"I know I get selfish in bed sometimes. Is that it? I'll slow down, but you gotta tell me what you like."

"Scott, you're a good lover. You know that has nothing to do with it."

"I know I'm kind of a slob, but when we get married, we'll get a maid. You won't have to pick up after me."

"We're not getting married, Scott."

"Why not? What did I do? I thought we were such a perfect couple. Everyone said so. Hell, my mother even likes you, and she's hated all my girlfriends."

"Scott, I can't take much more of this. It has nothing to do with you or your mother or your friends. It's over. That's all."

"Is it because I never said 'I love you'? I do, more than anything. I'll say it over and over again, ten times a day. I love you I love you I love you."

"I love you, too, Scott."

"But not that way." His tone turning sarcastic, nasty. "You fell out of love with me. Is that it?"

"Stop badgering me. It's over, that's all. Please accept it."

"Because of a fucking dream?"

"I know you don't understand, but I can't be with you."

"It isn't fair. I can match a rival, I can change my habits, I can read sex manuals, but I can't compete with a dream. I know you've got that *Rules* book that tells you to play hard to get, but this is ridiculous."

"I'm not playing hard to get, Scott. It's simply over."

"But why?"

Sometimes she wondered if she had been unfair to Scott, parsimonious in her explanation. Part of her saw what she'd done as abrupt and heartless, almost vindictive. Scott was, after all, intelligent and perceptive; he claimed to love her; perhaps he would understand. But how could she explain something she didn't fully understand herself? She had no words to describe the painful terror of her revelation, a darkness as piercing as the sun, a reverberating emptiness that left her aimless and depressed. Her dream had made her fear Scott, but it was more than that. She began to doubt not only the ideas of marriage and of male/female relationships but also the very possibility of connecting with another human being. Her dream, and Scott as an actor in the dream, robbed her of any desire to reach out to people. It stripped her of some essential humanity. And this frightened her.

It was better, she decided, to be ruthless, to cut him off cleanly, irrevocably, to catapult him from her orbit like an unwanted satellite. She felt she needed to do this to save herself.

Laura read in a pamphlet one of her friends gave her that she should alter her routine to be less predictable, less vulnerable. So she drove a different way to work, shopped at a different supermarket, used different ATMs, came home at different hours.

A week later, her boss cornered her in the kitchen. He sneaked up behind her while she was rinsing out her coffee cup. "I could take care of that boyfriend for you," he said. She stepped away quickly—"I was just leaving, Mr. Johnson, I'll see you in the morning"—as if she hadn't heard him, hadn't felt his sweaty hands on her hips, his breath on her neck. She practically ran to her desk to get her purse, feeling dirty and revolted, furious at herself for being such a coward. Johnson had a reputation, and she'd always been careful around him; but now he was swooping down on her as if she were an injured bird, easy prey.

She hated that instinct in her to cower, to flee, to be a victim. She was tired of feeling vulnerable.

She signed up for a course in self-defense. She disliked it at first, the punching and thrusting. It seemed so mean. During the first class, she cried, feeling horribly embarrassed, until the instructor said it happened to lots of women. They weren't used to striking out, he explained. She skipped the second session. It took her two weeks to gather the courage to go back.

One night when Scott was at her door demanding that she open up, his frenzied pleas escalating, her landlord chased him off with a golf club.

She knew she would have to do something soon.

Scott was sure she was seeing someone else. After all, that was the most reasonable explanation for why she'd broken up with him, wasn't it? But why didn't she simply tell him? He could handle it. He couldn't imagine her liking anyone more than him, but if there was a rival, at least there'd be someone to hate.

So he followed her, first in his BMW, then borrowing the

beat-up Datsun owned by his youngest sister, Pat, who was spending a semester in Europe. It was twenty years old, green and rusty. He knew Laura would never dream he'd drive such a thing.

He couldn't figure out why she was driving all the way into Venice to go shopping, or to Culver City to use the bank, or to the PowerHouse Gym that was almost in Westwood. Was that where she met her new boyfriend?

On Wednesday nights she drove to a studio on Washington Boulevard and got out of her car with a sketchbook. Since when was she into art? She was a dancer. Dancers don't have talent, not creative talent like that. He became convinced that was where she met her lover.

He watched closely as she came out of the studio, but she didn't talk to anyone. None of the guys who came out looked like her type. In fact, the class was almost all middle-aged women, a couple of real old guys who probably got off on seeing naked models, and some punk kids Scott figured were digital animators. It had to be the teacher, then.

So he waited.

The teacher came out of the studio fifteen minutes after the last student. As soon as the man leaned over to lock the door, Scott knew it was him, the mystery lover. So she was fucking an artist. Not even an artist, an art teacher, which meant he didn't have enough talent to make it as an artist. He was tall and thin, with long blond hair. He wore black jeans, a black leather jacket, and cowboy boots. When he got on a motorcycle, Scott snorted in disgust. It figured that she'd fall for someone like that.

Scott followed him down Venice Boulevard and left on Fairfax. The artist drove a few blocks, then parked his bike in front of an Indian fast-food restaurant. He came out five minutes later with a large paper bag, which he strapped to the back of his bike. So he was bringing her Indian food, a late-night snack at his place before they fucked.

A nasty, itchy rage ripped across Scott's chest like a brush fire. He followed the bike up Fairfax—he couldn't help himself—then to Crescent Heights, across Sunset up into the Hollywood Hills. He had to follow more closely than he wanted because the narrow road twisted as it climbed, but the artist didn't seem to notice him. The bike turned in to the driveway of a Frank Lloyd Wright knockoff at the top of the hill.

So she wanted a house. That must be the attraction. He cursed himself. Of course that was why she'd dumped him. Every woman wants a house. Dammit! He was a fucking Realtor. He could've gotten her a house without even trying.

The artist parked his bike underneath an overhang by the garage. Scott pulled up to the curb, leaving the engine running, and unfastened his seat belt. He watched and waited. As the artist pulled off his helmet, Scott leaped out of the car, charged across the driveway, and slugged him on the side of the head. The artist fell backward into some ferns, his eyes wide with terror, covering his head with his arms as Scott kicked his thighs, chest, and stomach. "You leave my girlfriend alone. She's mine, you fucking faggot."

The front door swung open. A middle-aged man, muscular and clean-shaven, with close-cropped hair, stepped out. "Hey, what's going on here?" he asked, his voice high-pitched and strained. "Tommy, are you all right?"

In an instant, Scott realized his mistake. He staggered back, aghast at the blood on his hand, the crumpled figure on the ground, the sweat dripping in rivulets under his jacket, the rank smell of fear seeping from his body.

He turned and ran back to his car.

"There are laws against gay bashing, you fucking Nazi," the artist's lover yelled.

Scott's car was screeching down the hill.

Something was changing in Laura, and she liked it. By altering her routines, she realized how stuck she'd become. She'd forgotten how to see, how to be alive to her surroundings. Now she was developing a new life, trying new activities, finding new friends. She had more energy. Life seemed filled with opportunities. She dashed across parking lots, afraid yet exhilarated, and she thought it must have shown in her face, because people noticed her, regarding her with interest, as if a chance meeting with her might suddenly catapult their lives in a new direction.

She enjoyed her drawing class so much that she signed up for creative writing. She threw herself into it as if making up for lost time. There was a whole world out there of things to do and learn. Just waiting for her.

She thought about getting a new job, something more challenging, more creative. A woman in her drawing class worked in the marketing department at one of the major movie studios and offered to arrange an interview for her.

Despite this new empowerment, she sensed sometimes that she was being watched, a tingling, chilling feeling, as if a light fog surrounded her. It was scary and exciting at the same time. She thought maybe Scott was following her, but she never saw him.

During her self-defense classes, she continued to break down into tears. She could see that Reggie Brooks, her instructor, was concerned. He worked with her; he didn't let her stop when she began to cry, his deep voice encouraging her, gently demanding compliance. So, with tears blurring her vision, she kicked and punched until the ache in her muscles usurped her concentration. Fueled by emotion, disciplined by exercise, she learned to let her body instruct her mind.

One day after class, Reggie asked if there was anything he could do to help. He explained that during the week, he was a detective with the LAPD. He was a powerfully built black man; his gravity, bulk, and patience made her feel safe. He seemed very sympathetic. Over ginger tea at a juice bar next door, she told him her story. He offered to give Scott a call, to warn him off. Later, he helped Laura with filing the paperwork for a restraining order.

That seemed to take care of things, or so she thought.

Still, she seemed to sense Scott's presence. Maybe it was only the memory of him, a threat lingering in her imagination, like fear of the ocean after seeing a movie filled with terrifying shark attacks.

Maybe she missed him.

Many times after work, Scott drove by her house to see if her light was on. If she wasn't home yet, he parked in the alley and waited.

As he sat drinking a beer, watching, he remembered that when they first started spending nights together, she wouldn't sleep in the bed with him; after sex, she would pull a quilt out of the closet and go to sleep on the couch in the living room. She said she couldn't fall asleep in the same bed with anybody, but after a few months, she began dozing off beside him, and he remembered how warm and happy that made him feel.

All it took was time and patience, he told himself. He fingered the ring box in the pocket of his jacket, the old leather soft as suede. He'd carried the box with him ever since the dinner at Geoffrey's, because he knew, when the time was right, she would agree to wear it.

This was a Friday night; he knew she didn't have a class. The front house was dark, and he figured the sculptor must be out. It got to be ten-thirty, and she still hadn't shown up. She must be on a date, he guessed, and the more he thought about it, the angrier he got. She'd be sorry if she brought anyone home. The bruises he gave that faggot art teacher were just a warm-up.

As it got to be around half past eleven, he became worried. He finished his third beer, his last, and wished he had another, even though it didn't taste good anymore. Maybe she was already there in the house, injured. Maybe she'd fainted and hit her head, or maybe she'd taken too many sleeping pills and suffocated in her pillow. All at once he felt incredibly anxious, as if crabs were trying to scratch their way out of his stomach.

Fuck the restraining order. He was going in.

Just as he was about to flip open the car door, he saw her headlights turn up the alley.

She closed the front door to her apartment, but instead of turning on the lights, she opened the blinds to let in the moonlight. She wanted to savor the magic of the evening, that slightly tipsy feeling after a first date: aroused, knowing he'd been interested, but not yet hot with lust; she was intoxicated with the possibility of desire. It was her first date since she'd broken up with Scott, a blind date with a guy named Kevin, set up by a friend from work. At first glance she'd thought she could never be interested in him, but by the end of the evening, after an extended hug that neither of them seemed able to break, she was surprised by a powerful attraction.

She pulled off her clothes, leaving them in a pile on the living room floor, then slid open the glass door to the balcony. The cool ocean breeze played over her naked breasts, neck, and shoulders. It felt soothing and exciting. Soon she was cold;

she walked into the bedroom to get a white T-shirt from under her pillow.

In the kitchen, she poured herself a glass of iced tea from the refrigerator. She looked out the windows as she sipped her drink, watching the moon glisten on the channel water. She loved the stillness, the ripples, the slow creep of moonlight; it completed her like a mate, as if it were all she needed, this solitude.

When she walked back into the living room, she noticed the light on her answering machine flashing red. Scott hadn't called in a while, but she still dreaded listening to her messages. It might be her friend Vivian in New York; Laura had called her earlier about the blind date, and Vivian probably wanted the latest. Laura braced herself, then pressed the play button.

"This is Stacy"—Laura didn't know a Stacy—"I'm Kevin's girlfriend. I want you to know that Kevin and I plan to get married, so you better keep your hands off him. Don't even think about dating him again, or you'll be sorry. Find your own fucking boyfriend."

Laura shook her head and pressed rewind. A chill passed over her; her heart beat rapidly. The woman's angry voice shattered her tranquil mood, reverberating in the still night. She felt violated, as if she'd been splashed by an SUV racing through a dirty puddle.

Laura had been warned. Halfway through her date, when they began to realize they liked each other, Kevin mentioned his ex-girlfriend.

"I tried to let her down easy, but she won't listen." He told her how Stacy came into the camera store where he worked. "She kind of latched on to me. She's young and sort of sweet, but she has some real problems. She demanded so much attention. It was too much, you know. I'm not a psychologist or a social worker. She was draining me. So I broke up with her. Does that make me sound terrible?"

Laura liked the way Kevin seemed to care about the girl's feelings. "It's hard. Not hurting people."

"She causes problems. I thought you should know. She might call you. Once she—" Kevin broke off.

"Once what?"

"I was dating this really great lady from Santa Monica. Stacy showed up at her house. She had to call the police."

Laura's stomach dropped. Another stalker.

"I'm sorry," Kevin said, his eyes soft, hopeful. "It doesn't make me a very attractive prospect, I know."

Laura knew he'd warned her because he imagined them dating again. That made her tingly and warm. It was nice to have a date without the heaviness of a relationship, of feeling responsible for another person's happiness. "I have that problem, too," she said. She told him about Scott and the restraining order, and noticed how easy it was to talk to him, as if they were old friends.

"Do you think it's our fault? Something in us?" she asked.

"No," he said thoughtfully. "People get confused about what love is."

"Exactly! Why do people want to own you? That's not love, is it?"

So there they were, on a first date, talking about love. It felt nice and natural.

As Laura sat on the couch finishing her tea, remembering, she enjoyed the dark and the moonlight through the blinds, casting stripes across the floor. But Stacy's shrill voice hung in the air—her neediness, her hysteria, her fury at not being in control. Laura stood and shook her body all over, trying to rid herself of that cloying, itchy, sullied feeling. The shaking seemed to loosen up her own anger.

What was it with these people? Couldn't they leave her alone? Scott was obsessed with her; her boss looked at her like a horny ape, calling her into his office, always touching her elbow or shoulder; and her landlord was acting like some possessive Neapolitan godfather, as if her affairs were any of his business. Who was next? She thought her self-defense instructor might be getting a crush on her. And what about that Mexican she'd caught spying? Even Vivian, wanting to know her every move. Didn't these people have lives? And now some crazed girlfriend threatening her?

God, it made her mad. What did they want from her? She wished sometimes that she could just disappear.

Yes, it was time to make some changes. It occurred to her that she might like to own a cat, something furry to stroke on her lap in the evenings. She recalled her new creative-writing teacher advising them to do something every day that was different from their normal routine, and she thought that perhaps this weekend she would rent a kayak, like she saw in the channel every morning, because maybe if she conquered her fear of water, she would be less afraid of simpler things, like talking to strangers or parking in underground garages or using the phone. She thought again about sending out her résumé, then realized that after a few months a new job would be just like what she had now, so what she really needed was a new sort of work altogether, not a new career, just a job, like maybe at a small boutique or a flower shop, someplace with no pressure, and maybe if she did that for a while, she'd discover something she really wanted to do.

No. She needed something more dramatic. Perhaps she should leave the country and start again somewhere fresh. She had enough money now. She could live the life of an expatriate in Mexico or Italy. There she would have the freedom of an outsider.

Her body was tingling, and her feet wanted to flex and point. As she stretched, she arched her back, enjoying the feel of cold air rushing down her esophagus. She felt hungry but didn't want to bother with eating. Besides, she liked the feeling of being a little hungry. It made her more energized, more alive somehow, stronger, sexier.

Finally, fatigue melted over her. She dragged herself to the bedroom, climbed into bed, and pulled the down quilt up to her neck. As soon as her body was still and she could feel her heart beating, she longed for the ocean breeze. She got out of bed, threw open all the bedroom windows, then crawled back under the covers. The cold air chilled her face, and she kicked her feet until they warmed up. As she relaxed and watched the white chiffon curtains move gently, she thought of the Andrew Wyeth painting of a field and a girl with a breeze blowing her skirt and hair, her body poised in expectation.

For a long time Laura lay awake, reliving her date. Maybe she would see Kevin again despite his ex-girlfriend. His conversation at first was strained and dull, but she'd let him talk and discovered he had other interests, in geology and scuba diving, and after their hug, she'd let him kiss her. The kiss felt good, as if she hadn't been kissed in a very long time, new and a little scary, and she realized this person didn't know anything about her, and she didn't want him to know anything about her, thinking, too, that usually the better-looking a man was, the worse he kissed and made love, and the man she was kissing was nice and a little goofy-looking, and his arms and shoulders were wonderfully strong.

She cleared her mind of his image and listened to the silence of the marina, a car passing, the plaintive hoot of a mourning dove. She suddenly felt fortunate to be awake while her neighbors slept, as if their sleeping gave her more room to breathe, more room for her thoughts, for her being.

Then she heard a thud against the side of the house, footsteps on her balcony, and the glass doors in the living room sliding open. She sat up quickly, her skin all gooseflesh, a cold stab of regret shooting up her spine, for she knew immediately that *he* had climbed up to the second floor and was there in the dark.

"Laura? It's me." His voice was light and querulous, like that of an adolescent boy, the hard leather soles of his shoes scraping across the living room floor, his palms slapping the furniture. He posed in the doorway to her bedroom, his hand sliding up the doorjamb, his body still and tense, like a dancer waiting for the curtain to rise. "There you are," he said.

She couldn't see his face but saw the angle of his jaw, set like an eel that was ready to strike. "You've been drinking," she said, remembering that alcohol made him petulant but not violent. "Go away, Scott."

"Why'd you come home so late? I was worried about you. Wait. Don't tell me if it was a date. I just wanted to make sure you were all right."

Laura used her feet to push herself back until her hips touched the headboard. "I'm calling the police," she said, reaching for the cell phone by her bed, though not dialing.

"You don't need to do that. I just want to talk. Can I turn on the light?" He walked toward her.

"No," she shouted. An urgent instinct to hide in the dark made her pull the cord to the bedside lamp, then scoot to the other side of the bed.

"Jesus, Laura. I'm not going to hurt you. Why are you being like this? Can't we just talk?"

"Don't come near me." She grabbed a wooden hanger from a chair and brandished it like a weapon. "I want you to leave, Scott."

He walked slowly toward her, and she swiped back and forth with the hanger until he lunged and grabbed it out of her hand. "Did you think you could hurt me with that?"

She realized she was cornered. She leaped onto the bed and across to the other side, then began dialing, knowing it was taking too long. Scott rounded the foot of the bed, grabbed her wrists, and slammed her down on the mattress. "For chrissake, Laura. Would you relax? I just want to talk to you."

The entire weight of his body lay on top of her, her arms pinned to the bed, his moist beer breath on her neck. She went limp. He took the phone from her, then sat back, straddling her hips. "I miss you something awful, Laura. You're the only girl for me. Don't you see? Weren't we good together?"

"Get off me," she said firmly, trying hard not to tense her body. "Please, Scott. You're frightening me."

He seemed not to hear, but leaned over and kissed her neck. "Baby, I love you." She struggled, pushing him away, wiggling out from underneath him; he let her go. She jumped out of bed and ran into the living room to her other phone, a land line; as she lifted the receiver, she dialed madly. The receiver slipped out of her hand. As she bent to get it, Scott came up from behind; she darted away, carrying the phone with her. The telephone cord pulled tight.

Scott yanked the cord from the wall. He advanced slowly, circling the room until his back was touching the front door.

"Scott, please leave. We'll talk tomorrow if you want. At a café or something."

"Like a date?" he said bitterly.

"Scott, please."

"I want to talk now." He inched toward her, then lunged, grabbing her hand. She turned and kicked his head, her heel landing hard on his jaw. He staggered back, clearly shocked, and put a hand to his chin. Tasting blood, he pulled his hand away, staring at the streak of sticky warm ooze on his fingers. He looked up at Laura, who was crouched in the fighting stance she'd learned.

"Okay, Laura. I'll leave, if that's what you want."

"Yes. That's what I want," she said firmly.

He walked to the front door, holding his jaw with one hand. She approached cautiously. As he opened the front door and stepped out, he turned and wedged his body against the doorframe, so she couldn't slam the door behind him. "I love you, Laura. I always will."

Filled with disgust, she pressed her lips together and lowered her chin. Scott plunged back through the doorway. She was ready for him. Grabbing the inside doorknob and doorjamb, she launched herself, kicking his chest with both feet. As he stumbled back, she slammed the door shut and bolted it.

She slumped against the door, her heart pounding wildly, sensing him on the other side. She expected him to pound the door and yell, but he didn't. She ran to the balcony, slid closed the glass panels, and locked them, then pulled the blinds. She ran back to the front door and waited. She heard nothing but silence for nearly a minute, and she worried that he'd fallen and hit his head, that he might lie there unconscious until morning. As she contemplated opening the door to check on him, she heard his footsteps descend the wooden staircase, pause, then crunch across the gravel driveway.

Scott staggered down the steps, acid burning in his chest. As a cool breeze hit his face, a horror took hold of him, as if life held no more pleasure, but was a black bottomless pit crawling with snakes and insects. He caught himself on the post at the bottom of the stairs. He hung there for a moment, his body shaking uncontrollably, his eyes tearing, a deafening rage roaring in his ears so that he could hardly see. He squeezed shut his eyes; burning lava shot up his spine, whipping it like a dragon's tail.

He parted his lips in a silent scream, forcing out air until his lungs hurt. He refused to breathe until his chest jerked in spasms and he gulped for oxygen.

Then all was still. A light mist chilled his skin. A foghorn moaned a distant summons as if from another world.

When he opened his eyes, he saw the sculptor's ax driven into a stump, its red handle purple-gray in the moonlight, its sharp, wedge-shaped blade glinting, beckoning, luring him to reach out and set it free.

PART TWO

LAUDS

Detective Sergeant Reggie Brooks, LAPD, Pacific Division, age forty-two, African-American, six foot three, 220 pounds, married with two sons ages nine and twelve, part-time self-defense instructor, and recently a devout Catholic, knelt on the bare cement in the cool sanctuary of Saint Ignatius. The church, undergoing a restoration, smelled of sawdust; the worn red carpet had been taken up and wouldn't be replaced until after the scaffolds came down.

Reggie bowed his head and buried his face in his hands, surprised by the feeling of his thick, smooth palms against his face. The sensation quickly passed, and again the guilt that ached deep in his bones, spine, and neck flooded his being, making him feel old and bruised.

He tried to pull himself together. He pushed up on the pew and looked around. He saw several other parishioners scattered among the pews waiting for Father John Ortega, mostly Mexican women, one black woman, and a few white teenagers. He wondered what these women had to confess, looking so contrite, like they'd stolen from the collection basket, and the kids, who probably made up sins, as he had when he was their age.

It had been a long time since he'd been to confession. He had wanted to, desperately, for years, but after dealing with killers and drug dealers and liars and prostitutes and pimps day in and day out, the uneasiness he felt, the sleepiness of his soul, the knot of despair in his stomach hardly seemed worth confessing. Was it a sin to feel numb? To feel nothing, no outrage, no love, no empathy? To shrug at every humiliation, every display of hatred? To prefer the silence of unspoken lies to confrontation?

He didn't know. All he knew was he felt so guilty that he felt deaf, and when he looked into the eyes of his wife and sons, they seemed like strangers to him. He felt he was a sinner, but he didn't know what to call it, a sinner in a way undefined by the church. He didn't want to waste the priest's time. There were so many others who needed a priest's comfort. So he avoided the confessional.

But now he had something real to confess.

He wanted her. So bad he couldn't sleep at night. He'd never wanted a white girl before. Sure, he'd desired them, wanted to fuck them. But he'd never wanted one to love, to take care of, to fold into his arms and caress. Maybe if he'd had daughters instead of sons, he wouldn't have this urgent need to protect her, to save her, but it was a craving stronger than anything he'd ever known before. Since the day she walked into the self-defense class he taught on Saturdays at the Tae Kwon Do Studio, he'd thought of little else.

Lots of women wandered into Reggie's classes, some who'd just moved to the city and sought urban survival skills, some who'd been mugged or raped, some who were afraid of ex-boyfriends. All were distrustful of men. When they first stepped into the classroom, they looked frightened, their eyes wide, taking in the mirrors, the mats, and the other students stretching in silence. They looked empty, he thought, as if some part of them had been stolen. They made him think of cornstalks after harvest—dried up, brittle, still standing, but dead inside. His job, as he saw it, was to wake them up, to make them feel life again, to convince them that there was something worth fighting for, that *they* were worth fighting for.

Others came as well: shy adolescent boys who had no fathers, gays tired of feeling threatened, fellow police officers who wanted to subdue suspects without ending up in court. He loved the old ladies who joined up, feisty, full of jokes, wearing white sneakers and baggy sweatpants borrowed from their grandchildren. They were often amazingly strong and focused. Yet it made him sad to think his city had become so violent that even old ladies were compelled to learn how to kick a gun out of an assailant's hands.

Reggie developed his own set of exercises, mixing tai chi, self-assertiveness role-playing, karate, boxing, and self-defense moves. The women—especially the young ones accustomed to aerobic classes—did well with the warm-up exercises, but when it came to pairing off to practice punches and blocks, they lost it, deflating like balloons. Invariably, at least one woman would break down in tears.

These women tore at Reggie's heart, and he wondered what humiliations they'd suffered to collapse at their first defensive punch, as if knocking through a dike they'd built to protect themselves. In a moment, these women unleashed a reservoir of rage, hurt, and a fearsome need to be loved. He figured if he were a smarter man, a psychologist or a priest, he could help them, listen to their hurts, mend them. But he stuck with what he knew—that disciplining anger through exercise would bring them courage.

When Laura first peeked into the studio, he thought she looked timid and mousy, in an oversize nylon jacket, carrying several books in front of her chest like a schoolgirl. But as soon as she saw the mirrors and the hardwood floor, confidence took over. She put down her books, slid off her jacket, then braided her dark hair into a single plait down her back. She strode across the room as if she owned it, and when she took a place on the floor and spread her long legs to stretch, Reggie pegged her for a dancer.

There was something tremulous about her, like a deer alerted to the smell of a hunter, delicate but powerful, intelligent but innocent. This was his first impression, and it surprised him that his original sense of her never changed.

Reggie heard footsteps and looked up.

Father John walked in from the rectory, counted the people waiting for him, then beelined into the confessional. The black woman went in first, then the Mexican women, then the others. Reggie wanted to wait until last. He was embarrassed, and unsure what to say.

Restless, he walked to a side chapel, lit a candle, and knelt under a statue of the Virgin Mary. As he gazed up at her, he saw Laura's image pass over the statue's face, her eyes and mouth settling on the sculptor's rendering like a butterfly on a flower. Anguish gripped his heart. He stood and wiped his eyes. The Virgin's face returned to its insipid Barbie-doll blandness.

Finally, it was his turn. There was no one else.

The confessional, made from old walnut, had probably been designed with the average-size Mexican in mind. The antique wood was finished with linseed oil, which had collected odors over the years; it smelled of nervous sweat, soap, and something like clover honey. There was hardly enough room for Reggie to kneel. The dark interior and his uncomfortable crouch made his sin sting like needles under his skin.

The fabric over the iron grille moved faintly as Father John breathed in and out.

"Bless me, Father, for I have sinned. My last confession was . . . years ago." Reggie listed the sins he could remember: impatience, anger, apathy, despondence. Then he mentioned the girl who had wandered into his self-defense class.

"Have you committed adultery?"

"No," Reggie said too loudly, then more softly, "No, Father."

"Do you lust for her, son?"

It seemed like such an old-fashioned word, *lust.* He had to translate it: *Do you want to fuck her?* "I'm not sure. I want to make her feel safe."

The priest was silent. The walls of the confessional seemed to dissolve, and Reggie imagined the two of them beside a cold stream in a vast subterranean cave. He heard Father John scratch his scalp. "By its nature," the priest began, "desire grows, feeds on itself, and becomes what it wants. The desire for God reaches for goodness, truth, and beauty. Desire in the wrong direction takes over our lives and the lives of others. It can destroy that which it desires."

The fabric of Reggie's slacks bound his thighs, and his head felt as if it were submerged under water. What was Father John saying? That he might destroy Laura? No, that wasn't it, was it?

Father John interrupted Reggie's backfiring synapses. "Have you told your wife about her?"

"No."

"How is your relationship with her?"

"Who, the girl?"

"No, your wife."

The word that came to mind was *cool.* Audrey Carol-Brooks was a driven, capable supermom, a paralegal going to law school at night, always after her sons to do their homework; she was a dynamo, one of those beautiful, powerful black women so sure of herself that in the early mornings, when she wanted tenderness, Reggie felt pressured, resentful that she made herself soft and available for twenty minutes a day and he was supposed to respond. But that, too, made him feel guilty because he knew she tried so hard and had sacrificed so much to be his wife, a sacrifice he neither understood nor thought he deserved. "We're okay," Reggie said finally. "We love our sons. We are . . . good partners."

"Do you have relations?"

"You mean sex?"

"Yes."

"We make love . . . when we have time," which, he realized, was not frequently. "I love my wife," he added lamely.

"Good. I'm glad to hear it." Father John paused to blow his nose—a real honker—then said, "The two of you need to set aside time to be together, to remind yourselves why you married, to feel grateful for what you have together. The vulnerability that draws you to this girl is there in your wife as well. She needs you, especially when she is busy with so many responsibilities."

The priest told Reggie to pray to the Virgin Mary, to avoid seeing the girl, and to come to mass every Sunday and bring his sons. He gave him ten Our Fathers and ten Hail Marys as penance.

Later, after he knelt in a back pew and recited the prayers, Reggie felt better. Yet he realized he hadn't been completely honest with the priest. Did he want Laura? He wasn't sure. He thought about her a lot, especially since she'd skipped his last two classes. He wanted to watch her. He wanted to see her dance. He wanted to hold her in his arms and to stroke her long, dark hair.

He recalled how, after he telephoned her ex-boyfriend and

helped her get the restraining order, she had made this gesture that was almost like sign language: She rubbed her palms together four times, then placed her hands on opposite shoulders and slid them down her arms in a self-embrace until her fingers stretched toward her feet. It was so eloquent. It said, *Thank you for helping me do what needed to be done.*

As he remembered this, Reggie realized he was in love.

I have a cousin on the police force in East L.A., so I know that the day shift starts at seven A.M. When I'm coming back with my fish, I often see one or two cruisers at the end of Marina Point. The cops inside drink their coffee and look out over the channel, watching the sun rise over the purple water. I can understand how it's a nice way to start the day, filling their hearts with peace before they face a city that hates them. They never get out of their cars, so one morning, when I saw a black plainclothes detective climb out of a slickback and wander down the jetty by himself, looking around the sand like he'd lost his keys, I figured he was searching for clues.

Back when I first realized who the arm belonged to, I considered calling the police and leaving an anonymous message. But it wasn't my business, and with my luck, they'd track me down, and the sculptor would tell them about the time he caught me watching her, and they'd think I was the one who chopped her body into pieces. Every day I scanned the papers to see if they'd identified the arm or found a suspect, but after they reported finding the second arm, there was nothing.

So I was surprised when I saw the same officer a few days later, talking to the crazy-haired sculptor. I knew from one of the early-morning dog walkers that the sculptor spent his summers in France. It looked like he was fixing to go. His tools were all locked up in the shed, and his half-finished sculptures sat around the sandy lot, looking like pilings from the old piers that burned down in the fifties.

The officer walked around the house slowly, pacing out measurements. He stirred the gravel in the driveway with the toe of his shoe and picked up something. Then he walked over to the Japanese boxwood hedge, right where I used to stand and look up at her kitchen window.

My first thought was that the sculptor had told him about the Mexican fisherman he'd caught watching her, so I made back to my truck fast, cutting around houses, checking over my shoulder to see if the cop was following, but he wasn't.

When I got to my truck, I circled back through Speedway, the alley by the beach. It was a dumb thing to do. If he looked, he could've taken down my license number. But at that time of day, there's lots of Mexicans in trucks going up and down the alley—gardeners, construction workers, plumbers—so I figured he wouldn't notice me. Nah, that's not true. I didn't figure nothing. I just wanted to see what he was up to.

Now he was inside in the kitchen. He slid open the window and looked out over the bougainvillea toward the ocean. He had a face that looked like a scarred-up rottweiler, but you could tell there was something gentle about him. His expression moved me, sad and troubled, and I was surprised, 'cause when you know someone's a cop, or he wears a uniform, you don't expect him to show emotion, just like you expect him to be honest and to know what he's doing.

He stood there a long time. I could tell he was thinking about the girl. He picked a feather out of the bougainvillea, held it for a moment, then blew it in the air.

Someone called him from inside. As he turned, he glanced over at my truck. I don't know if he saw me or not, or if his head was filled with images of the girl, but I decided to get out of there.

* * *

"Well, I'm glad you're finally over her," Scott's mother said from the kitchen. She rocked a cleaver back and forth, mincing a mound of onions, cilantro, and serrano peppers, then shoveled them into a Japanese rice bowl.

Scott poured himself a gin and tonic from the wet bar and ambled into the kitchen. He leaned against the black granite countertop and drew a spider out of a spill of tomato sauce. "I thought you liked her," Scott said.

"She was much too skinny. Weren't you afraid of snapping her in two when you had sex?" The cleaver thunked into the butcher block, halving a hot Italian sausage.

"Mother, I wish you wouldn't talk about her like that."

"I'm sorry. I forgot. My thirty-year-old son is still a virgin," she quipped, waving the cleaver in his direction.

Despite the fact his mother had married and divorced three times, she was not normally sarcastic or bitter. It was a state she wound herself into when she spent time with her ladies' support group, women in their fifties, invariably wealthy, who, now divorced, felt cheated of youth and romance. They were by turns polite, amusing, and ruthless. They were the kind of women who might, on occasion, hire a gigolo and then boast about it. Scott's mother called these women her *girlfriends,* although they were a long way from being girls and were as friendly to one another as rival bidders at Sotheby's. Scott always noticed a change in his mother after one of her luncheons with the gals: She turned into a bitch. "What are you so mad about?" he asked.

"I'm not mad," she said. Scott saw something stretch and snap in her like an elastic band. She put down her cleaver, and he caught a glimpse of the mother who once greeted him after school each day with milk and cookies. "I'm just tired."

He expected her to say more and sensed dark secrets shimmering beneath her skin. Then she looked at him coldly, blaming him for being male, he supposed. She turned to dig out the veins from a pile of tiger shrimp.

His sister, Samantha, a short, athletic blonde, barreled through the kitchen to the refrigerator and grabbed a Diet Coke. She was one year younger than Scott and resented it. Or maybe she resented his status as the only son. Whatever her grudge, it seemed to Scott that she had spent her entire childhood trying to get him into trouble. He wasn't sure she'd outgrown it.

Samantha popped open the tab on the Diet Coke, took a swig, then arched her back, swishing her hair back and forth like a schoolgirl showing off her tresses, a habit Scott found irritating. "Have you asked him, Mom?"

His mother glanced at her as if suddenly becoming conscious of a distant barking dog, then resumed chopping tomatoes. Using that stagy clear-as-a-bell voice that she affected to ask about a broken vase or a scratch on her Mercedes, she said, "Scott, since you're not using Grandmother's engagement ring, would you mind if Sammy wore it?"

Scott jumped, startled, wondering what she knew. Perhaps that was why she was acting so strangely. But she couldn't know anything, could she? Would she care? "Grandma wanted *me* to have it," said Scott plaintively.

His mother dumped the shrimp in with the chunks of raw tuna and salmon. "She wanted you to have it for your wife. A lot of good it does anyone in your sock drawer. Why don't you let your sister wear it?"

Scott looked out the French doors to the pool shimmering in the yard. His mother had been the first in the neighborhood to design her garden according to the principles of feng shui, with clumps of trees, rock groupings, and winding paths. The pool had a yin-yang mosaic in the bottom, which her Chinese consultant had assured her was worth the twenty-thousand-dollar cost in the good fortune and harmony it would bring. Scott thought it was gaudy. Yet he had to admit there was something soothing about the view. It tended to make him reflective.

That damn ring. What a nuisance. Laura hadn't protested when he slipped it on her finger that night. She had no choice. He knew at the time it wasn't the wisest thing to do and was bound to cause trouble, but he was so full of love for her, he wanted something of his to be with her. For a moment it made her his.

He jumped at the sound of the cleaver, the blade bisecting another sausage. He turned and saw his sister staring at him. The fish smell seemed to be mixing with the smell of the women, and it was nauseating him. "The ring is the only thing I have to remember Grandma by," he said. "Besides, I'm thinking of getting married soon, and I want my fiancée to wear it."

"Really?" His mother twisted her neck to look at Samantha, her expression sarcastic, her tone mocking, superior. "Sammy, have you ever heard Scott use the word *fiancée* before?"

Samantha leaned against the countertop, propping herself on her elbows, breasts thrust forward, chin angled up. "Nope. I'm shocked it didn't choke him."

His mother peered at him curiously, then over at Sammy. "I'm glad my son bounces back so quickly from heartbreak. I wonder when he'll let us meet this new girlfriend?"

Speaking about him as if he weren't there—it pissed him off—was a trick his sisters used to tease him, and their mother borrowed it whenever she was feeling nasty. At that moment Scott hated his mother, her face unnaturally wrinkle-free, her thighs surgically thin, her clinging blouse and capri pants, casual yet expensive, the costume of a woman thirty years younger. With effort, he kept his voice relaxed and pleasant. "She's on vacation right now. I'll bring her over for dinner one of these days, after she gets back."

"Does this young lady have a name?" asked his mother.

Scott flashed over the names of ex-girlfriends he could ask for a favor. His mind went blank, and he couldn't put a single name to any of their faces. "Really, Mother. I hate being interrogated like this. I'll bring her over, and you can ask her as many questions as you like."

"I hope she's not a snob like Laura," said Sammy, stuffing a slice of raw red pepper into her mouth.

Anger pressed down on Scott's chest. He felt his neck telescope into his shoulders. He forced the air out of his lungs in a long hiss until there was no air left in him. He breathed deeply, struggling for control, like a man without arms treading water. "Laura wasn't a snob," he said softly. "She was quiet, that's all. Do you have to make a comment about everyone?"

He caught a malevolent glint in his sister's eye. "Ha! She dumped you, but you're still in love with her. You guys love abuse. You eat it up, don't you?"

"Shut up, Sammy." He stood clenching his fists, with specks of spit bubbling at the corners of his mouth. Both sister and mother recoiled, chins tilting up, eyes wide, frozen like coyotes feasting on a carcass, alerted to hungry predators.

The motor for the Jacuzzi rumbled on. A blue jay squawked in the eucalyptus. A block away, a leaf blower whined and sputtered.

After several moments, his mother, cool and steady, went back to chopping tomatoes. "Well, Scott, until we meet this mysterious new love in your life, I want you to give the ring to Samantha."

His anger melted into a dull, throbbing boredom. Why did women become such bitches when they got together, ganging up to get their way, taunting and nagging until they broke him? All for a stupid ring worth what, a few thousand? He couldn't wait to get out of there. He didn't even care that his mother was making his favorite dish. "I don't want Sammy wearing it. She ruins everything."

"I bet he lost it." Sammy was doing calf stretches on the step to the living room, which annoyed Scott. As if that would help her lose the ten pounds she complained about.

His mother arched her left eyebrow and stared him in the eyes. "Did you lose it, Scott?"

He seethed inside but kept his voice even. "No. Of course not. I can bring it over and show you if you want."

She paused in her chopping, then smiled as if recalling something cute one of her children did when small. "Yes. Why don't you do that."

Sammy grinned smugly.

Seafood paella or not, he couldn't take any more. He wanted desperately to leave, but knew if he did, he'd be starting a family drama, a battle of wills. A war he could never win.

He grabbed two Heinekens from the refrigerator and went into the garden to wait for dinner.

As Reggie Brooks walked around Laura's empty apartment, he saw no evidence that a crime had been committed there.

The place hadn't been cleaned yet, and there were dusty outlines where furniture had been moved. The sculptor who rented to Laura said that she had flown back east to care for her mother.

"You talked to her?" asked Reggie.

"No. I noticed she was gone a few days. Then her boyfriend came by to move her stuff into storage. He told me that Laura's mother was very sick. He said that Laura wasn't sure when she'd be able to return and wanted to give up her apartment. She had asked him to take care of things."

"You mean Scott Goodsell?" asked Reggie. He recalled printing the name on the paperwork for the restraining order, how incensed it had made him.

"Yes. He's the only guy I ever saw her with."

"You kept track?"

The sculptor gave Reggie a withering look, then harrumphed, his thick mustache vibrating as he exhaled. He said he'd be up front if Reggie needed him.

The floor of the foyer was white marble. The air smelled of new paint, which seemed odd. But then Laura hadn't counted on her mother getting sick, so it wasn't unreasonable to think she had recently redecorated. Near the baseboard, Reggie noticed tiny dark splatters showing through the new paint. Probably mud she'd missed, then painted over.

In the living room, he discovered several slivers of glass between the floorboards near the balcony. He pulled on a plastic glove and brushed the minute pieces into a small offering envelope from church. They made good evidence bags in a pinch.

He found a broom in the closet off the kitchen and swept the bedroom. In the pile of dust and sand, he recognized Laura's long dark hairs. There were short coarse hairs as well. It gave him an odd sensation to imagine where those came from. He picked up a small yellowed strip of paper from a Chinese fortune cookie. *A wise man turns adversity into a fortune.* He imagined her long fingers breaking open the cookie, reading the fortune, then, in a vague desire to hold on to the thought, slipping it into her pocket, and later, the paper, forgotten, floating out of her jeans as she undressed, hiding in the dust beneath her bed, lying there as she slept.

He brushed the hairs and the fortune into another offering envelope.

The bathroom was the cleanest room; sparkling, even. The

tub looked like it had never been used. She must be a shower person, he decided. He imagined her graceful silhouette behind the white shower curtain, arching back, massaging her scalp, steam billowing over the top. He turned and looked at the floor. He noticed green garbage-bag fasteners under the sink, the heavy-duty kind, six stuck together as if they had fallen out of the box when she pulled out a bag. He slipped them into an envelope.

On the balcony off the living room, Reggie noticed the lattice that held up the bougainvillea was broken in spots and loose, as if someone had climbed it. He recognized it as the cheap stuff Audrey bought at Home Depot, not made for scaling or even for heavy vines.

He walked into the kitchen and stood over the double sink. The view of the channel was incredible. Catalina Island, faint blue and misty, sat on the horizon. Reggie imagined her standing there eating strawberries, dipping them in whipped cream, first licking the cool, slippery foam, then wrapping her tongue around the tart sweetness of the berries, dreaming about love on an exotic island, Jamaica or Madagascar, folded into the arms of her young black lover, his dreadlocks tickling her neck . . .

"Excuse me." The sculptor's barrel body filled the doorway. "I need to run some errands. Do you mind locking the door on your way out?"

Reggie slowly pulled himself away from the view and turned to the sculptor. "That's all right. I'm done here," he said. "Will you be renting out the apartment soon?"

"I hope so. I have several people stopping by to take a look at it this evening. I want to get a tenant settled before I leave for Europe. Is that a problem?"

Reggie wanted an excuse to keep it vacant. He sensed she'd left something here for him, but he didn't know what it was or where to look. He had no cause to ask the sculptor to keep it empty. It wasn't a crime scene after all. "No. Go ahead and rent it. If Miss Finnegan contacts you, would you please ask her to give me a call?"

Reggie handed him a card and left.

The third time I saw the cop was on a Saturday morning. He was off-duty and was wearing long cotton shorts with a Hawaiian print. He looked even bigger out of his suit. His shoulders looked as strong as a railroad trestle, and his calves were the size of my thighs. He had his two sons with him, and they were playing in the waves with Boogie boards. They tried to drag him in, but he shook them off. He sat down and dug holes with his toes. He stared out at the ocean, running sand through his fingers like he was thinking 'bout something.

I was fishing close to the end of the jetty. The Salvadoran beside me hooked a big one. We were all helping to bring it in, four or five of us, arms around one another's waists in a chain, yanking hard, laughing, so I was surprised after it was over and the Salvadoran was mugging with his twenty-pound fish when I turned and the cop was climbing onto the jetty. As he passed, the muscles in his back quivered like the haunches on a buffalo; he turned at the very end, then walked back toward us. I was the only one who knew he was a cop, and he must've sensed I was nervous, 'cause he came up beside me.

"That's a beautiful fish," he said. His voice rumbled through the ground like a passing freight train.

The Salvadoran didn't speak English, so I answered, "It's a bonito. That's a type of tuna."

"He's full-grown?"

"No way. They get to be a hundred pounds. But you have to go out to sea to get the big ones."

He really seemed to admire the fish, like he was touching it with his eyes. "You fish down here a lot?" he asked.

"A few times a week."

He looked down into my pail. "What kind of fish you got there?"

"Sea bass. They haven't been around here for a couple years, but they say the warm currents shifted, and it's bringing them up close to shore."

"El Niño?"

"Probably."

We were talking like this for a while, about different kinds of bait and stuff, when he turned and looked at the girl's house back up on the sand. The sun was glinting on her windows and making it look like there was a fire inside. He kept watching, as if he expected her to wave. He had this expression on his face like I've seen in churches in Mexico, like after the '85 earthquake, when people prayed to statues of the Virgin of Guadalupe as if she could do something about it. I knew the girl meant something to him.

He turned and caught me watching him. My ribs squeezed around my heart. It was like running into someone you grew up with who knows the clay you're from, and no matter what you've made of yourself, he remembers why you left the neighborhood. At that moment, I knew we were linked.

"You know who lives there?" he asked, almost whispering.

I told myself to be cautious. "Sure. Some famous artist. A sculptor or something."

"Not him. The girl who lives in back, over the garage."

I felt my face turning red. "Really? A girl, you say?"

He knew I was lying. His stare felt like a tongue depressor shoved down my throat, and I knew that if he ever got me in one of those interrogation rooms with the fluorescent lights and the one-way windows, he'd have me pissing on myself in seconds.

"Her name is Laura Finnegan," he said. "The sculptor who rents to her told me she left a few weeks ago. Apparently, her mother had a stroke, so she flew east. I was wondering if she was back yet."

I realized he didn't know she was dead. "That's too bad," I said. "About her mother, I mean."

"You haven't seen her?"

"Nope."

He gave me that look again, and I felt like an egg being tapped on the edge of an iron skillet. I should've told him then. I should've said, "You know those arms they found on the beach? They belong to her." But I didn't. I don't know why. Maybe part of me still wanted to believe she was alive, standing beside the bed of her sick mother, head bent to one side with that gentle smile she had when she fed the birds out her kitchen window. Or maybe I didn't want to cause any more sadness for this man whose eyes said he'd had plenty. Or maybe I was still afraid they'd peg me for a Mexican psycho killer.

He knew I was holding back something. He handed me his card, white with blue letters and the LAPD insignia. "If you ever see her here again, would you give me a call?"

As he climbed back down to the beach, grabbing each of his sons around the waist, charging into the water, the boys squealing and giggling, excited by their father's strength, I knew he was trying to forget her.

Scott turned left off San Vicente Boulevard on to Twenty-sixth Street, up to Sunset Boulevard, then left again on Mandeville Canyon Road. He took the first left and wound up the Santa

Monica foothills to a ranch house on top of a crest, nestled behind cypress trees. The house was one of the least expensive and oldest homes in Mandeville Canyon, a solid three-bedroom that still smelled of the old woman who had died in it. It didn't have the granite countertop kitchen or the Jacuzzi or the master bedroom or the marble tub or the DSL hookups, but it did have a great view of Will Rogers Park and, in the distance, the blue horseshoe shape of Santa Monica Bay. In most other neighborhoods, it would be considered a modest home, but here he hoped to get at least a million dollars for it.

His clients were late. He parked his BMW by the curb and opened the car door to let the cool breeze blow through. He leaned back in the seat and tried to relax.

As he waited, he calculated that he had a 60 percent chance of getting the asking price for the house. Scott organized his life around percentages. He enjoyed rattling them off to his clients: 80 percent of the neighborhood incomes were over two hundred thousand; 2 percent of the neighbors were Asian, 1 percent African-American; real estate values had risen by 14 percent last year; there was a vacancy rate of 3 percent; 95 percent of the local children went to college. He had a 15 percent chance of selling the house to this couple, and a 65 percent chance of selling them one of his own listings. The market was hot, and the percentages were in his favor.

Knowing the odds gave him a sense of security. Like a gambler, he never questioned the importance of winning.

He'd read somewhere that only 33 percent of L.A. County homicides resulted in a conviction. If there was no murder suspect within forty-eight hours of the killing, there was only a 10 percent chance that the case would be solved. So far, only the arms had been found, which remained unidentified, and no one had questioned Laura's disappearance. Everyone accepted the sick-mother story. As each day passed, he began to feel more optimistic, revising the probability of life incarceration downward.

He tried out the story first on the sculptor, whose own mother had fallen ill a few years before and who had made numerous trips back and forth to Belgium until she passed on. Scott knew this, and he knew the effectiveness of a lie depended on knowing your listener. The sculptor even helped load up the truck. Scott drove straight to the Salvation Army with the stuff. He saved a box of paperwork so he could cancel her car insurance, utilities, and magazine subscriptions. He found the pink slip to her car and sold it for cash within days through *The Recycler.* He became proficient at forging her name. He sent a letter of resignation to her boss, using the same ill-mother excuse for her hasty departure. It wasn't the kind of job where anyone was likely to check up on her. He disconnected her phone but kept her message service in order to monitor anything that might crop up later and cause problems. He forwarded her mail to a post-office box where he could pick it up at any time, day or night, without being observed. He figured he'd need it only for a month or two.

Luckily, both of her parents were dead. She had a younger brother somewhere, but she hadn't spoken to him in ten years. She had few personal friends. Her acquaintances from work would get word of her sick mother. He supposed there was a chance she'd told friends that her mom was dead, but he knew Laura was reticent about such things, and he was counting on her not having told anyone.

She did have one close friend, a roommate from college named Vivian Costanza with whom she'd toured Europe after graduation. From Laura's telephone bills, he saw that they talked at least once a week. Still, Vivian lived in New York, and he didn't think she'd create a problem.

Scott figured he could explain almost everything away if he had to, even the forging of Laura's signature. He could say she asked him to handle things for her. He wasn't writing checks to himself, after all; he was merely taking care of her business affairs.

At first, when the arms showed up, he panicked. He immediately thought of buying a ticket to Brazil, but then he decided to wait and see if they identified the body. Just in case he had to make a quick getaway, he packed a suitcase and spent the week at his sister Pat's apartment. He called his neighbor every day and asked if anyone had been by. No one had. After two weeks, he began to relax a bit. The arms remained unidentified, and the rest of the body never showed up. He got no surprising messages on his answering machine, no unexpected visits from police.

He was amused that everyone seemed to accept Laura's abrupt departure, but he supposed that was the kind of town L.A. was: People came, spent a few years, then disappeared. It happened all the time. No one thought twice about it.

His only problem was the ring. He should have told his mother he lost it, but now it was too late. He'd have to try to find a replica, and that was going to be a pain in the ass.

Scott watched a black Mercedes wind slowly up the hill. His clients had finally arrived.

When he first met the couple, Sara and Ted Brighton—wife, studio executive; husband, small-business owner of several copy shops downtown; second marriage; no children—he'd thought his chances at a sale were pretty good. The wife liked to garden, the husband wanted to be close to a golf course. They both wanted that feeling one got in the Santa Monica Mountains—of being far away from Los Angeles yet close to town. But as he watched them climb out of their car—the husband forgetting his cell phone after he locked the car, unlocking it, setting off the alarm, getting the phone, then, after the car was locked a second time, the wife deciding she wanted her nylon running jacket after all, unlocking the car, getting the jacket, locking it again, all this in a neighborhood that hadn't seen a car theft in five years—Scott wasn't sure he had the patience to see it through. He felt an insufferable boredom, a hysteria, building inside him. He figured he could force politeness for about half an hour before he'd start to lose it, before he'd have to hustle them out, jump in his car, and screech down the hill.

Sara Brighton wore running tights and sneakers and probably thought she looked good in them. She marched around the house quickly, as if looking for someone; Ted Brighton shuffled along behind. When they got to the overgrown garden, Mrs. Brighton pulled her husband off to one side for a private consultation. Scott stepped back into the house and wasn't surprised when they returned for another look, this time going through the rooms slowly.

They had so many questions and those irritating comments bargain hunters always make: "Looks like it could use a new roof. How old is the water heater? Isn't that a crack in the foundation? There's no air-conditioning, you say? Just to make the place livable, the kitchen will have to be redone."

Scott detested them. He was trying his best to be patient, but he was starting to get the jitters. He let them wear themselves out poking and nitpicking before he gave them his spiel. "The house was built twenty years ago by a building contractor for him and his wife. As you'd expect, the construction is fabulous. He made it strong enough for a bomb shelter." He added a friendly chuckle. "Instead of two-by-fours, he used two-by-sixes, and the studs are placed every twelve inches instead of every sixteen. They haven't done that since the fifties. He even used steel beams bolted into bedrock. You don't have to worry about earthquakes with this baby." The built-by-a-contractor-for-himself story worked well as a guarantee of quality. No one ever questioned it.

The husband seemed impressed. "What was the last offer?"

"The owners turned down nine-twenty-five." That was almost true. They probably would turn down that offer if they got it. "They were hoping to get a million."

"A million! That's a hell of a lot of money," the husband said anxiously.

"Considering the neighborhood, it's an absolute steal." Scott made his voice sound folksy, as if he really cared about saving them money and was letting them in on a good deal. "You're not going to find anything close to that price range around here."

"It's a bit small," said the husband.

"I think it's charming," said the wife.

"It certainly has charm, all right." Scott flashed his Hollywood smile, and Mrs. Brighton smiled back, appreciating a man who, unlike her husband, understood charm. "The foundation is built on a ten-inch poured concrete slab. You won't have any problems adding a second floor if you want," he assured them, not mentioning that building permits were difficult and costly to get.

"The view *is* incredible," said the wife.

"Sure is solid," said the husband.

"Yup. It's solid, all right," said Scott, smiling to himself, sensing that he had a sale. His commission, 3 percent less incidentals, would be an easy twenty-five thousand.

The night-watch commander called Reggie at twenty minutes after twelve. By the time he got to San Juan and Sixth in Venice, four patrol cars were double-parked on the street, along with a van from SID, the scientific investigation division.

Squad-car radios crackled with dispatches, and on both ends of the block, orange flares hissed. The street was unusually dark: The streetlights were shot out, and the neighbors had turned off their lamps to peek between the curtains.

He heard voices: SID technicians already inside the ramshackle Craftsman, collecting fingerprints, fibers, and blood samples. Outside, two night-watch detectives secured the block with yellow tape, and two investigating detectives, Sanchez and Gates, were hunting down shell casings and interviewing neighbors. Reggie could tell by the way the mothers were shaking their heads that no one was talking.

He sighed heavily, grabbed a flashlight, and climbed out of his unmarked squad car. Jasmine perfumed the moist coastal air. It might be a tropical paradise, except the trunks of the palm trees had bullet holes.

Detective Velma Perkins was primary on the case, a hardcore, hard-bitten black woman, six feet of solid muscle, with a mean mouth and a meaner sucker punch. She was the best Reggie had. She met him at the front gate, whipping her thigh with a half-finished diagram of the crime scene.

"What do we have so far?" asked Reggie.

"It's a fucking mess inside. Five vics, black, two children under five, one grandmother, two male teenagers. Looks like a drug kill turned into a massacre."

"A drive-by?"

"No. They entered the house."

"Any witnesses?"

"One neighbor said he saw a white Cadillac pull up to the house and one guy enter the place. He's down at the station giving a statement."

"Keep him for me. I want to talk to him," said Reggie. "You get an identity on the vics?"

"Looks like the targets were the boys in back, known as T-Bone and Viper, or Sam and Teddy Ellsworth, fifteen and seventeen. I ran their prints from the squad car. Both have arrest records: auto theft and possession."

"Gangbangers?"

"Looks like it."

Reggie shook his head. This forty-block area of Venice, Oakwood, was a gang-infested neighborhood of subsidized housing complexes and run-down stucco boxes with yards of naked dirt and hurricane fences. Land developers had been trying to gentrify the area for thirty years. Around the edges, a few brave artists had set up house until the evening serenade of gunfire drove them out. It was a nasty hive of evil surrounded by some of the most expensive real estate in California.

You couldn't drive through Oakwood without feeling the currents of venom, everybody overcharged, wary, and watching, the asphalt itself vibrating with tension. Every few years the gangs heated up. Reggie remembered the long, bloody summers of '94 and '97. This time around, the war was between the Venice Shoreline Crips and the Culver City Boys, fighting over the Westside drug trade. They used bullets the way dogs pissed to mark their territories.

Captain Clive McBride gave Reggie a six-man task force of investigating detectives to clean things up. Things weren't going well. Since the beginning of the year, Reggie's men had investigated twelve murders in a ten-block area between Brooks and Westminster. Two cases had cleared. With the addition of these five, that made seventeen murders, and the summer hadn't even started. Reggie was under serious pressure to get results.

He walked up the cracked cement steps into the house. The air smelled of cats, old bacon grease, and the metallic stench of fresh blood. Two SID technicians crouched by the corpses in the living room, collecting fingerprints. The rugs were stained; the furniture, sparse and worn, looked like it had been stolen from a cheap motel. The grandmother was splayed back on the couch, her jaw blown away. Two children lay at her feet, collapsed over their toys.

White plaster dusted the floor as if someone had exploded a bag of flour. The walls were dimpled with fresh bullet holes. Bullet shells lay scattered across the room like chicken feed. The television was shattered, with a dime-size hole in the center of the tube.

Reggie noticed the outline of a shoe in the plaster dust. "You guys got this print?" he asked.

"Yeah. We're done with the floor. You can walk on in."

Reggie stepped around the print anyway and walked into the bedroom. Piles of rock cocaine lay on a card table in the corner, along with stacks of plastic bags. One boy lay on the bed, a bullet hole in his chest; his hand, half under the pillow, gripped the stock of a .44 semiautomatic. The other boy sat in a ratty overstuffed chair with a .38 under the cushion. The top of his head was blown away.

As Reggie returned to the living room, the coroner showed. Reggie watched as he turned over one of the children, a little girl, pink barrettes at the bottom of four stubby braids, her arm over her face as if to protect herself. Such little hands, thought Reggie, recalling his own sons as babies, their tiny, grasping hands that you could never imagine growing to adult size. These hands wouldn't.

It hit him—all at once and hard. He felt like he was shrinking, his mind plunging down through his center. He fought nausea, trying to focus, searching the wall for something to lock on. Pockmarks of plaster formed hundreds of faces from corpses he'd seen on Los Angeles streets, cyes and mouths wide open as if in surprise.

He felt exhausted, like he'd been forced to watch a marathon newscast on a bank of television screens, like his brain couldn't process any more images. He felt too tired to care anymore. What did it matter when tomorrow there would be faces of more dead children, their killers children themselves, arrested perhaps, sent to prison only to make rage their master and to learn better ways to destroy their minds and souls, better ways to rob, rape, and murder? What did it matter?

For a moment he saw Laura's face flicker over the raw plaster holes, smiling. It seemed she was trying to tell him something. Then she was gone.

"Are you all right, Sergeant?" asked Sanchez, beside him, who looked a bit green himself.

"Fine." Reggie stood, grateful for his height so Sanchez couldn't see into his eyes. "Have we located the mother yet?" he asked.

Before Sanchez could answer, Velma blustered in and glanced down at the toddlers. "I'm gonna find this motherfucker and fry his ass. I want these predators off my streets, fuckin' outta my neighborhood. This shit has gotta stop."

"This isn't your neighborhood," said Sanchez.

"Every neighborhood is my neighborhood," she snapped. She knelt beside the coroner as he stripped the bodies to examine exit and entry wounds and to take body temperatures. She flipped to a new page on her notepad and jotted down the findings.

Reggie looked at her with curiosity—her facial muscles contorted, jaw forward, eyelids lowered, ears stretched back like those of a pit bull ready to attack. Reggie understood her rage yet felt nothing.

He began to realize that ever since Laura had disappeared, he'd been in this fog. He had no concentration. Nothing seemed to matter. He felt as if he were acting in a play and didn't know his lines, staggering aimlessly across a stage. If only he could see Laura again, it all would make sense, and if it didn't make sense, maybe he could at least feel something—even pity would do.

Around two o'clock, the mother of the two toddlers came home all dolled up, hair curled and ironed so it looked more like a hat than hair, skirt slit to her crotch, breasts—stretch marks and all—popping out of a leopard-print top. She stumbled on her three-inch heels toward the yellow tape, nearly knocking down a uniformed officer. She clung to his arm, staring blankly at her house until it sank in. No words came out, only screaming. She screamed until she choked, spit and vomit dribbling out of her mouth, a piercing, ragged sound that grew shriller with each gasp, like a buzz saw hitting granite, a scream not of love and loss but of self-loathing and guilt.

As her scream ripped up the potholed street, a cool mist penetrated and numbed Reggie's heart. It wasn't his job to absorb her pain; it wasn't his job to comfort her; it wasn't his job to wonder how many other children would be murdered on the streets of Los Angeles that night. He yearned for stillness. He approached the mother and gently squeezed a pressure point at the base of her neck; she percolated down to a whimper and stopped fighting the two patrol officers who held her back.

When Reggie asked her to come down to the station, she nodded. He led her to his car.

Scott jumped out of bed. He was late again. He needed to dash to the office and finish the offer for the Mandeville Canyon house before the Brightons showed. He dressed in a hurry, but just as he was locking up, the telephone rang. Scott raced back into his apartment and grabbed the phone.

"Scott here."

"So . . . did you find it yet?"

"Hi, Samantha. How ya doing?" Impatiently, he glanced down at his watch. He had no desire to talk to his sister.

"You pawned it, didn't you?"

"I can't imagine what you're talking about, Sammy."

"Don't be a dickhead."

"Oh, you mean the ring. It was never lost. It's sitting right here in my drawer, between my jockstrap and my condoms."

"I want it now, Scott. Mom said I could have it."

"Jesus, Sammy, you sound like you're twelve years old. Why don't you find a boyfriend to give you your own ring?"

Sammy chuckled bitterly. "Guys don't want to get engaged anymore. They don't even want sex. They'd rather jerk off and go to the gym than have a relationship."

"Are you saying you can't get a date?"

"None of your beeswax," she snapped. "Just give me the ring, why don't you?"

"Why is it so important to you, Sammy? If you've got a problem, you can talk to me. Let me guess. I bet you want it to cover for some lie you told. You trying to impress someone? Make someone jealous?"

He heard silence on the other end. Then she said, "I want a piece of the family history."

"What crap. Can't you come up with something better than that? Besides, didn't Mom ever tell you? You're adopted."

"I'm not kidding, Scott. If you don't give it to me, I'll tell Mom about the silver."

Scott got a sudden nasty taste in his mouth, like when a bum won't stop pestering you. Sammy was referring to the silver and jewelry he had stolen from their mother when he was twenty. It was their mother's fault. She had agreed to pay for his college, so he had enrolled at USC, an expensive school. She stopped paying after the first year, not for any financial reason but because she felt Scott, as the male in the family, shouldn't rely on handouts. She told him just a few weeks before the fall semester began, so he didn't have time to apply for a scholarship (which he probably wouldn't have gotten anyway) or to hustle up dough from his dad (if he could find out where in the South Pacific his yacht was). It was even too late for a student loan. So he burgled the house and made it look like a robbery. He sold the stuff for tuition, stuff, he justified, that his mother didn't use or like. Sammy found out about it. He couldn't remember how. She had promised to keep it a secret. "That's ancient history," he said. "Mom would just laugh about it now."

"Oh, really? You don't know Mother very well, do you?"

Sammy was right. There was no statute of limitations on their mother's vengeance. He had only to look at her ex-husbands; she found many ways to make them pay. "I've got to go, Sammy. I'll call you later." He hung up. His heart was beating fast. She was a persistent irritation, an eczema that wouldn't go away. Sooner or later, he'd have to deal with her.

After talking with Father John, Reggie resolved to spend more time with his wife. For him and Audrey, that meant sailing.

As they turned in to Burton Chase Park and drove into the lot reserved for members of the Santa Monica Windjammers Yacht Club, Reggie recognized Susie Edmunson and her husband, Ralph, and several others he knew by sight. They all waved, with big grins. Paul Axelrod, a crusty old sea dog, shuffled over and offered to help get their boat down from dry dock; it was the part of sailing Reggie didn't like much, but it was cheaper than paying rent on a slip and having to scrape the bottom of the boat.

It was Audrey who had taught Reggie to love sailing. She grew up in Washington, D.C., a member of the old-moneyed black elite. She gave it all up to marry Reggie—a tar-black

Catholic cop completely unacceptable to her family—but the summer sailing lessons with her father in Martha's Vineyard at the Sunshine Club, an exclusive East Coast yachting club for black physicians and attorneys, had not gone to waste.

Even before they bought a house, Reggie and Audrey purchased *Amazing Grace,* a thirty-foot Coronado with a small but comfortable cabin. It was their escape—from the city, the department, her job, the kids, the constant stress of trying to cram too much into one day. When Reggie and Audrey were out on the boat alone, just the two of them, time jumped back and they became as they were when they began discovering each other, during long nights of whispered confessions and sweaty sex in Audrey's dorm room at UCLA, nights made sleepless as they struggled to keep from rolling off her twin bed. The boat was their refuge, a return to their tenuous intimacy that existed in its own time and space. It was on the boat where Reggie and Audrey talked. It was on the boat where they had conceived their two boys.

"You guys headed out to Catalina today?" asked Paul. His face, tanned and leathery, twisted to the horizon to see if the island was visible. It wasn't. Too much haze.

Reggie attached chains to the hoist, then he and Paul lowered the boat into the water. Audrey dragged over the hose to wash down the deck. "We thought we'd spend the night and come back tomorrow," Reggie said.

"Good weather for it. Wind's at thirteen knots. You should make it in four and a half hours or so."

"We're not in a hurry."

Amazing Grace slapped into the water, bobbing up and down. Reggie thanked Paul, and he and Audrey hopped on. Reggie opened the hatch, pulled out the mainsail, and began attaching the genoa and the other rigging. Audrey started the motor. As

Reggie hoisted the jib, *Amazing Grace* puttered around the docks into the main channel.

Scott kicked himself. He never should have told his mother he was engaged. But there it was, popping out of his mouth like it was true. Now he had to find someone who would play along. He unearthed his address book from beneath a stack of bills and magazines. He'd never thought of it as his little black book, but he supposed it was. He sat down in a worn, overstuffed chair, his legs over the armrest, and flipped through the pages, running his fingers over the names of women he had dated. Some had moved or married or, he suspected, would not appreciate a call from him. Some names he couldn't remember. One had become a lesbian.

Then he came across Connie Philips.

Connie was an all-around great girl: pretty, with a band of freckles across her nose, athletic, adventurous, and sweet. She was famous—well, almost famous, a kayaker at the '96 Olympics in Atlanta, used in a couple of commercials because she was attractive, and even though she brought home only the silver, she won enough media time to launch her own line of women's athletic wear. She loved more than anything to spend the weekend kayaking, mountain biking, sailing, or hiking. A real tomboy, but sexy as hell.

Scott couldn't remember why they broke up. Maybe she was too easy. Frank and open. She was never moody and didn't seem to need anything from anybody. Not that she was tough. Not at all. She was just so reasonable. Like one of his buddies. She wasn't mysterious, like Laura. That hardly seemed like a good reason to break up with someone, but that was the best he could come up with.

Actually, he recalled, they never really broke up. After their last date, he simply let several weeks slide before calling her, then chatted her up without asking her out, a technique he used to deflect the awkward conversation when he'd have to say he wasn't ready for a relationship or some other lie. Like most girls, she got the picture.

He rang her up and left a message on her machine. He was pretty sure she'd call back.

Anchored in Catalina, *Amazing Grace* rocked back and forth, the waves lapping her hull, gulls screeching outside, the orange sunset peeking through the portholes. Reggie and Audrey lay collapsed on top of each other.

"Let me get this straight. You're confessing to me that you feel concerned about this girl?"

Wearily, Reggie propped himself up on an elbow and admired his wife. She lay on the bunk between brown satin sheets, her skin almond, her negligee pink-orange. She looked like a tropical fruit hidden beneath a dark forest canopy, behind orchids and ferns. She smelled of musk and ripe cantaloupe. The sheets shimmered, and as he rested his cheek on her stomach, he imagined the two of them floating on a raft down the muddy Amazon.

"I guess that's about it," Reggie muttered, marveling at his wife's clarity. She would make a great lawyer. His own thoughts were a muddled mess of half-formed feelings and fears that he couldn't articulate. Often he'd ramble on for ten minutes and still not know what he was trying to say. But with scalpel precision, Audrey would find the topic sentence. He suspected she understood his interior life better than he did.

"You say she's the delicate sort, without any family nearby, and she was being stalked by her ex-boyfriend?"

"Yes."

"You think he murdered her?"

"There's no evidence of that."

"But she's gone. Just disappeared."

"Yes."

Audrey ran her fingers over his massive forehead, his oversize nose and lips, smoothed his eyebrows over his huge sleepy-cow eyes. "I would be angry with you if you *weren't* concerned about her."

Reggie exhaled deeply. He found her hand and kissed her fingertips. "You're making it too easy for me. I'm not sure it's that simple."

"You didn't sleep with her, did you?"

"God, no!"

"You didn't kiss her?"

"No."

"Do you want to sleep with her?"

"No. Not really."

"Not really?" She lifted an eyebrow skeptically, then let it pass. "What do you feel so guilty about, then?"

"I worry about her. I wish more than anything that I could protect her. And now she's disappeared. I feel like I should've done something."

"She sounds smart to me. I think she figured the only way to be safe from her ex-boyfriend was to disappear without a trace. It's what I'd do. I bet you she's fine."

"Maybe," he said. Perhaps she was fine. Perhaps it was merely his own desire to see her again that left this raw knot in his stomach. But that wasn't usually what the knot meant. It showed up when he listened to a plea for help on a 911 tape, or when he saw fresh blood on a playground in Venice. He always hoped he was wrong, but the knot didn't lie. It meant someone had died. "I have a feeling about it."

Audrey sighed, exasperated. "Reggie, you can't keep anyone safe, you know. Not me. Not the boys. You've taught them to look around, to stay away from drugs and guns and the kids who'd like to mess with them. You've taught them how to fight if they have to. But if they're walking down the street and some kids drive by shooting guns, there's nothing you can do. You have to trust in God."

"I do trust in God. I guess maybe not enough." He felt a squeeze in his throat and a tingling behind his eyes. He couldn't help himself. "I feel like I'm supposed to do something, but I don't know what."

Audrey kissed his eyes and his forehead. "Only good people feel guilty about such things. I know you'll do what's right."

She didn't get it. How could she forgive him if she didn't understand? If she understood, how could she love him? Fury shook his body like a sudden fever. He couldn't breathe.

He realized she was aroused, running her hands over his buttocks and back, pulling herself to him, and as much as he wanted to shake her off, he couldn't. He needed her so much. As she ran her tongue down the ridge between his ribs, over his penis, between his thighs, he felt the knot in his stomach melt into passion.

By the time Monday morning rolled around, all the gentleness and harmony nurtured during their trip to Catalina had dissipated like water in a desert.

They had argued this morning, he and Audrey, the worst ever, after the boys left for school and they could really let loose. "You're not the man I married," she'd said plaintively. "You've changed." She said his depressions were pulling her down. Reggie knew brothers who slipped back into dialect or ghetto-speak when they got mad. Audrey went to the other extreme, articulating like a snapping turtle, spitting out SAT words: *indolent, solipsistic, melancholic, anguished.* "I'm tired of your self-indulgent angst," she'd said. He figured she wanted to fight, to make him talk, to make tangible this coolness that drifted between them like morning mist, to burn it off with anger. "I bet you don't even know what classes your sons are taking," she'd said. "Do you know what Luther is building for the science fair? Do you know that Leon's baby teeth haven't fallen out yet? Do you care, Reggie? Do you?"

Reggie did care. A lot. But he never thought to ask, which was something he couldn't explain. He couldn't bring himself to fight with Audrey, and caved in. When he didn't fight, Audrey got even madder and stomped out of the house.

She'd be early for work, he thought. He imagined her using the extra time to eat a bran muffin and coffee, bending over her desk so as not to get crumbs on the floor, a hard lump of anger in her throat, the muffin tasting like grit. She'd choke down her tears, determined not to let feelings mess up her day.

She was right. He was depressed. He knew what she wanted, but he couldn't seem to give it to her, as if she were an apparition reaching out to him from a foggy swamp. He loved his family. He loved Audrey. But there was this thing, wrapped around his heart like plastic.

Audrey suggested he go to a shrink. But as much as a shrink might try to convince him he wasn't to blame—that it was the fault of his Catholic upbringing; or of losing his father and his little brother to a car accident that he survived, then later, his mother to cancer; or of his body chemistry; or of giving himself entirely to his job in a city that hated cops—a shrink could not absolve him. A shrink could not take away his nagging guilt.

He stopped for early mass at Saint Ignatius, and as the host melted on his tongue, he felt the steady throb in his head melt into the unfinished cement floor of the nave. For a moment his grief abated. He felt forgiven and strong.

But by the time he slipped behind his desk, he was again heavy with despair.

His desk was rough terrain, valleys and precipices of paperwork—subpoenas, murder books, witness statements, suspect interviews—and he imagined toy trains winding up the mountains of reports, under pencil trestles, around lakes of coffee. Today he had to tackle stacks of sixty-dayers from his detectives, updates on unsolved homicide cases, each one thirty pages of meticulous details, cases that had almost no chance of being cleared. Then there were the cases they were working on now: a twelve-year-old boy killed during a carjacking; a double murder after a dope house rip-off; another double murder between gang members during a street fight; two more drive-bys and two body dumps.

And then there were this week's murders in Oakwood.

Before he'd even sat down with his coffee, Reggie's supervisors, Detective Lieutenants Newcomb and Blake, dragged Reggie into an office. Burnout, they said, not unexpected. Reggie was over forty and still working homicide, when most of the other detectives were in their twenties and thirties. Reggie was one of their best, they said, and commanded respect from the other officers, got them to do their jobs quickly and efficiently. But the Venice Gang Task Force had solved only two out of seventeen cases. Crime wasn't down, it was up. Reggie was late on all his paperwork, and his follow-up on older cases was lousy.

The crack-house killing of five people on Thursday night, now called the San Juan murders, was high priority. Councilwoman Pauline Parker was breathing down their necks, expecting results from the millions she spent on antigang detail in her district. Her constituents were scared, complaining, writing letters to the editor, and she was up for reelection in six months.

"We've got to see results. Now!"

"Tell us if it's too much for you, Reggie."

"We'd hate to replace you, but if we don't see some perps in custody fast, we'll reassign you to robbery or community outreach, or maybe another bureau that isn't so demanding."

Nothing like being reamed on a Monday morning.

Reggie had begun looking over the notes from the San Juan murders when Velma Perkins poked her head into his office, her overbite smiling, her muscular body and her breasts busting out of her uniform.

"Hey, Reggie. You asked to see me?"

"Yes. Come in."

Velma flopped down in a chair in front of him. "You look bummed. What did Newcomb and Blake want?"

"They're thinking of putting me out to pasture."

"No! They can't do that! They're blowing up their own assholes. They oughta take their hands off their dicks long enough to see what it's like out there."

"Thanks, Velma." She was in attack mode. Reggie pulled a package of Fig Newtons out of his desk drawer to calm her down. "Where are we on the San Juan murders?"

She squeezed a Newton and sucked out the fig before picking at the cake. "A few people in the neighborhood said they knew someone named Li'l Richie who drove a white Cadillac. No one seems to know his last name."

"You search the computerized moniker file?"

"Yup. There's a half-dozen Li'l Richies on the Westside, a few in jail. I made up a few six-packs with their mug shots. Our only witness, James Floyd, didn't recognize any of them."

"You get anything from the mother?"

Velma sighed. "She denied that her brothers were in a gang. I asked for names of her brothers' friends, and she says"—Velma, imitating the woman, swiveled her head from side to side with serious attitude—"'They's my family. I ain't gonna rat on no family.' Some family! I swear, Reggie, I nearly lost it with her." Velma mimicked herself: "'Your brothers were running a rock house under your nose, and you're telling me you knew nothing about it? Your two babies got blasted all over your living room. Wha's wrong with you, woman? Maybe you don't care 'bout your mother and your kid brothers, but your babies? Damn, you're cold! Now talk to me!'"

Reggie laughed. It felt good to laugh. He hadn't in a while. "What else?"

"Well"—Velma chomped another bite of cookie—"we have patrol units keeping an eye out for a white Cadillac in the neighborhood, but nothing so far. We got one witness who says Li'l Richie bought his Cadillac from a used lot over on Jasmine and Washington. I made a visit and looked through their paperwork for Cadillac sales. There was only one with Vogue Tyres—sold to a woman, Tina Dupres, about six months ago. I ran the plates. Bingo. A guy named Charles Richard Cole III, resident of Mar Vista, got a traffic ticket in the car last month."

"Charles Richard Cole III. Sounds aristocratic. Does he have a record?"

"No. But one witness said he was a member of the Bones."

"That's in Santa Monica. Why would he be over here in Crip territory?"

"Turns out the Ellsworth boys weren't gangbangers. The Crips were pretty ripped that they were dealing drugs, and so were the Culver City Boys. There was a contract out on them."

"The Culver City Boys and the Santa Monica Bones have been talking merger. You think Li'l Richie did the competition to get in good with the Culver City Boys?"

"Could be."

"Any sign of the murder weapon?"

"Nope. Ballistics says it's a thirty-eight. He didn't dump it in the area, so I bet he still has it."

"This Tina Dupres is his girlfriend?"

"Looks like it. I put twenty-four-hour surveillance detail on her apartment. If he comes near it, we'll have probable cause to get a search warrant. We might find the gun there."

After Velma left, Reggie felt overwhelmed with fatigue, as if some poison were seeping out of his bones into his muscles. Burnout. Maybe Newcomb and Blake were right. What had Father John called it? *Acedia?* He'd said monks call it the noonday demon. A listlessness, a mild despondency, a feeling that all the sacrifices you make aren't worth shit. It's when you ask yourself why you bother working the long hours, missing sleep, meals, your family. Life itself!

Then the guilt follows. Guilt over slipping on the job and not caring, over neglecting those you love.

Reggie thought of Laura walking meekly into class for the first time. She had come to him for protection—at least that's the way he saw it. He realized he felt less guilty for loving Laura than for not making her safe.

He knew he had to do something about these feelings that kept him from breathing right. There was no choice.

He had to find Laura. He had to know she was safe. He had to see her again, to test what his feelings were for her. He had to know if maybe she had these feelings, too.

Scott looked at his watch. It was one-fifteen P.M. He thought he might catch a matinee. He opened the *Los Angeles Times* to see what was playing when the telephone rang.

"Good afternoon. May I speak to Scott Goodsell?"

Scott had expected this call sooner or later, but the voice on the other end made his breath short; sweat exploded on his temples. The rich bass resonated with wide vibrations that Scott could feel even over the phone line, and the words had the rounded articulation of a black man, a big black man. It made Scott think of a whale deep in the ocean.

"This is the man. Speak to me." Scott reached for chipper, even though he guessed what was coming.

"This is Detective Reggie Brooks from Pacific Division. We spoke once before. I wondered if it would be possible to meet with you."

"What about?"

"I'd like to talk about Laura Finnegan."

Scott tried to keep his voice relaxed. "What about her?"

"We can go into that when we talk. You're not far from the Cow's End Café. Could we meet there at three P.M.?"

Scott felt some relief that he wasn't being asked to go to the station. That probably meant he wasn't going to be arrested. Not yet, anyhow. "Do I have a choice?"

"We all have choices."

"Then this is not in any official capacity."

"No. But if you have a few minutes, I would like very much to talk with you."

Scott's first instinct was not to meet with the cop. No one had to talk to a cop unless he was charged with something. Even then, he had a right to legal counsel. But maybe it would be better to answer the cop's questions as if there were nothing to hide. He'd write out his story beforehand so his facts would be consistent, then a quick workout so he'd be relaxed. Maybe he could get the cop to like him. Most people did.

"Sure, I'd be glad to meet you. How will I recognize you?"

"You'll know who I am." The cop hung up without saying good-bye.

The Cow's End Café was a rustic coffeehouse at the end of Washington Boulevard, near Venice Pier. A black-and-white Holstein-patterned sign with a cow's udder hung over the door. The bottom floor had several small tables and torturously uncomfortable wooden stools; the upstairs looked like a fraternity lounge, with tattered couches and wingback chairs.

Screenwriters and students worked upstairs, while the dog walkers, tourists, and Web designers hung out below.

When Scott walked in, he had no doubt who Officer Brooks was. The only African-American apart from the Jamaican behind the counter, he was huge and looked rock hard. He wore khakis and a polo shirt and had that compressed Superball look of off-duty cops—calm on the outside, but get them agitated and they'll start bouncing all over the place. He wore half-lens reading glasses like librarians wore; he took them off when he saw Scott.

"Let's go upstairs," he said, raising his cup to the Jamaican for a refill.

Scott stood close to six feet, but he felt like a child, following the sergeant. As the detective sat on an old couch, the sides bowed in, like a gondola. Scott took a rickety chair on the opposite side of the table.

"I ordered you a decaf mocha cappuccino. I hope that's all right."

"Sure," said Scott, wondering how the officer knew what he'd order. The thought that the cop had been making inquiries about him made him uncomfortable. But no doubt that was his plan, to make Scott nervous so he'd say something stupid. Then it occurred to Scott to ask. "How'd you know that was my drink?"

"Just figured."

So that's the way it was going to be. Fine. "What is it you wanted to talk about?"

"When was the last time you saw Laura Finnegan?"

"Months ago. You should know. You're the one who got the judge to expedite the restraining order."

"And you haven't seen her since then?"

"No, sir."

"But you've talked to her."

Here Scott knew he had to be careful. "A few weeks ago, she called me from upstate New York. She told me her mother had a stroke and she was going to stay on and take care of her for a while."

"She called you at home?"

Cautiously, Scott replied, "I don't remember. Could've been at work."

"How long did she say she was going to be away?"

"She didn't know. That's why she asked me to clear out her apartment. She's never been close to her mother, and she thinks maybe now she should spend some time with her." This last part was true. Laura once mentioned that her mother, before passing on, was a religious nut, borderline crazy, whom she had avoided visiting.

"She asked you to take care of her affairs even though she has a restraining order out on you?"

"Yes. She doesn't have many friends out here. No family. We've had our differences, but we're still very close. She trusts me completely."

"Why didn't she ask her landlord to put her stuff in storage?"

"I don't know how well you know Laura"—Scott thought he saw the cop flinch—"but she's a very private person. I'm sure she didn't want to bother him with her problems. The truth is, I think he annoys her. You know, a bit of a busybody. I wouldn't be surprised if he has a thing for her."

"Where did you store her stuff?"

"In a storage locker in Culver City, on Overland." Scott realized he shouldn't have dumped Laura's belongings so quickly. But his sister had a locker that he could show if he had to.

"Do you have a number for her mother?"

"No. She said she was at one of those nursing homes where each patient gets a little cabin to herself, but they were moving her to a more intensive-care facility, and she didn't know the new number."

The Jamaican came with their coffee. Scott noticed that the cop had ordered it black.

"Is she staying at a motel?"

Scott knew he was talking too much, giving too many details that might haunt him later. But the cop kept shooting questions at him, trying to rattle him, he supposed. "She didn't tell me. Maybe she thinks I'd bug her or something."

"What's the name of the nursing home?"

"She must've told me, but I don't remember."

"Did she tell you the name of the town?"

"No. But she said it took her about three hours to drive from Albany."

"North?"

"I don't know."

"You have no way of getting in touch with her?"

"No."

"And she trusts you to take care of everything?"

"Yes."

"She didn't leave you a number to call if you had questions about what to do with things such as her car and her mail?"

"No. I figure she wants to have contact kind of one-way, if you know what I mean. So she has control."

"I see." Officer Brooks handed Scott a card. "When she contacts you again, would you ask her to call me?"

"Sure." Then Scott added, "She likes you, you know."

"She said that?"

"Sure." Scott suddenly grinned from ear to ear, pleased as punch at making the tough cop blush. So the cop carried the torch for Laura. Well, perhaps Scott could use that if he had to.

Without saying another word, the cop stood and left the café.

* * *

Reggie didn't like Scott; he found him obsequious and annoyingly amiable, bobbing up and down, saying yes on the outside and no on the inside. When Reggie saw brothers acting like that, he felt ashamed, but in a white man the trait was revolting. What made Scott more pathetic, Reggie thought, was his confidence that people believed his lies.

Reggie didn't.

Something made him curious. Usually, when a cop asks about someone, the first thing a person says is "Why, has something happened to her? Is she in trouble?" Scott hadn't asked. As if he knew.

Other things didn't make sense. People flew home to take care of parents all the time, but they didn't stop their lives or give up their apartments and jobs. If Laura were using her mother's illness as an excuse to get away from Scott, why would she have him take care of her affairs? Why couldn't he remember where the nursing home was? If Scott knew Laura so well, he'd know that from previous conversations. He said she'd told him the nursing home was three hours out of Albany. Reggie looked at a map. He figured three hours was about a hundred and fifty miles. Three hours west, she would've flown into Syracuse; three hours south, Newark; three hours east, Boston. If she'd been going north, it would make more sense to fly into Burlington, Vermont, unless the place was smack in the middle of the Adirondack Mountains. That shouldn't be too hard to track down.

When Reggie got back to his office, he pushed aside all the paperwork on his desk and reached for the phone. His legs were quivering like when he'd been to the gym after a week-long layoff. He had no legal authority to do what he was doing, and he certainly didn't have the time.

By calling in a favor, Reggie managed to get Scott Goodsell's and Laura Finnegan's telephone bills for the last three months, but they proved disappointing. There were no calls between the residences. Neither revealed any numbers to upstate New York. On Laura's bill, there were several calls to a number in New York City, which Reggie discovered belonged to a Vivian Costanza. Something told him she might merit a call.

He ran a credit check on Laura. She hadn't used her credit cards in the last three weeks. But that was not unusual. She appeared to often go months without using a credit card, a tendency that probably came from doing other people's finances and seeing how much trouble they got into. Reggie figured he'd check in another few days to see if there was a charge.

Reggie shoved aside a white Styrofoam tray of Chinese take-out, of which he'd eaten less than half. It didn't taste quite right; maybe he was coming down with something. He picked up the phone again and called Laura's supervisor at work. Reggie had spoken with him once regarding the restraining order, asking him to call if Scott showed up at Laura's office. In talking to him briefly, Reggie pegged him for someone with something to hide.

Mr. Johnson said Laura had quit without notice but sent in a letter of resignation after missing a few days of work. He sounded sore, like he'd taken it personally. Sounded like he might've had an interest in her. But then Laura seemed to be the kind of girl who starred in a lot of male fantasies.

"Do you have a copy of her letter of resignation?" Reggie asked.

"I sent it down to human resources. They would've put it in her personnel file."

"Could you make a copy and fax it to me?"

From his hesitation, Reggie could tell Johnson didn't want

to be bothered. Maybe he'd lied and had ripped up the letter. Maybe he'd taken it home and kept it under his pillow.

"Is she involved in some kind of crime?" Johnson asked.

"Not as far as I know."

"I'll have to ask the legal department," said Johnson. "We have to be very careful these days. There might be procedures, like needing a warrant or something. You know how big companies are. I can't just make a copy of something from an employee's file and send it on to the police."

"Ex-employee."

"Same difference."

Reggie knew he couldn't get a warrant. There was no crime. "Could you read me the letter, or at least tell me the date it was written?"

Johnson hesitated, then said, "I suppose so. If you really need it. It's the hard-copy stuff that they're paranoid about."

"Did she leave any personal things at the office?"

"A few things, not much. I had one of the girls pack her stuff in a box. Her boyfriend came and picked it up."

"Ex-boyfriend."

"Same difference."

"Don't you find it odd that an ex-boyfriend would bother to pick up a box of her things from the office?"

"Nah. I'd do the same for any of my ex-wives."

"You have more than one?"

"Two. Number three coming up."

"I'm sorry."

"Don't be. Marriage is fun for a while, then it isn't."

By the time Johnson called back that afternoon to read him Laura's resignation letter, Reggie had discovered a sexual-harassment suit pending against the man in the Court of Appeals. A similar suit had been settled out of court a year before. Reggie asked how he got on with his female employees, and Johnson, taking the hint, faxed Reggie the letter.

The letter was dated April 15. The DATE RECEIVED stamp said April 17. There were notes written in the margins—Reggie assumed by people in human resources—regarding termination date and unused vacation days. It was difficult to tell from the fax, but Reggie thought a dot-matrix printer had been used. The language in the letter was formal, almost legalese: "Due to the declining health of my mother and her long-term health-care needs, I hereby resign my position at Thompson & Thompson." She went on to say that she'd enjoyed her experience working there, found it "challenging and invigorating," and was grateful for "the nurturing guidance and unflagging encouragement of my supervisors." Was that sarcasm? Or was it the overblown courtesy of a form-letter book, like Reggie had seen Audrey use in job hunting?

Reggie tried to remember if Laura had ever been sarcastic. He recalled a conversation in which he had reported to her a snide comment Johnson made about the restraining order. Johnson couldn't keep his hands to himself, she'd said, then added, "Gentlemen such as Johnson generally get what they deserve. One of these days." Was that a threat? Or merely wishful thinking? What did she mean?

Reggie decided she could have written the letter. He wondered if he might have her signature on file at Tae Kwan Do Studio; all the students had to sign a release form limiting liability in case they hurt themselves. He'd drop by later and check.

Something seemed odd about it all. She hadn't first called her boss, then followed up with a letter. That would be normal. Maybe she didn't want to talk to Johnson? She could've talked directly with human resources. It occurred to Reggie that Johnson might be worth a visit. Maybe Reggie could talk with some of Laura's fellow workers and see her desk.

As he reread the letter, Reggie got a sick feeling in his stomach as he imagined Johnson fingering Laura's shoulder, his flabby, lecherous lips breathing down her neck, pretending to review her work but getting ready to drop his hand on her thigh.

Men pushing themselves on women—it made him sick. Then he *was* sick; he bolted out of his office, between the rows of desks and busy cops, into the restroom, where he, weak-kneed and shaky, vomited out the Johnsons of the world.

PART THREE

TERCE

They call it June gloom even when it's only May. It happens every year. Fog and wet clouds hang over the shore. Maybe the sun comes out for an hour at noon, maybe it doesn't. It's depressing and a little spooky. The fish swim near the surface, so the fishing's good. But it's hard to get up early, and when I get down to the marina, all the houses are still dark.

The guy on TV who gives the weather says it's caused by a layer of cool air above the water that's trapped by hot air, but that May it felt like something else to me. It felt like the sun wouldn't come up because she wasn't there. When I walked down the jetty, I stopped and looked for her. Her window was closed and dark. The bougainvillea and roses looked wilted. The birds weren't singing, and all you heard was the foghorn sounding like it was crying.

So one day I got to thinking about a news story about some lady hikers who were raped and murdered up in the Sierras, and I thought about the arms and the girl in the window and wondered if she was raped too. I got this bad feeling, and thought of all the women I see alone at Home Depot and at the nursery, and worried if the guy who chopped off her arms was out there and was gonna do it again.

All of a sudden I got panicky—like if I didn't do something, nothing would ever be the same, like someone else would get hurt, and bad feelings would cling to this place forever.

You know how I feel about cops. They're not the way we Mexicans handle things. If something bad happens, we usually let things slide. It's what fate has brought us, our miserable *pinche vida.* But there always comes a time when something changes your mind and you end up doing the opposite of what you always say you'll do.

I found the card the cop gave me under the mat in my truck and put it in my pocket.

After missing confession one morning, Reggie called Father John and asked to see him. The priest met him at the door to the rectory wearing a white shirt and black pants. His breath smelled of red wine.

"I'm glad to see you taking such an interest in the Church," he said. "You're making me work for a living."

Reggie detected a smirk. No, not a smirk really, but a tired smile. Even priests had their cynical days, he supposed. Father John led Reggie back into his office and placed his stole around his neck. He sat down in a worn leather chair by his desk. Behind him, a large lead-paned window looked into a rose garden.

Reggie was about to kneel when Father John flipped his hand at a chair. "Have a seat, Reggie." The priest observed him for a long moment, tilted his chin to his chest, and closed his eyes. He sat like that for over a minute, motionless, silent.

Reggie heard children playing down the street and two male voices from somewhere in the rectory.

Father John sighed ponderously, rubbed his eyes, then pushed back in his chair. He took off his stole and folded it. "There are all kinds of sin, Reggie," he said as if answering a question. "The majority aren't big sins. Most people wouldn't even think to confess them as sins. But sin, any sin, is nothing more than a thought that keeps you from opening your heart to God. We all live in perpetual sin, even the most devout monk, because it is impossible for us to constantly keep our thoughts in God. But we try." He smiled wistfully as he ran his hand over the folded stole. "Now, tell me what you came to tell me today."

Reggie was confused. "You aren't going to hear my confession?"

"No, not today. Let's just talk."

Reggie felt his face flush and swallowed hard. He opened his lips and the words flowed, the story of Laura: the first time he met her, the vulnerability that had attracted him, her disappearance. He said he wasn't sure if he should continue with his unofficial investigation, but he felt himself irresistibly drawn into it. He referred to Laura by name, describing her in detail, trying to pinpoint why he couldn't stop thinking about her.

"A woman of modest reticence and great physical beauty. A rare combination." The priest sighed as if after a sip of a particularly good brandy.

"Yes," said Reggie, embarrassed, glancing up at the priest. He saw a faraway look in Father John's eyes and wondered whom he was remembering: his mother, the Virgin Mary, or maybe some woman he knew before he became a priest. Perhaps it was the idea of female perfection that had drawn him away.

"Do you know what *laura* means in the Church?" the priest asked.

"No."

"It was a type of early Christian monastery. Each monk lived as a hermit in his laura, then got together from time to time with other brothers. In their laura, the monks dedicated their lives to silence, solitude, and prayer."

Reggie wasn't sure what the priest was getting at. "Is it wrong for me to try to find out what happened to her?"

"Does the investigation keep you from loving God?"

"No," Reggie said, unsure. He searched hard for the right words before he continued. "It's like I have this feeling I'm supposed to find her . . . like it's my assignment."

Father John nodded. "Does the investigation close you off from your family? Your wife?"

Again Reggie hesitated. "I think I'm afraid to talk about it with my wife."

"Afraid?"

"It's like"—Reggie paused, looking down at his hands—"it's like we're walking on an ice crust over snow, and if we start talking, the ice will break and someone will fall through."

"I've never seen snow," said Father John wistfully.

"What?"

"I've never seen snow. Except in the distance, in the San Gabriel Mountains. I've lived in California my whole life, and I've never been to the mountains to see the snow."

Reggie was confused. Had Father John been listening? Was Reggie supposed to understand something here?

"Everyone hears God's call in a different way, Reggie. For some people, it comes in a flash. For others, it unfolds over a lifetime. I was already in seminary before I heard it. At the time I thought I wanted to be a monk, but He called me to be a priest. Once you hear the call, you spend the rest of your life trying to answer it."

Reggie felt a pulse of impatient anger that dissolved instantly. He frowned, squinting against the sun. The afternoon light poured through the window and made the priest into a dark blob. "Are you saying Laura is my calling?"

"What I'm saying is for you to open your heart. God calls

you through your desires. Where you find desire, sin, and guilt, you will find God seeking entry into your soul."

"You're telling me to have an affair?" Reggie asked, flabbergasted.

Father John smiled. "The soul will not stand being neglected, Reggie. Your desire for this woman is your soul demanding attention. If you don't do work on your soul, it pops up symptomatically, in loss of meaning, obsessions, and adultery. When sex creates a problem, it means something else needs to be addressed. Do your soul work, Reggie. You'll be fine."

"How do I work on my soul?"

"You do nothing. You open yourself up and observe the world uncritically. You watch your thought. You listen to your dreams. You pray. You wait."

"You mean I have to quit my job?"

"Could be. Nothing needs to change. Or everything can change dramatically. I know that I am going to drive to the San Gabriel Mountains. I'm going to find a huge pile of snow and bury myself in it. I'm going to taste it and rub it in my face. I'm going to let it melt on my skin. I'm going to make a snowball and throw it."

"For your soul?"

"Precisely. For my soul."

Reggie didn't understand. Or maybe he did. It was just so hard. But the ache in his shoulders was gone, and his head felt better. He thanked Father John and left.

As Connie Philips pulled her canary-yellow kayak onto the white sand of Malibu Beach, her legs wobbled; her arms felt heavy and throbbed. She grabbed the bow rope and, with the last of her strength, yanked the kayak beyond the reach of the waves. Then she collapsed.

She knew it wasn't merely muscle fatigue that made her limbs shake.

She lay on the sand, her head spinning from the abrupt change to solid land. Slowly, the world settled in one place. She closed her eyes and relaxed.

She decided then not to answer Scott's call immediately. Maybe she'd let a day go by. She didn't want to sound overly enthusiastic, and she didn't trust her voice not to reveal too much. Her surprise, her hurt, her anticipation.

She didn't know what to make of Scott Goodsell. Last time they'd been together, they had a great time. Great laughs, great sex. She thought they were falling in love. She hadn't liked someone that much in years. Maybe never. She was excited about getting to know him. It felt so right. For weeks she stumbled about in an erotic daze, writhing in a sleepless sweat at night, refusing to relieve the burning coiled tension herself, waiting for him, letting it build, savoring the agony. She couldn't eat, couldn't swallow anything but fruit and juice.

He didn't call.

She would have rung him up, but she waited for him to call her, like the dating books tell you to do, and after three weeks she knew it was too late—he'd hear desperation in her voice. So she waited by her phone on Saturday nights, feeling stupid to be wasting her time but not really wanting to do anything else. After a month, she realized she couldn't remember exactly what he looked like and made herself go out dancing alone.

She didn't get it. How could you experience that kind of emotional intensity with someone, then not call?

Now, six months later, he calls.

Connie looked out at the water, the gray mist hanging over the glassy surface, the algae blooms rising and falling with the waves. Maybe she shouldn't call back at all. Why disturb the tranquillity of her life? Why accept a date from a man who was too rude to make a follow-up call, too cowardly to tell her he had another girlfriend, too diffident to admit he didn't want to get involved? Hadn't she learned anything from those weeks of suffering?

Apparently not. Disgusted with herself, Connie brushed the sand off her bottom and prepared to drag her kayak up beneath her balcony, where she would rinse it off with a hose. She broke down her paddle into two pieces and tucked it beneath her seat. As she hoisted the kayak up on her hip, stepping carefully over the sharp rocks, she knew that despite the hurt, despite the voices that told her no, despite an inexplicable yet lingering apprehension, she would call him back.

Thompson & Thompson Accounting covered eight floors of a turquoise glass skyscraper in Century City. Reggie waited behind bulletproof glass in the reception area and marveled as the receptionist ate a doughnut, painted her nails, opened e-mails on her computer, and answered the phone all at the same time.

Employees arriving to work used electromagnetic swipe cards to let themselves in. They were mostly young; a large number were women and minorities. Dress was casual, although a few of the women were doing the stockings-and-heels routine. After ten minutes, Brian Johnson clicked open the door and led Reggie back to his office.

Two hundred identical blue-gray desks between identical blue-gray partitions lined up eight across, twenty-five deep. Along the sides, glass-enclosed offices for the executives. Many were already behind their desks, hard at work. Apart from the mountains of paper, stuffed rabbits, Gumby dolls, and toy cars cluttered the desks. Exotic landscapes, Laker pendants, and pictures of movie stars torn from magazines wallpapered the five-foot-high dividers. Two hundred dorm rooms in need of cleaning.

Johnson wasn't at all what Reggie expected. He was tall, with a square midwestern-farmer face, thick brown hair with gray temples, a soft belly, and an easy laugh. He stopped to say hi at each desk, slapping the partitions, making goofy comments: "Hey, Phyllis, didn't you hear? New regulations. No coffee drinking." "Hey, Tom, off to the gym? Or did you bring your laundry to work?" "Hey, Laticia, don't we let you go home anymore?" He was the kind of guy who needed to touch—things and people—needed to be noticed. Such guys often seemed to get plugged in to middle management, Reggie thought, whether they were right for it or not.

"This is where she sat," Johnson said, pointing to a gray cubicle. There were a few personal items scattered about—a sweater on the chair, an empty coffee cup, a box of Kleenex. "The desk was reassigned a few days ago."

Reggie was appalled. It hurt to think of Laura working there. The place was so bleak and anonymous.

As they passed the conference room, Reggie noticed men dressed in suits. Computers were set up on the conference table beside huge volumes of computer printouts. Walking through the maze, they met other suits carrying mugs of coffee and more printouts. The suits seemed to come in groups of three.

"What's going on?" asked Reggie.

Johnson shrugged. "Just our annual audit."

"Accounting companies get audited?"

"Of course. Every year. Don't cops police their own?"

"Sure. Internal Affairs."

"Same thing. It's no big deal, but it always makes the employees a little jumpy." Johnson swung open the door to his office. "Come on in."

Johnson handed over Laura's original letter of resignation. "While you check those signatures, I'll hunt down Amy Chow. She was Laura's closest friend here."

Reggie compared Laura's signature on the letter to her release form from Tae Kwan Do Studio. Although he wasn't an expert, they looked identical.

"Amy, this is Detective Reggie Brooks." Johnson gently pushed her forward.

Amy was petite and birdlike. She looked scared, as if she might cry.

Speaking softly, Reggie asked her to sit down. "Don't worry. Laura's not in any trouble. We simply would like to locate her. We need your help."

Amy nodded.

"When was the last time you saw Laura?"

"The Friday before she quit. We went out for a drink at Typhoon."

That, Reggie knew, was a restaurant-bar at thc Santa Monica airport. "To celebrate?"

"No. Well"—she smiled—"maybe to celebrate getting through the week. We went for margaritas on Fridays once or twice a month."

"Did she seem agitated or upset?"

"No. Laura doesn't upset easy. Laura is Laura."

"Did she ever mention her mother? That her mother was sick?"

"No, she never mentioned her family."

"Did she give you any indication that she was planning to quit her job or leave town?"

"No. Well . . . she always had travel brochures on her desk. Every vacation, she was off someplace different—New Zealand, France, Morocco, the Virgin Islands, Hawaii. But she didn't mention anything in particular."

"Did she have a boyfriend?"

"Only her ex-boyfriend. Scott."

"Did she seem frightened of him?"

"More annoyed, I think, like he wouldn't leave her alone. But I don't think she was scared of him."

"Any close personal friends outside of work you know of?"

"No. She was kind of a loner, I guess."

"Was there anything different you noticed, how she looked, how she acted?"

"On that Friday?"

"Anytime."

"Well . . . maybe there's this one thing. No, forget it. It's too stupid."

"That's okay. Tell me."

"Well, she kept an action figure of Bruce Lee on top of her computer monitor, you know, one of those little toys." Amy pointed to the left corner of Johnson's computer. "When I came in on Monday, it was gone."

"Was anything else gone?"

"Not that I noticed."

"Was the Bruce Lee toy special to her?"

"Like would she take it with her if she was going to split? I don't think so. No more than the photos and other stuff that I put in the box."

"What exactly did you put in the box?"

"Oh, you know, personal stuff. Hand cream, photos—like I said—nail files, gum, her desk calendar."

"Who were the photos of? Her family?"

"No. They were of her and people she met on vacations. She really liked to travel."

Reggie would have liked to see Laura's desk calendar. When he ran out of questions for Amy, he asked Johnson if he could look at the files on Laura's computer. Johnson hesitated, then said as soon as someone quit, their computer was stripped. All accounting files were stored on a mainframe. Reggie didn't believe him, but without a warrant, he couldn't check.

"How was your relationship with Laura?" he asked Johnson as he closed his notepad.

Johnson turned beet red. "She was a model employee. Human resources can tell you whatever else you need to know."

Reggie figured he'd pushed Johnson as far as he would give. For now. He thanked Johnson for his time and left.

Scott glanced at his watch. He had a date to play racquetball with Peter Flynn at three. He changed quickly into his gym shorts and sneakers and hurried toward the door. He locked up the apartment and jumped into his BMW.

He raced down Santa Monica Boulevard, then headed south. The marine layer was thick, the air moist. Scott wondered how far inland he'd have to drive to find sun. This kind of weather always left Scott feeling muddleheaded, but at least it would be cool for his game.

He pulled up to the intersection of Colorado and Eighteenth, by a large building-supply store. He frowned. Mexican day laborers lined the sidewalk, looking anxiously at cars slowed by the light. Scott resisted an impulse to roll up his window. A truck pulled over and was suddenly mobbed by twenty squirming bodies, children's bodies, not even full-size men. Their desperation made Scott sick. How could they let themselves get like that? Breeding like rabbits. Too ignorant to use a condom. Taking our air. Our space. Our city.

He revved his motor and raced through the red light. Fuck it if he got a ticket. He wasn't going to stop near all that.

He had to concentrate on not speeding as he turned east down Ocean Park, the last stretch before the gym. As he pulled into the 24 Hour Fitness parking lot, he saw Peter's ass hanging out by the trunk of his blue Volvo station wagon. He was changing into a T-shirt and sneakers right there in the parking lot. What a strange bird he was. He wore basketball shoes and ratty shorts, the elastic all shot, with his butt crack showing like trailer trash. Still, he was the nicest guy Scott knew.

He'd been spending a lot more time with Peter since Laura went away. That's how Scott thought about it—Laura going away, as if she were on vacation. Peter was easy to be around. He never asked personal questions and didn't need favors. Cheerful and deferential, Peter made Scott feel like the high school football hero who befriends a nerd; he gave Scott an odd sense of security.

They checked in at the front desk. They were ten minutes early, but the racquetball room was empty, so the musclehead at the desk said they could go ahead and take the court.

The racquetball court was a box of gleaming yellow wood with a Plexiglas wall that looked out into the lobby. The room made Scott think of a padded cell—the crushing claustrophobia, the amplified noise, the bleaching white light—and it occurred to him that one of the reasons he played so hard was the jolt of panic he always got in the room. That and showing off for the people glancing in from the lobby.

Peter served. He was a consistent player, strong, methodical, reserving his final burst of energy for the end of the game. Scott, on the other hand, was erratic, which in itself worked as a strategy, keeping Peter guessing, never knowing how hard a ball was coming.

Scott balanced on his toes, nervous, like a white mouse in a maze. He slammed back Peter's serve again and again, hitting the ball as if it were an evil thing out to get him, an odious eye, relentless, vindictive.

The ball ricocheted against the Plexiglas like a bullet. Peter seemed more aggressive than usual; the room vibrated from the impact of his serves. The men scrambled past each other, smelling the other's body, feeling his heat. Sweat dripped down their faces and limbs, flipping off their arms as they clobbered the ball.

The air began to press down on Scott; a hysteria took over, like an enormous bat swooping down on his back, biting his neck, driving him insane. The ball was a thing of pure hate; barely seeing it, he swung madly, bashing it away to save himself.

They both played as if possessed, like pit bulls from adjacent yards finally getting at each other.

After a half hour, Scott smashed a rebound that slammed into Peter's leg. Peter sank to the floor, dropping his racquet and grabbing his calf, rocking back and forth in silence. The room echoed with their heavy breathing, the walls spun around them, the air was heavy and damp.

Scott felt a stab of erotic, malevolent victory. He stood dizzy, jubilant, above his enemy. After a moment he realized, reluctantly, that this wasn't the correct response. "Jesus, Peter. I'm sorry." He picked up Peter's racquet and squatted beside him.

"I didn't expect it to come so fast."

"I'm so sorry. Are you okay?"

"Sure. It's my fault. My concentration's a little off today. I guess I'm tired."

"Are you kidding? You were a maniac!"

Peter grinned at the compliment. Wounded but a warrior still. He stood and hobbled across the court, rubbing his calf. "I'm okay, but I don't think I can finish the game. I'm sorry."

"I'm the one who should apologize," Scott said. But the only thing he really felt bad about was his own lack of compassion. He felt annoyance, not empathy. What was wrong with him? "I was pretty much ready to quit, anyhow. How 'bout if we grab a late lunch?"

"At four o'clock?"

"Yeah. My treat."

"Sure. Why not?"

On the way to the car, Peter slowed in the middle of the parking lot. When Scott turned around, Peter said, "There's something I've been meaning to ask you, Scott."

Scott noticed Peter's knees, knobby, white, and wrinkled, and suddenly felt embarrassed to be seen with him. "Can't it wait until lunch? I'm starved."

"No. I don't know if I'll have the nerve to ask you once I cool down."

"What's up?" said Scott, using his most chipper voice, hoping to prod Peter on.

"If you feel at all uncomfortable about this, I want you to tell me, okay?"

"Sure. Speak, my friend."

"Well . . . I was wondering . . . you've been broken up with Laura for a few months, right?"

"Yeah."

"Well . . . I was wondering if you'd mind if I asked her out?"

Scott froze; the air between them pulsed with hostility.

"I know it might be a little weird for you," Peter added quickly. "But she always seemed like such an interesting person. She has such good posture."

"You want to date a woman because she has good posture?"

"No, of course not. I'm not good at expressing . . . Hell, I like her. There's something special . . . well, you know. Of course, if it would make you feel at all uncomfortable . . ."

Scott was speechless.

"I guess it's a bad idea," said Peter, disappointed.

"It sure is. It's a fucking terrible idea." Scott was furious. He found Peter detestable and couldn't bear to look at him. He stammered, uncharacteristically. "You know . . . I just r-remembered something I n-need to do at work. I'll have to take a rain check on lunch."

"I'm sorry, Scott. I didn't know you'd be so—"

"Forget about it. See you next week."

"Next week. Sure."

Scott got into his BMW and screeched out of the parking lot. In his rearview mirror, he saw Peter standing there like an idiot, not moving, watching him drive away.

After his anger faded to a bitter scum in his mouth, Scott wasn't sure if he felt worse about Peter bringing up Laura or the fact that now he'd have to find another racquetball partner.

Reggie feared the trail on the San Juan murders was getting cold. Li'l Richie's girlfriend said she'd let him have her car, but she hadn't seen him for a month. Whatever she knew, she wasn't telling. Patrol units were still stationed outside her house. So far, Li'l Richie hadn't showed.

"You won't believe this," said Velma, charging into Reggie's office. "I went down to Parker Center to do a background check on Li'l Richie's mother. She was arrested in eighty-seven for prostitution. She's got family down in Texas. Turns out Li'l Richie's half brother lives in Houston."

"You figure Li'l Richie's skipped town?"

"I'd bet on it. Officers found the Cadillac abandoned in South Central. He's gone."

"Why don't you call the FBI Fugitive Task Force and give them the addresses of his relatives. Guys like that don't just disappear."

Sanchez poked his head around the doorjamb; he looked like he'd been up all night. "Hey, Reggie. There's a Mexican out front who wants to see ya. You want me to show him back or give 'im the brush-off?"

"Show him back, would you? And ask Simmons to hold my calls. Unless it's Audrey."

"Right," said Sanchez. His wink to Velma said he thought Reggie was pussy-whipped. Reggie ignored them both.

"I gotta get going on the body dump we got last night," said Velma as she got up to leave. "I'll catch you later."

The distraction was welcome. Reggie had a coffee burn in his stomach and was having a hard time sitting still; he needed a break from the mess of paperwork in front of him.

When he saw the little man standing shyly in the doorway, wearing black slacks and a starched white shirt as if for church, it took him a moment to remember the Mexican fisherman from the marina. Reggie was both surprised and not surprised, as if he had been somehow expecting him but had given up hope.

"Come in," he said. "Please have a seat."

The Mexican took a chair on the other side of Reggie's desk. He sat straight, making himself as tall as possible, like a schoolboy in the principal's office. He had a wide, pleasant face, and it looked like he'd used water to comb down his hair.

"How may I help you?" asked Reggie, pulling off his half-glasses and laying them on his papers. The Mexican didn't offer his name, Reggie didn't ask it.

"I'm sorry to bother you, but you told me to call if I saw the girl . . . Laura . . . again."

Reggie almost leaped out of his chair. "You've seen her?"

"No, no. But I have something to tell you."

"Go on. What?"

The Mexican proceeded to tell his story about the arms, the one he'd found and the other one in Malibu, and how he didn't see Laura after that, and how he knew the arms were Laura's.

"What makes you think they were Laura's arms?" Reggie vaguely recalled the case, a body dump that went nowhere.

"I just know. But there's something else . . ."

A number of things flashed through Reggie's mind: first, the Mexican was crazy; second, he was making some bizarre confession; third, he was one of those guys who wanted to be a cop and used any excuse to talk to cops; fourth, how quickly could Reggie get him out of his office. "Yes?" Reggie tapped his pencil impatiently.

"Well, the sculptor who owns the house she lived in—"

"Yes?"

"He leaves his tools out sometimes. He has an ax, and sometimes he leaves it in a log, sometimes leaning against the shed."

"What about it?"

"That's what he used."

"Who used?" said Reggie, frustrated.

"The guy who chopped her up."

"What makes you think that?"

"I just know. Ask the sculptor guy if it's missing."

Reggie's heart was racing. The image was outrageous—Laura being chopped . . . no, it was too much. Reggie didn't know if he felt so irritated because the Mexican was talking about his Laura as if she were a salami, or because of the remote possibility that there was truth to what he was saying. A painful throbbing started at the base of Reggie's neck, shooting down his rhomboideus muscles and through his shoulders. The Mexican looked so earnest, so sincere. But it was impossible.

The Mexican continued. "I know that you can't open up an investigation unless someone reports her missing."

"That's true."

"I want to report her missing."

Reggie stifled a smile. "It has to be someone related to her, or someone like her boss. You're a complete stranger to her." Reggie regretted the way that had come out. He could tell he'd hurt the Mexican's feelings.

"Then why don't *you* report her missing?" the Mexican asked.

Reggie pressed his lips together to keep from laughing, but it came anyway, a nervous giggle tickling his throat, then bursting out of his mouth like a hiccup. He clapped his hand over his mouth, alarmed by his sudden hysteria. He excused himself and went on in a somber voice. "Then I couldn't work on the case. I would be considered too closely involved to be objective."

"I know what I say is true, and I want to help." The Mexican spoke deliberately.

"Help? How?"

The Mexican propelled himself forward in his seat, palms beneath his thighs. "I could, like, investigate for you or something."

"This isn't television. I can't simply start an investigation because I want to," although in truth, that was exactly what Reggie had been doing.

"That's how I could help. I'm good at watching."

That hysteria almost erupted again—the idea of Laura and the arms was too awful. But what if the Mexican was right? What if Laura had been murdered? Hadn't Reggie feared that all along?

He regarded the Mexican's wide face, his black eyes shining like pools in a cave. He seemed honest and was smart enough to have guessed that Reggie cared enough about Laura to break a few rules. "Where were you from Friday, April twelfth, to Monday, April fifteenth?" he asked.

"Big weekend." The Mexican smiled broadly. "My youngest daughter's first communion. Lots of family stuff. Barbecues and church."

If that was true, the Mexican would have plenty of backup

for his alibi. "I'll tell you what," said Reggie. "Let me take a look at the case file on the arms. Then I'll give you a call."

The Mexican gave him a number. "Then I'll be your detective?"

"No, that's quite impossible."

The Mexican looked disappointed. "One more thing," he said as he stood to go. "There was a ring on the arm's left hand."

"A ring?"

"Yeah. On her third finger, like an engagement ring."

As the Mexican turned and shuffled out of the office, his words settled over Reggie and seeped into his skin. *I just know.* Reggie had a feeling, too, that kept him awake at night and gnawed at his stomach. Wasn't that how God talked to you? A clear, undeniable feeling? Or maybe it was through a Mexican fisherman.

What had Father John said? *God speaks, but rarely in full or coherent sentences.*

Reggie sat staring into his palms. The question was where to begin.

Since the arms had been found on the beach, Reggie figured the case would be handled by the sheriff's department. Later, he'd call around and find out for sure.

If the Mexican was right, then Reggie could try to match the DNA from the arms' tissue samples and the hair samples he'd bagged from Laura's apartment. But he couldn't get authorization for the DNA tests unless there was more evidence that Laura was a victim of a crime. Even then it could take half a year to get back the results. A low-profile case without a suspect would get the lowest priority.

It would be difficult to work officially on the case, even if the LAPD and the sheriff's department would cooperate. And someone had to report Laura missing. Someone other than Reggie or a Mexican fisherman.

Shit.

Scott knew Samantha had seen the ring only once, when she house-sat at his place and snooped through his drawers. His mother had seen it, of course, but not since Grandma gave it to him fourteen years before. He had it appraised for apartment insurance, so he knew the cut and size: two-carat solitaire. He also had a Polaroid of it. The diamond would be simple to duplicate, he figured. The hard part would be the setting.

Scott turned off the Santa Monica Freeway by the convention center, at the Union Street exit for downtown. He turned down Sixth Avenue, then to Broadway, to the jewelry district. Within a block, the lavish glass skyscrapers leased by lawyers and stockbrokers deteriorated into crumbling three-story brick buildings with broken windows, electronic and textile stores with signs in Spanish and English: NOVEDADES, LIBREIA, LA CATEDRAL WEDDING CHAPEL, GIROS A MEXICO, LATMOS JEWELRY, BENNY'S JEWELRY, BROADWAY JEWELRY MART, and the omnipresent CHECKS CASHED. There must have been more than a hundred jewelry stores. The street smelled of urine and dirt. The sidewalks were thick with garbage; bums camped out on collapsed cardboard boxes; drunks staggered into pedestrians; punks sold dope; hookers scanned the passing cars.

Who would ever want to sleep with something that looked like that? Scott wondered.

Warily, he parked his car in front of a jewelry store. He had an alarm, and the store was right there, but he figured there was a 30 percent chance his car would be broken into before he came out. As he locked up, a bum asked him for change. Scott gave him five bucks and told him to bang on the window of the store if anyone bothered the BMW. The bum said he'd do it, but Scott didn't really expect to see him when he came out.

The store was called Gems Galore. A colleague had told him about the place; it was supposedly reputable and would give you a good deal. It was a two-story building with grimy windows and heavy grating that the owners didn't bother to pull back during the day. Scott wondered if it wasn't worth spending an extra thousand dollars not to have to come here. It dawned on him that this was why people were willing to pay Rodeo Drive prices.

Inside, a Middle Eastern guy, about Scott's age, dressed in a sharp white Armani shirt and slacks, was waiting on two Chinese women. Scott noticed coarse black hairs like two paintbrushes sticking out of the salesman's nostrils, clipped but not recently. He was grateful the clerk had enough sense to keep his shirt buttoned.

The other clerk was with a young Hispanic couple. In the back were two scurrilous-looking fellows in black leather jackets. Scott couldn't tell if they were buying or selling.

There was no obvious danger in the store, but, like a bus station at night, it wasn't a place one felt particularly comfortable. Scott detected the vague smell of a men's locker room wafting across the counter from the direction of the clerk.

He fought the impulse to clamp his hand over his nose. The place was revolting. He couldn't help himself. In a sudden panic, he backed up and bolted out the door.

He drove a few blocks, then pulled in to the underground parking lot under Pershing Square. He decided to try the California Jewelry Mart, an eight-story modern building on Hill at Sixth. He'd have to pay more, he figured, but the prices should still be wholesale.

He took the elevator to the third floor, which was divided into separate shops by narrow corridors and glass partitions that gave the diamond exchanges a look of openness and efficiency. The halls were soundless, the air still and heavy. Scott stopped at a store called the Diamond Factory. The door was locked. A man who looked like an Irish prizefighter buzzed him in.

To the right as he entered was a large glassed-in room where two heavyset men sat cutting diamonds. At first glance, they appeared hunched over, but then Scott realized that the tables were built to come up close to their chins. A machine that looked like an old phonograph was polishing a large diamond.

Scott showed the clerk the ring appraisal and the yellowed Polaroid.

"I'm sorry. There simply isn't enough information here to go on." The man's accent was South African. "I couldn't possibly make you a duplicate." He had a nose that looked like it had been broken a couple of times; his eyes were the color of sapphires.

"What do you mean?"

The clerk smiled, his manner relaxed, like he wasn't worried about making every sale and found the bargain hunters who wandered into his shop mildly amusing. "The photo tells me only that it was a pretty ring. The appraisal tells me the general cut and size, and the appraiser's value assessment, but it doesn't describe the clarity or color grades. And there's no diagram of interior flaws."

Scott kicked himself. He should have gotten a professional jeweler's appraisal instead of using Peter's friend. Fucking Peter. "Flaws? I don't understand."

The clerk looked pleased with himself, like an evangelist before an apt pupil. "Almost all diamonds have inclusions, which are little flaws or crystals in the stone. They make each diamond completely unique."

"So you can't make a duplicate?"

"It's impossible. If I had more information, I might be able to replicate the cut. From the appraisal I see that you had a two-carat solitaire with forty-nine facets. That tells me it's old. Most round diamonds now are cut with fifty-eight facets: thirty-four facets above the girdle and twenty-four facets below."

"The girdle?"

The clerk pointed to a wall diagram of a solitaire cut. "That's this narrow rim at the largest diameter of the stone. What you probably had was thirty-three facets above the girdle and sixteen facets below."

"Can you cut a stone like that for me?"

"Sure. But there's nothing here about the color, the height of the crown, the depth of the girdle, the size of the table—"

Scott began to lose patience. "Do you have some two-carat diamonds I could see? Maybe you have something that's close enough. I don't need an exact match."

"Just good enough to fool the wife?"

"Something like that."

The clerk smiled as if he'd anticipated this revised request from the beginning. "Let me make a selection of two-carat white solitaires, brilliant cut." Moments later, he returned with a black velvet tray holding three diamonds.

To Scott, they all looked the same. He found himself pressing his fingers on either side of his temples, trying to remember what his grandmother's stone had looked like. "Are they all about the same price?"

"Goodness, no. That one is eleven thousand, this one is forty-five hundred, and the other thirteen hundred."

"Why is this one less expensive?"

"It is a white, color grade L, with many crystal inclusions in the pavilion, and you'll see the girdle is slightly thick. That affects its brilliance." The jeweler handed Scott a loupe. "Here, take a look. You'll see the difference immediately."

"Never mind. I'll take it," said Scott, annoyed. He didn't want to become a gem expert. He simply wanted a damn diamond.

"It's a lesser quality than your appraisal, which sets the diamond value at about five thousand."

"That's fine," said Scott. He felt a headache coming on; he didn't want to hear any more. He hated salespeople who made you feel guilty about taking the cheapest item. The diamonds were simply shiny rocks to him. He couldn't imagine what all the fuss was about.

The South African recommended a store upstairs for the setting. Scott figured the guy was getting a kickback, but at this point, he didn't care. He took the elevator to the sixth floor and a place called Dornbirn Jewelry.

Multicolored wax casts sat in the window like Halloween candy: rings with dragons, lizards, flowers, even a miniature suspension bridge. A round Bavarian woman buzzed Scott in. She wore glasses, and two gray braids wrapped around her head like a halo, and had round red cheeks like lollipops. Behind her stepped out her son, a lanky kid with a long greasy ponytail.

The woman was a chatty sort and told Scott a story about bringing home a young German tourist she'd met and feeding him stuffed cabbage, the point being, Scott surmised, that they were honest folk. Her son, who hung back at the door between the showroom and the workshop, chuckled as she told the story, like a punk kid sniggering at fart jokes. Scott began to wonder if the German boy had made it back to Europe or ended up in a dill sausage.

He showed them the Polaroid and asked if they could duplicate the setting.

"We can do anything, anything at all," the woman said, pulling out a thick portfolio of photos. "People even bring in pictures of their dogs, and we make pins out of them." She flipped to a picture of an Irish setter, gold, encrusted with diamonds and rubies. "The lady who ordered this was a judge for the Westminster Kennel Club. Very nice lady."

The son nodded and repeated, "Very nice lady."

Scott imagined a fiftyish woman who wore a Pendleton suit that hung below her knees, thick stockings, and those funny walking shoes they wear at dog shows. He thought the pin was hideous, but the quality of the craftsmanship was obvious.

"Do you have the stone?" the woman asked. Her son continued to lurk at the doorway, his long fingers playing arpeggios on the doorjamb.

Scott shook out the diamond from a small white envelope into her palm. She popped a loupe in her eyes, then sighed, disappointed. "Your setting is going to be more expensive than your diamond, I'm afraid."

"Doesn't matter," snapped Scott, losing patience.

She gave a chuckle. "Mothers aren't always so easily fooled."

"What?"

"You lost the ring, no? You're not trying to fool a girlfriend. No. First time you have a fight, a girlfriend will run to a jeweler to find out how much the ring is worth. But a mother will take you at your word . . . usually." She smiled at her son, who then disappeared into the workshop.

"Can you make it up?"

"Certainly." She peered at the photo again. "I can't tell from the picture if it's white gold or platinum . . . it's so yellowed. Your diamond even looks greenish in the photo."

"Whatever is cheapest," said Scott.

"Well, we don't use anything less than eighteen-karat gold."

"Fine, fine," said Scott. "How long will it take?"

She estimated about a week. He wrote a check for a thousand, and she gave him a receipt for the deposit and the diamond. The setting would set him back three grand.

As he pushed through the lunchtime crowd back to his car, Scott thought of his grandparents, trudging along in the alpine snow, spending all their money on a ring, unsure if they'd even live another day, yet wanting this symbol of hope and commitment as they embarked on a new life in a strange country. What had Grandma said when she gave it to him? "You carry with you all the riches you'll ever need." She'd probably meant love, or talent, or ingenuity.

Scott began to regret giving up his grandmother's ring. But the moment Laura rejected him, he lost all illusions about love, a love that would redeem him, a love so absolute she would flee across continents with him to start life anew. She killed his love and left him a cynic.

No, it was better that the ring had disappeared with her.

Reggie called Ronda Wiley, an officer he knew at the LAPD detective headquarters division who handled adult missing persons for Los Angeles County. He asked her to see if there was a missing-persons report on Laura Finnegan. Ronda was in the middle of something but promised to call back. Reggie began the search for who might be handling the arms case, which was not as easy as it sounded.

Los Angeles was a jigsaw puzzle of police jurisdictions. Some parts, located in unincorporated zones outside the city limits and therefore serviced by the Los Angeles County sheriff's department, had L.A. in their addresses and seemed more part of the city than places like Simi Valley, which was serviced by the LAPD. When a crime happened in two jurisdictions, the decision on which department handled it was a toss-up based on who had time and resources available. Then there were those cases co-opted by Robbery and Homicide, downtown, because they were important or glamorous. Venice Beach was LAPD, but Malibu Beach was the sheriff's department. Since the arms had washed up on the beaches, the crime presumably happened at sea: the sheriff's department.

Reggie looked in his state law-enforcement directory and called the homicide bureau of the sheriff's department down in Commerce. For whatever reason, the detective bureau at the Malibu/Lost Hills station was handling the arms case, so Reggie called Malibu and asked to speak with the lead detective. "Oh, you mean the *empty embrace case,*" said the female officer who'd answered the phone with a chuckle in her voice. "That'd be Detective Mike Morrison. He's not in, but I'll leave a message for him. What division you with?" Reggie gave his division and telephone number. Detective Morrison called back in twenty minutes and told Reggie to come on out that afternoon.

Just before Reggie left the station, Ronda Wiley called back; no one had reported Laura Finnegan missing.

Reggie drove toward Malibu on Pacific Coast Highway, a narrow ribbon of asphalt that ran up the coast. On one side, the turquoise sea; on the other side, perilous cliffs that scattered rocks across the road at night like termite dust, reminding Los Angelinos that the process of deterioration continued, unabated, at the edge of the continent.

The view made Reggie contemplate mortality. It made him think of Laura. How many others like her, he wondered, escaped to California to re-create themselves, to begin new lives as if they had no past. How many others would vanish without anyone ever knowing or caring, disappearing like an inspired thought someone forgot to write down. Thousands, tens of thousands? Actresses, runaways, parole violators, college dropouts, those who'd had enough of dead-end jobs, abusive boyfriends, and oppressive families, escaping cold weather that no longer gave them joy, reminding them of the coldness in their hearts. But in escaping these things, they were left with no one to give a damn, no one to file a missing-persons report.

Reggie understood because he was one of them. After he lost his father and brother, and after his mother died, Reggie had become a foster child of the Boston projects, passed between parents who housed him for money. When he won an athletic scholarship to UCLA, he kept no ties to his childhood. He, too, reinvented himself. He took diction lessons, studied martial arts, and practically lived in the library. He attended classes in art history and Chinese. But he yearned for family, and as soon as he and Audrey knew they wanted to spend their lives together, he began convincing her to have children right away. When their first son came, Reggie felt reborn.

Reggie knew where gangbangers were coming from—calling their homeboys *family,* their loyalty and obedience to their gang more visceral than to blood relatives. Their need for family was so strong that they made one up.

As he crested the hill by Pepperdine University, Reggie realized he was now endangering the one thing he treasured above all else—his family—placing it if not in jeopardy, then in a state of ambiguity. But his searching—if that's what it was—wasn't something he felt he could stop. Nor did he want to.

Reggie parked his car next to a gleaming red Dodge Ram. Out here, all the cops drove trucks to work as if they were cattle ranchers. The insides of the truck beds were unscratched and spotless; Reggie suspected they were used for little more than picking up potted plants at Home Depot for their wives, or occasionally moving a sofa for a buddy.

Mike Morrison turned out to be a young, round-faced fellow

who looked like he spent a lot of time mountain biking. He showed Reggie to an empty interrogation room. A blue three-ring murder book and a small evidence box were already set out on the table.

"We figure this is one of those cases that'll never get cleared, so any help you can give us would be great. If you get bored, I've got twenty others like it sitting on my desk. Can I get you coffee or anything?"

"Is it any good?"

"Are you kidding? It's the best. One of our guys has a wife who imports the stuff. We get freshly roasted Colombian every day."

"In that case, I'd love a cup."

After Morrison brought the coffee, he left Reggie alone. Reggie opened the murder book: lists of evidence and preliminary reports, statements from witnesses and patrol officers, photos of the arms, photos and crime-scene diagrams of where they'd washed up, a photo of the ring. He took the ring out of its double clear plastic envelope and passed it back and forth between his palms. He didn't know anything about diamonds. It was bigger than Audrey's ring but nothing fancy.

The detective's reports revealed little. Worse than a body dump, there was no evidence whatsoever from the crime scene. No witnesses. No murder weapon. Almost nothing to go on.

Reggie turned to the medical examiner's report. The bones in the right arm were bigger than those in the left, so it was assumed that the victim was right-handed. The medical examiner was 90 percent sure it was female because of the size of the arms and the fingernail polish. They could, however, be the arms of a small man, a transvestite, perhaps. The report estimated the height based on the length of the arms as being between five-two and five-eight. Weight based on height and frame was estimated at 110 to 140 pounds. Age anywhere from twenty to fifty. The hair on the forearms was fine and brown. A small scar on the left elbow. No tattoos or moles. Blood type was A positive, the second most common blood type. Tissue type was inconclusive. No fingerprint match.

The medical examiner found no fiber or skin under the fingernails, which wasn't surprising considering how long they'd been in the water. To rule out drowning as cause of death, the bone marrow was tested for diatom skeletons, a microscopic algae that penetrated lung tissue, then moved into the organs and bone marrow. The test was negative.

She'd been killed, then dumped into the ocean.

Reggie forced himself to look at the photographs. Both arms had been roughly severed by a sharp instrument; the medical examiner suggested a machete or a butcher knife. It must have made a terrible mess. Reggie didn't think the arms looked like Laura's. He remembered her striking out tentatively in class, then, as the weeks progressed, with more assurance, her triceps and deltoids gaining muscle mass. The arms in the pictures resembled chewed-up pieces of plastic. However, the medical examiner's profile was vague enough to include her. Reggie would see if he could find out Laura's blood type. Maybe in her employee records, if she'd participated in an office blood drive. He would ask Johnson. It was a long shot, but he couldn't get access to her medical records without a warrant.

Half an hour later, Morrison peeked into the room with freshly baked muffins. "Find anything interesting?"

"How far did you get with this case?" asked Reggie, taking a muffin. It was warm and smelled of cinnamon.

"The ME estimated the arms were two to six weeks old at the time they were found. We checked with Missing Persons for a Caucasian female in the previous three months. We thought a teenager from Torrance might fit the bill, but the blood types didn't match. We didn't take it much further. We've been kind of preoccupied."

"With the Westlake shootout?" Reggie had heard about the hostage situation at a bank three weeks before, when several cops and two suspects were shot. The suspects who had survived were now suing the county for racial profiling and excessive force.

"Yeah." Morrison's face assumed an expression that Reggie recognized, a look that said maybe the hassles of the job weren't worth it.

Reggie shook his head. "Any idea where the body was initially dumped?"

"Well, the currents at that time of year flow north. Assuming the arms were out there for three weeks, they could've been dumped down in Orange County, by the coast, or drifted in from miles offshore. We got maps of the currents from the Coast Guard, but they didn't really help much."

"Could I have copies?"

"Sure."

"Do you have any idea why the arms were found so far apart?"

"Again, two possibilities. Either they were dumped separately, or the parts got caught up in different currents. There were fish bites on both arms, so it's not inconceivable that fish carried the parts in different directions."

"Any attempt to locate the rest of the body?"

"We asked the Coast Guard to keep an eye out, but that's the most we could do. We can't dredge the ocean. We're not talking about John F. Kennedy Jr., after all."

Reggie shrugged. The inevitable and unmentionable truth—that the death of one person could be vastly more important than the death of another. At one time, black bodies were at the bottom of the list. Now it depended on the media. If television reporters took an interest, so did police. The arms had been newsworthy for a day.

"An unidentified body, no crime scene, no suspects. That pretty much sums it up?" Reggie took a bite of the muffin. He couldn't remember the last time he'd tasted something baked from scratch; it was great.

"Yup."

"How about this ring?"

"There's no inscription or initials or date. Looks pretty much like your average engagement ring. Matter of fact, it looks like my wife's."

"Mine, too. You didn't have it appraised or anything?"

"No. I guess we were kind of waiting for the rest of the body to show up. Without more to go on, it didn't seem like the ring could help us much."

"Could I keep the ring for a day or two? I'd like to take it to a jeweler. See if he might have an idea where it came from."

"Sure. Sign it out. I'll give you copies of anything else you want. This is not really what you'd call a hot case."

When Reggie got back to the office, he asked Velma to find out which appraiser the department used. She came back ten minutes later with the address of a guy on Fairfax.

That pleased him, because he thought he'd have a chance to stop by the farmers market and get some Ring of Fire hot sauce from a store called Hot, Hot, Hot. A peace offering for Audrey. She loved spicy sauces. It was starting to hurt his stomach, but he'd never tell her.

Connie wasn't the kind of girl to fuss about what to wear on a date, but there she was sitting in the middle of her bed in a white camisole and underpants, staring into her open closet, feeling completely defeated. It would help if she was sure what kind of date it was supposed to be. She hadn't gotten any real sense of what Scott expected. A date between friends, or did he want to start something up again? Should she wear sexy or casual? Makeup or no makeup?

Even when she called on clients, Connie seldom concerned herself about what to wear; she wore what she was selling—workout clothes. In a way, she thought of her muscles as clothes, something she put on to hide her true self. When people saw muscles, they saw discipline, drive, and determination. She knew it was a costume of strength over the pathetic weakness that she called herself.

Only another athlete could understand how weak she was, could know what it was like to swim the two-hundred-meter butterfly in 2:06:58, slower by a hundredth of a second than the winner, her will failing in the final nanoseconds, pulling back in despair, a secret even her coaches never knew, assuming it was fatigue when it was a weakness of another kind entirely. Only another athlete could understand the terrible ennui that had overtaken her in those moments before her hand slapped the side of the pool; it all seemed so pointless. She gave up swimming and took up kayaking, a sport in which, competing with nature, she was propelled across the finish line by a survival instinct. Now that, too, was over, and who was she but a girl with overdeveloped muscles who, as a teenager, didn't have time to date or socialize and never really learned how?

She scrutinized her shoulders, wondering if she should cover them or show them off. Did guys find muscles sexy? Or did they find them intimidating?

Finally, she decided on black satin pants and a clingy maroon top. She put on mascara and lipstick but ended up wiping off her mouth because she couldn't get the line right.

She had a fluttering in her stomach that she used to get before a meet; her fingers were trembling. Did she really like Scott that much? He was just a guy, charming, yes, good-looking, yes, but like many others. It made her mad. Here she'd spent almost her entire life, at least since she was eight, training her body to do what she commanded; then, at the prospect of a kind-of date with a sort-of-average guy, she completely lost control. She considered calling Scott to cancel. But out of some peculiar logic that came, she supposed, from years of living by workout schedules, she decided since she hadn't been on a date in several months, she needed the practice.

Because her house—perched on a ledge between the ocean and Pacific Coast Highway—was insulated from traffic noise, she didn't hear Scott's car drive up. When he tapped on the sliding glass doors to the deck, she jumped back in surprise. He was dressed in white slacks, a white V-neck sweater without a shirt, and expensive tan shoes with tassels. She didn't recognize him at first, grinning at her ear to ear, almost demented-looking. Through the double-paned glass, he mumbled something about the door being locked. When she unlocked the door and slid it open, a large wave crashed on the rocks below, distracting her for a brief moment, like a distant warning shot.

Scott walked in without kissing her. "Hey, sport. You ready to go?"

"Almost. Let me put on my shoes." She hurried into the bedroom and slipped on black patent-leather evening sandals with heels. Did he actually call her *sport*? Like he was somebody's uncle in a fifties sitcom? She stood and wobbled across the room, hoping for momentum to carry her through.

Scott paced back and forth, marveling at the view. That pleased her, but at the same time she felt vulnerable, as if she were revealing something intensely private. Yes, the view was great, but it meant so much more to her: the ocean, the waves, the dark storms, the tangerine sunsets, the dolphins and whales. In sharing her view, she revealed her soul, like an artist showing a painting that has taken months to finish. She felt dangerously exposed.

But he didn't sense any of this. He thought it was merely a spectacular view of the ocean. It seemed to her that a man who could love her would look out at the ocean, then turn and gaze into her eyes, understanding that she and this landscape were one. She reprimanded herself; she expected too much.

"Do you ever get water on your deck during storms?" Scott asked.

"Yes," she said nonchalantly, not for a moment revealing how the storms frightened and exhilarated her. "Where are we going?" she said to change the subject.

"It's a secret. You look great, by the way." He got that odd grin again. He helped Connie on with her sweater. She grabbed her purse and locked the sliding glass door. Then they went out the side door and up the stairs that climbed the hill to the garage.

They drove in silence. It was a little cool for the convertible top to be down, and Connie wondered whether Scott wasn't intentionally postponing conversation, or if it was some kind of macho vanity, showing off for the cars coming in the other direction, a proclamation that he was single, free, cruising the California coast with a babe at his side. She pulled her sweater tightly around her, fists under her armpits, getting mad, but not exactly sure why.

They cruised down Pacific Coast Highway, the sun setting over the ocean on the right, the Palisades pleated with dark shadows on the left. As the colors bled to gray, a mist rose from the surface of the water. A mile out, a light from a single sailboat running its motor, trying to make the marina before fog set in.

Scott and Connie made good time. Rush-hour traffic was headed in the other direction. Scott turned up the California Incline and stopped at a light before pulling on to Ocean Avenue in Santa Monica. At the next light, he turned to her and asked, "How would you like to be engaged?"

"Engaged in what?"

He laughed. "Engaged to be married."

"To you?"

"Yes. Who else?" He turned right on San Vicente. "I told my mother I would bring my fiancée over for dinner. You're my fiancée."

When she realized he was serious, a wave of anger crashed over her. The date was apparently a ruse. Her head wobbled in confusion. He was using her, asking her—for some reason he had yet to reveal—to impersonate a fiction, to lie to his mother. She, no doubt, was getting him off the hook for something. Yet despite her anger, another part of her was curious, perhaps even flattered. He had chosen her, after all. "Why me?" she managed to say.

"Because if I were ever to marry, you'd be the type of girl I'd ask."

A bucket of ice water couldn't have surprised her more, her fury quick-freezing to doubt. Had she misread him? There it was: sincerity, a gentleness in his face, his crooked, abashed smile. He thought that much of her? No, he had to be lying.

Perhaps if she were a better-looking girl, a more feminine girl, perhaps if she had a job that gave her more of an opportunity to meet men, perhaps if she were not twenty-nine and had yet to have a relationship with even a remote possibility of growing into marriage, perhaps if she didn't have three siblings, all married with children, perhaps then she would have asked Scott to stop the car, and taken a taxi home.

But she didn't.

In a matter of seconds, she swallowed her pride and convinced herself she was game, up for a lark, a good sport, ready to pull a caper. "Sure," she said. "Why not?"

His mother's house was a large Mediterranean affair in Bel Air, bubblegum pink with a front lawn the size of a golf course. They rang the doorbell. Scott's sister Samantha answered it. The look she gave Connie was not particularly kind.

Scott's mother sashayed toward them from the living room with a gin and tonic in hand. Connie's impression was of a woman working hard to hang on to her youth, her dreams, her sexual appeal. The impression was anything but appealing. It wasn't her obvious face-lifts or her silicone implants or her thick makeup that made her so appalling, but her aggressive chattiness. Connie saw in her everything she disliked about women, everything she hoped never to be. Then she scolded herself for being so critical: Mrs. Goodsell had not been born this way; surely she'd been driven to create this Medusa by a life of crushing disappointments, by Madison Avenue marketing campaigns and bogus Hollywood images. Mrs. Goodsell wasn't shallow; she was the product of a woman's deepest despair.

Connie resolved to find a way to like her.

"I'm so glad to meet one of Scott's girlfriends." Mrs. Goodsell sang her words, like a librarian reading to a circle of preschoolers. "He keeps them secret, you know. I'm afraid he's ashamed of us." With both hands, Mrs. Goodsell clasped Connie's extended hand. Her fingers were thin, her skin shiny and unnaturally smooth, like an old woman's. Her grip was tight.

"Mother, don't be rude. Besides, it isn't true. I'm sorry, Connie." Scott put his arm around Connie's shoulders, then said, "Mother, I want you to meet the girl I plan to marry."

Connie couldn't tell if the look Mrs. Goodsell gave her was

skeptical or pitying. Whatever it was passed quickly into an effusive warmth that felt as impervious as a pink vinyl raincoat. Connie supposed this must be normal social behavior for a woman of Bel Air.

Social grace was not one of those things Connie—a farm girl from Wyoming—felt she understood very well. Like Mrs. Goodsell asking her to call her by her first name, Bunny. How could she possibly call her Bunny? But if she called her Mrs. Goodsell, the woman would be sure to take offense. Connie decided to solve the problem by avoiding the need to address her at all.

"Has he given you the ring yet?" asked Mrs. Goodsell.

Connie glanced over at Scott, not sure how to respond. She suddenly became aware of Samantha standing behind them, listening intently, and it occurred to her there was something more here than a simple question. Scott answered for her. "Of course, Mother. At Geoffrey's, in Malibu. I got down on one knee and everything."

"Ooooo . . . Let me see it," Bunny said enthusiastically, like Connie's best girlfriend.

"Sorry, Mom. It's being repaired. I guess it had been so long since it was worn, the diamond fell out of its setting. I had to take it to a jeweler. It had to be resized, too. Grandma had big hands, you know. Should be ready in a week or so."

"You should've told me, Scott. I would have sent you to my jeweler on Rodeo Drive."

"Don't worry, Mother. I found someone good."

"Are you sure he's reputable? I've heard of jewelers switching diamonds with fakes."

"He's very reputable, Mother. My boss's wife recommended him." Scott knew his mother would respect a woman's opinion in such circumstances.

Connie saw Mrs. Goodsell and Samantha exchange looks. It didn't occur to her until they had finished dinner and were eating dessert—a tiramisu from Beverly Hills, ladyfingers soaked in espresso and brandy, slathered with marsala-laced mascarpone and chocolate, all of which melted on her tongue like twilight over a hot sandy beach—that this whole painful charade had something to do with the ring.

Scott knew he'd been somewhat unfair, bringing Connie into this viper's den, but she handled it well, answering his mother's annoying questions with ease: "What is it you do, Connie? Where are you from, Connie? What do your parents do? Where did you go to school? Wasn't it hard to do all that training and have a social life? They cut you from the swim team, so you took up kayaking? Wasn't that hard, dear?"

Connie fielded the questions brilliantly, briefly answering each, then spinning off into a short amusing anecdote. She didn't even know she was being charming. He couldn't have asked for a better performance. He was beginning to feel like they really were engaged, and to feel oddly protective of her.

"Do you need to ask so many questions, Mother? You have a whole lifetime to get to know her."

"But she's so interesting. I can't imagine how you managed to snag such a gem."

Scott was so used to his mother scooping on an insult along with her compliments that he hardly heard it. For some reason, he thought of a fairy tale about two sisters: Whenever the older sister opened her mouth, out popped a toad. It occurred to him that he had been raised in a family of toad-talkers.

Samantha was being uncharacteristically quiet, eyeing Connie and his mother as if she were plotting something. He decided to ignore her.

After two glasses of wine, his mother started in on questions about their impending marriage, not, he suspected, to satisfy her curiosity but to embarrass him. "So, do you plan to have children? Where are you going to live? What religion are you, Connie? Will you get married in a church?" Bunny smiled, poised with a morsel of food on her fork. Then, after asking a question, she delicately rested the fork on her tongue while slipping the food off with her teeth.

Scott wanted to jam that fork down her throat. He'd have loved to see her eyes bug out in surprise as she grabbed her throat, gagging. He grew immensely bored and irritated. His eyes drifted around the dinner table as he imagined how he would kill each of the women. Poison would be the easiest. Get them all at once.

He felt himself drifting apart from his body, above the conversation: as if watching strangers, not people, even, but characters in a movie, cartoons, and as the director, he could move these globs of clay at will. Such a strange sensation he was having, floating above the dinner table. Was it the overhead lights, too bright for dinner? He wasn't drunk. He'd been careful not to drink much this evening—a beer, that was all. Maybe it was the air, all these women's smells, pussy, perfumes, and cosmetics polluting the air, transforming oxygen to ether, making him light-headed. Or maybe it was the food, his mother finally deciding to kill him off, to rid herself of any male in her life. He always suspected she hated him underneath all her doting and teasing. Whoever thought that the teasing that went on in families was a display of affection had never been teased. Teasing, he decided, was pure hate.

Finally, they were able to leave. As Scott said good night to his mother, he placed his arms around her shoulders, pulling her in, then kissed her on the left cheek, close to but not on her mouth, thinking for a moment of his college graduation, of seeing his buddies kiss their mothers on the mouth, how revolting he found it, and how his mother seemed shorter than she once did, and frailer, and it occurred to him that he could snap her like chicken bones if he wanted, and in feeling his power over her and imagining how delicious the crack of her neck would sound, he wondered why more people didn't murder their mothers.

PART FOUR

SEXT

Audrey announced that she was taking the boys over summer vacation to her family's estate in Oak Bluffs on Martha's Vineyard.

Reggie should have known then what was up. She'd always claimed she didn't want the boys anywhere near all that, and now she was proposing that they sail each day with the black princes and princesses of America. Hadn't he listened to her rant—for eighteen years—against her family, about how she despised the culture of elite clubs, coteries, and cotillions, complaints so far from Reggie's life experience that it seemed like something out of *Star Wars*. Hadn't he listened to her childhood story of riding in the back of the family Mercedes down K Street in Washington, D.C., of peeking out the tinted glass windows to see black children running through spouting fire hydrants, cooling off from the swampy summer heat that settled over the city like sludge, and she, chilled to the bone from the air-conditioning, begging her mother to stop so she could play with the other kids, longing to soak her clothes and splash and giggle, and her mother saying, as she said so many times before and after, *You play with your own kind of people.*

Audrey's childhood had included weekends with the Jack and Jill Club, a by-invitation-only social club for elite black children, and summers at Martha's Vineyard or Sag Harbor. She was a graduate of Georgetown Day School and a debutante presented by the most prestigious (black-elite-by-invitation-only) Washington men's club, the Bachelor-Benedict Club. Her father, Lawrence Syphax Carol, traced his descendants back to Charles Syphax and the illegitimate daughter of George Washington Parke Custis, grandson of Martha Washington. The Carols had been wealthy for over 150 years, a most important family of the Washington black upper class. They socialized neither with whites nor with common blacks but solely within a circle of established, elite black Washington families. Their children were expected to become doctors or lawyers; no other occupations would do. They were expected to attend one of three black colleges—Howard, Spelman, Morehouse—or perhaps Harvard. No other schools would do. They would marry within their own class, their own race, from a "good family," someone with skin no darker than a paper bag, hair straight as a ruler. They would marry an Episcopalian. No other religion would do. And don't even think—not in a million years—about marrying a white.

Few elite black children rebelled; they might whine and occasionally get wild, but to reject all that wealth, power, and history, to try to survive the urban jungle, to breathe the anxious anger of an underclass, to suffer the scorn of white trash? It wasn't done.

But that was precisely what Audrey did. Even at a young age, she preferred playing with the maid's little girl to the daughters of her mother's friends in their starched dresses, starched accents, and starched postures. At school she sought out the scholarship kids. She grimly attended the Jack and Jill black-tie dances and backyard tennis parties, but they seemed to her so phony, clinging to the manners and concerns of another era. None of it seemed to have anything to do with her or the life she saw around her. She spent most of her time reading in her room.

At seventeen, she chose to go to UCLA. Her parents were horrified. She would be mixing with kids from South Central Los Angeles? Hadn't she seen videos of the riots? No better than niggers. Did she really want to be around such people? Finally, they relented. UCLA was a good school, after all, with an excellent premed program.

There she fell in love with Reggie, tar black, kinky-haired, Catholic, ghetto-born and -raised, who wanted to be a cop. Wasn't that why she loved him, because he was the opposite of everything her family wanted for her?

But now she was leaving him.

It was only when she told Reggie she might interview at Georgetown University Law School that he fully understood. When he asked her to talk about it, she flew into a fury, saying she was tired of talking about how they never talked. She needed some time to herself, she said, and it didn't take a genius to see he was having an affair, and if he wanted to save their marriage, he'd better do some soul-searching himself while she was away. She hadn't given up her life to watch him drift away and dump her for a younger woman. A white woman, at that.

As usual, she did the talking. Reggie listened, astonished. His head spun, shards of glass scratching at the base of his skull. How had it come to this?

"I called for you at the Tae Kwon Do studio. They said you'd canceled classes for a month. That's not what you told me when you left the house this morning."

Reggie had canceled classes so he would have time to investigate. They had seemed so empty without Laura. His heart wasn't in it.

"I don't want any confessions," she said. "I don't want to

hear your denials. I don't want to hear anything about it. I just want you to figure out what you really want, Reggie."

He didn't bother denying an affair. He took her hands and kissed her fingertips, then pressed her buttercup palms against either side of his face and held them there. He felt such a terrible yearning in his chest that it almost creaked like a wooden hull. He reached across the deck of his boat to her, his prow banging against the dock, waves rolling beneath him, his stomach lurching, the tethers loosening; he was slipping away. He clung desperately to her, but he risked pulling her into the water. He imagined her sinking beneath the waves, her face upturned, gasping for air, then tranquil, transforming slowly into . . . *Laura?*

Laura's image jolted him, burned through the center of him like a torch. It was wrong. He must stop it. He needed to tell Audrey he loved her, needed her, but while this was true, and while everything that nourished him—air, food, light, love—was Audrey and only Audrey, he relaxed his grip and let go.

He looked up to see her angry eyes softening to worry. He held her gaze, seeing beyond her to a blank future. "I'll miss you, babe," he said, his voice husky with emotion.

That melted her.

She pulled him close, pressing her mouth to his so hard he cut his lips on his own teeth. She gasped as if pricked by a pin, her hands diving under his shirt collar, pulling off his clothes as she tore off her own, pressing against his skin as if she were trying to get inside, running her tongue down his chest and between his abdominal muscles, her thumbs massaging small urgent circles on the inside of his thighs until he was hard, his breath short. But after they made love, she started to cry, angry again, hitting him softly with her fists. She was sick and tired of having sex every time they ought to be talking, and sex didn't solve anything and she was still going and he'd better think about what his priorities were because she was ready to move on if that's how things were gonna be.

Now the house was empty. For the first time since he'd come out to Los Angeles twenty years ago, he was utterly alone.

He sat in the living room in the dark. His eyes were drawn to the Tiffany chandelier over the dining room table in the next room, a room they never used except to pass through.

Would he leave his family for Laura? No. That was ridiculous. She had never expressed interest in him that way. Besides, she'd packed up and disappeared. But what if Laura called him up, said she wanted to see him, reached out to him for comfort, her graceful white arms trembling with fear and passion? Could it work? Even in Los Angeles, mixed relationships were problematic, and she was ten, fifteen years younger than he, so East Coast sophisticated, and they couldn't possibly live here in Inglewood, and would his sons get teased at school, and . . .

Stop it! That wasn't how he wanted her. An affair. It wasn't like that, not at all.

But why couldn't he stop thinking about her?

Was this yearning merely a biological drive to spread his sperm among as many available females as possible? No. It was desire beyond lust, a yearning that made him jittery and hungry. It made him want to leap off the earth and fling himself into outer space.

He understood why Audrey had to leave. Her pain and frustration were like knives in his chest. Why couldn't he reach out to the woman he loved, who meant everything to him? It was something he couldn't explain. Part of him felt that if he gave in to Audrey, he would be settling; not in the sense of settling for a lesser woman—Audrey was the most beautiful and vibrant woman he'd ever met—but missing out on some unexplored aspect of himself. In a way, it felt wrong to succumb to Audrey, as if he would be neglecting his mission in life.

Laura was different. He imagined that Laura could see in him something Audrey never would: the man in him beyond the sexual man, the workingman, the political man. Man as he stands naked before God.

Why couldn't he reveal this man to Audrey? Perhaps she knew him too well. Perhaps he couldn't show such vulnerability (if that's what it was) to the woman who depended on him to be strong, the man in the family. Perhaps he couldn't risk her not liking this man.

He then understood that this was exactly what Audrey wanted, what maddened her, what drove her away. She wanted him to reveal his true self.

And yet he couldn't. It was to Laura he desired to reveal this man, not Audrey.

It was as if his life depended on it.

Scott was late for another showing. He locked up and was headed out the door when the phone rang. He dashed back to grab it.

"Hello, is this Scott?" a woman's voice asked.

"Sure is, sweetheart. What's up?"

"Listen, dickhead, I'm not one of your bimbos. You got that? So don't even think of using that Dean Martin women-melt-when-they-see-me voice."

"Who is this?"

"This is Vivian. Laura's friend from New York."

Scott suppressed a groan. "I should've recognized you by your lyrical phrasing." Scott had first met Vivian on a vacation he and Laura took to Manhattan. He thought her loud and bossy, and recalled that all through their dinner at the Russian Tea Room, she had grilled him hard. She had acted so possessive that later, he asked Laura if Vivian was a lesbian. Laura had laughed and said definitely not, but he suspected that

Laura was naively mistaken and thought it might be interesting to check it out for himself.

"Look, bastard"—that voice again—"I'm not going to waste my time with you. I want to know where Laura is."

"I haven't a clue." Scott knew he couldn't use the ill-mother story—Vivian knew Laura's mother was dead.

"She isn't answering her e-mails, so I called, and her phone's been disconnected."

"Maybe she's run off with her new boyfriend."

"She doesn't have a new boyfriend. She'd tell me if she did. Anyhow, she wouldn't go anywhere without telling me."

"She must've lost her head." Scott smiled to himself. "You know how it is when you're in love. Or maybe you don't."

"Fuck you. What did you do to her? Did she have to get an unlisted number because you were harassing her? She told me about you stalking her, shithead."

"I don't know where she is, and I don't care." That was half true; he often found himself wondering where she might've drifted. "I haven't spoken with her in months."

"That's not what she told me."

"She made it clear she didn't want to see me, and I respect her decision."

"You are so full of shit."

"They teach you to talk like that at Vassar?"

"Fuck you."

"I'm sure you'd like to; but alas, you're in New York, and I'm in Los Angeles."

"Listen, prick, I'm on the next plane out if you don't tell me where Laura is."

"Let me know when, and I'll pick you up at the airport. It'd be delightful to see you again."

Vivian gave a contemptuous laugh. "Yeah, right. I don't know what you're up to, but trust me, I'm gonna find out."

Scott was pretty sure she was blowing smoke. Even if she did come to L.A., what could she do? She'd get the sick-mother story. No one knew anything he hadn't told them. It had been a month since the arms washed up. The papers were filled with tales of new violence: a teacher in upscale Brentwood shot by an eight-year-old; a hostage situation on the pier; riots at the Democratic National Convention. The cops were busy. No one was likely to make a connection.

"I'm sorry I can't help you, Vivian. I'm sure she'll call and entertain you with the details of her new affair. Or maybe she's afraid you'll scare him off."

"Fuck you."

"It's so nice to hear your voice, Vivian. Feel free to call again."

Scott hung up thinking he had handled that pretty well.

Vivian slammed down the telephone, her body trembling. Something was wrong. She was sure Laura was in trouble.

She looked around at the SoHo gallery she owned. She was in the middle of hanging a new exhibit, and of course, Amaldo hadn't shown up to help her. The huge framed photographs leaned against the walls. The lights would have to be changed for photography. They would take until midnight to finish.

Vivian was excited about the new exhibit, a new batch of the highly erotic photography of Wendy Sharpe. This batch was full of dismembered mannequins, grotesquely arranged in pornographic poses, interposed with young naked models and fake blood. When Wendy first showed Vivian her new work, she said somewhat apologetically that she was going through a divorce. Vivian didn't need an apology. The work was brilliant. It was hot.

All of Wendy's work was highly controversial. Feminists called it misogynistic, others thought it liberating. One famous feminist accused Wendy of "trying to set back the women's movement to the time of the Salem witch trials." This stuff would knock their socks off. It made Mapplethorpe look like Norman Rockwell. Well, not quite. But controversy was good. Controversy meant big sales. Vivian would price them at thirty thousand apiece.

She admitted that she found the work disturbing. The composition and colors were beautiful until you realized what the pink chunks and red blotches were. The pictures made Vivian's heart hurt; they made her think of Laura. She'd been trying to get ahold of her since Wendy came in last week with her new work.

Vivian dragged the stepladder to the wall and lifted up a photo she particularly liked, a waifish model in a T-shirt and white socks, face streaked with tears, sitting cross-legged, genitals exposed, plastic body parts and fake insects strewn around her. It was pure Stephen King.

When Vivian stood back to see if it was hung right, she thought again of Laura. She didn't know why. Perhaps the model looked a little like her, straight dark hair pulled forward as if to hide her face. Not that Laura ever wore her hair that way, but there was something—a common woundedness.

Vivian remembered touring Europe with Laura one summer during college. Vivian had been hit with hepatitis in Florence. She had a fever for weeks, diarrhea, vomiting. She couldn't remember half of what Laura did for her. When the fever finally broke, she found herself in a bed beneath a window that looked out over an orchard of almond trees. It was an ancient one-story country house in Tavarnuzze, a tiny town just south of Florence, in rolling hills of olive groves and Chianti vineyards. It had cool red tile floors and thick stone walls. There was no glass in the windows, only thick wooden shutters they closed at night. On a rough kitchen table sat a vase of freshly cut daffodils and iris.

Vivian learned later that when she first got sick, Laura went to the American embassy and got the name of a doctor who taught at the American University in town. He diagnosed her and told Laura that Vivian couldn't travel for at least a month. The family of his Italian wife had a weekend cottage; he arranged for the two to stay there. Laura nursed Vivian for six weeks, fed her, helped her learn to walk again. When Vivian was well enough to ask Laura to keep track of the costs so she could pay her back, Laura dismissed it with a flick of her hand and ignored Vivian whenever she tried to bring it up again. As soon as Vivian was well, they traveled on to Greece and Turkey as if nothing had ever happened.

Vivian was sure Laura had saved her life. She felt a ferocious loyalty to her.

After college, when they shared an apartment in New York, Vivian became a maniac at the slightest perceived injustice against Laura. She was a pit bull sniffing out a crackhead, a grizzly bear guarding her cubs. The punk who whistled at Laura, the slimy landlord who made a pass, the doctors who said Laura could never dance again, none of them saw it coming, a whirling dervish of fury completely out of proportion to the transgression.

It frightened Vivian, this violent protectiveness that overtook her, even after Laura moved to California. If, when she called from Los Angeles, Laura complained about a boyfriend or someone at work, Vivian felt a madness smolder inside her. She would be preoccupied for days, wondering what she could do to solve Laura's problem. She jogged around Central Park, exhausted herself at the gym, but nothing gave her relief. There was nothing she could do, nothing she *should* do. Laura was a grown woman who could take care of herself.

Or could she?

Vivian knew Laura needed her now. She was in danger. Vivian could feel it. After the opening this Friday, she would let Amaldo run the gallery and do the follow-up. She could take a week off. She hadn't seen Laura in almost a year, and she missed her. Besides, she had some business to do in Los Angeles, clients to see, new artists to check out.

Vivian could already smell the jasmine, sage, and eucalyptus—the moist, fragrant air of Los Angeles.

Reggie felt a burst of energy, the energy of the righteous, the sheriff, the cowboy in a white hat. He drove up Fairfax Avenue to Third, then turned in to the farmers market parking lot.

That morning he'd woken from a fabulously sexy dream. Audrey was in it, and Laura, too. He was amazed at how a dream could set up your day and linger, even if you couldn't really remember it. Sometimes his dreams were so intense that he woke up more tired than when he went to sleep. Those were the dreams that replayed his day, the dead bodies and lying perps. Other times he woke up jubilant, kicking at the sheets like a kid, joyful to get out of bed. That was the way it had been this morning. He woke up diagonally across the bed, and his first thought was how great it was to have it to himself. He tried to dive back into that luscious luminosity, but the images grew faint, drying up as quickly as breath on a mirror.

Some of it he could remember. Audrey was grinding millet on a rock in a dusty desert village in Africa. Laura knelt beside her, rolling an oblong stone over the grain, back and forth, her braid swishing like the tail of a contented cow. Both were wrapped in bright red cloth with gold flecks. They chatted and laughed and seemed to be enjoying each other's company. When Reggie approached them, Laura stood up. "You found me," she said. "I've been waiting." She motioned him to follow her. She led him over rippling hills of hot sand, and as she walked, the red cloth unraveled from her body, and he walked over it like a red carpet. At the edge of a beautiful blue lake, she stood naked. She turned to him: her breasts small and round, her stomach dipping between her hip bones, swelling slightly above her pubic hair. She walked to him and unbuttoned his shirt, kissing his chest, slipping her hands under his shirt and pushing it aside as if brushing off a snowy windshield to peek within. Her long hair caressed his body, warming him like the winter sun, filling the air with her almond scent. She peeled off all his clothes and led him into the lake. Underwater, they swam past pink scaffolds of coral and tropical fish. He was amazed he could breathe, and she said, "Of course you can breathe underwater." As they swam, she slipped her hand around his penis and slid it inside of her, and then they were on the deck of a sailboat making love, the hot sun pouring down over them, and he had never felt so pure in his life, the white sailboat, the blue water, and Laura's red lips.

He woke to the sun pouring through the windows. Last night he'd been too tired to pull the curtains; it felt wonderful to bake under the sheets. As Laura's image faded, a feeling, more than a thought, flowed through his body: *I'll find you, Laura.* He was fully aroused and rubbed his hand over his penis; he groaned softly, then scrambled out of bed.

His arrested arousal propelled him through coffee and a shortened jujitsu routine. He showered and dressed quickly. As he shot out of the house to West Hollywood, he wondered why he didn't feel guilty for the fantasy. But he didn't. He felt great.

The farmers market was bustling with shoppers and tourists—mostly beefy white midwesterners with cameras around their necks. Older European immigrants chatted with their favorite vendors, stopping for a particular sausage or jam they could get only there. Reggie pushed his way through the crowd to a stand covered in red-and-white-striped awning called Hot, Hot, Hot. For sale were hundreds of small bottles with vibrant red and yellow labels depicting dancing devils, flames, and hot peppers with pitchforks, grinning malevolently. The sauces were rated on a scale of one to four for hotness. Reggie smiled, planning how he'd box them up and send them to Washington. He bought a half-dozen bottles rated four, a hot mustard, and a jumbo bottle of Audrey's staple, Ring of Fire. It was so hot that his fingers stung from the residue on the outside of the bottle.

He locked his treasures in his trunk, then drove down Fairfax to a small jewelry store between a Jewish delicatessen and an Indian restaurant.

In contrast to the dirt and grime of the street, the store was immaculate. A tall man in his mid-fifties raised his head. A loupe protruded from his left eye; when he focused on Reggie, it dropped neatly into his hand.

"Good morning. I'm Reggie Brooks, from Pacific Division. I called about an hour ago. Are you Mr. Feinstein?"

"Of course." The man said this without expression, without inflection. "You mentioned a ring?"

"Yes." Reggie pulled the evidence bag from his pocket, shook the ring into his hand, and laid it on the counter. He glanced behind Feinstein, noticing a dozen antique clocks that said exactly the same time, the second hands rotating in concert like the legs of synchronized swimmers.

With the solemnity of a priest, Feinstein washed his hands at a small porcelain sink behind him. He then cleaned the diamond with a cloth dampened in ethyl alcohol. He worked efficiently, his movements as measured as a metronome.

Reggie listened to the faint ticking of the clocks and to the ambulance sirens arriving at the hospitals nearby.

Feinstein took off his glasses, then placed the ring beneath a ten-power triplet loupe, which he had wiped with a lint-free cloth. As he worked, he sucked in air through his nose every twenty seconds or so, punctuating his thoughts. He switched on a fluorescent lamp and stood close to it as he looked through the loupe. He stepped back almost immediately, with a surprised expression.

"What?" asked Reggie.

Feinstein hesitated. "Let me look again." He peered for a long minute. He then took the ring over to a microscope. His little gasping sounds took on the rhythm of a spouting dolphin. From under the counter, he pulled out something that looked like a Walkman with a pen attached.

"What's that?" asked Reggie.

"This is a Gem pocket diamond tester," Feinstein explained. "Since diamonds conduct heat better than imitations, this little machine tests for a stone's thermal conductivity." He ran the pen along a facet of the stone. The machine beeped three times. "Well, it's real," he said, grinning. "Both of them."

His exaggerated triumph puzzled Reggie. "What?"

Feinstein shushed him, then placed the ring on what looked like a miniature set of white stairs. He set a master stone next to it for comparison. "See the color?"

"No."

"Precisely. It's colorless. A colorless grade D."

"Grade D? Is that like failing?"

"On the contrary. The GIA—that's the Gemological Institute of America—has a grading system from D to Z-plus. Grade D is the highest grade."

"Is it valuable?"

"Well, before I'd certify it, I'd want to run it by a spectroscope to see how it absorbs light. It's possible someone's come up with a substance that would fool the Gem pocket tester. I doubt it, but it's possible."

"But you think it's valuable."

"Let me put it this way: In this diamond, you have no cracks, no scratches, no blemishes, no crystals within the crystal, no inclusions—"

"Inclusions?"

"Internal irregularities. There are no grain lines, no laser drill holes, no clouding. Most diamonds have these little faults. It's not really a bad thing. They make each diamond unique, and it helps identify each particular diamond."

"Like a fingerprint?"

"Exactly. But this diamond is flawless, the highest grade of clarity for diamonds. In the GIA clarity grades, it's an F1. They are extremely rare and extremely valuable. In fact, flawless diamonds are seldom used in jewelry, because any wear might make them lose their flawless status, which would decrease their value. Combine a two-carat flawless, a grade-D colorless, an excellent cut, and we're looking at about fifty thousand dollars wholesale."

Reggie whistled and suddenly felt oddly nervous. "But it looks so simple. Even my wife's looks more expensive, and I bought it for her in college."

"If it were simply looks, people would buy cubic zirconia. They are more brilliant, more perfect, and, of course, far less expensive."

"You said something about both of them?"

Feinstein grinned. "May I take the stone out of the setting?"

"Sure, if you can put it back."

"That won't be a problem." Feinstein walked into his office and brought out a canvas roll of small hand tools. He put the ring in a vise, then popped out the stone with a tool. He peered at the setting and let out a triumphant laugh. He showed the ring to Reggie.

"You broke the diamond?" Reggie asked.

"No, no." The jeweler set one diamond on top of the other. "Incredibly clever, the way he lined up the facets, so you'd never know. Let me take a closer look." Feinstein removed the second diamond—which was smaller and bluish—weighed it, then set it under the microscope. He inhaled so loudly, so abruptly, that Reggie thought he might be choking. "It's a flawless, a rare blue, a little over a carat. We're talking a couple hundred thousand dollars."

"I don't understand," said Reggie. "The jeweler who made the ring was obviously trying to hide its worth. But why would he do that? And why would someone put so much money into a ring that looks so simple?"

"To transport wealth from one country to another unnoticed. To customs agents or anyone else, it would look like a rather ordinary engagement ring."

"Can you tell where it was made?"

"I can hazard a guess. The top stone has forty-nine facets, which places it as a European cut from the thirties or forties. Also, the table—that's the flat part on top—is large, perhaps sixty-five percent of the girdle diameter. A large table is preferred by Europeans. American tables are around fifty-three percent of the girdle diameter. The setting is platinum, which is more valuable than eighteen-karat gold. It's a prong-set solitaire designed for two stones, hand-fabricated rather than cast or die-struck. The inside is well worn, but I bet you anything that if you use an infrared camera, you'll find a faint outline of a jeweler's mark. Maybe even an inscription. I would guess that it was made in Switzerland or Austria in the early forties."

"It's an antique?"

"Not quite. My guess is that it was brought over by a Jewish family fleeing Nazi Germany who wanted to carry their wealth easily and inconspicuously."

"A family heirloom?"

"Possibly. It's a remarkable ring. An inexperienced appraiser might think it was a fake, because the gem is so perfect. He might even miss the second stone."

Reggie recalled once commenting on Laura's blue eyes and dark brown hair, and she had said that both her parents were Black Irish. So it probably wasn't an heirloom from her family. She was almost engaged to Scott Goodsell. But Goodsell wasn't a Jewish name, either. Perhaps the ring came from his mother's side?

Reggie realized he was getting ahead of himself. There was no proof that the arms were Laura's. "Anything else you can tell me?"

Feinstein put the stones back in the setting. "Be careful with it. If you get even a scratch on either stone, you lower its value by tens of thousands of dollars."

Reggie asked for a written appraisal, which Feinstein said he'd fax over that afternoon. Reggie gave him Mike Morrison's fax number, and Feinstein promised to send a copy to the sheriff's department as well.

Carrying around a ring worth several hundred thousand dollars made Reggie exceedingly uncomfortable. He wasn't sure if it was fear of losing it or temptation that made him sweat, followed by guilt, because he *was* tempted. Wasn't it only human to imagine, if only for a moment, possessing all that money, taking Audrey and the boys away from Los Angeles, maybe to Belize? Shame washed over him like a waterfall hidden beneath a jungle canopy.

As he drove down Wilshire Boulevard, he wondered what might be etched inside the ring. As far as he knew, Parker Center was the only forensic lab in town with a camera that could do an infrared test, and he knew he couldn't get access to it without going through official channels.

Then he remembered an expert witness, Françoise Augier, hired by the district attorney for a case he'd worked on several years ago. She'd used an infrared camera to authenticate a painting by Dosso Dossi, stolen in transit to the Getty. Art thieves were getting as clever as bank robbers; valuables were most vulnerable in transit, and unfortunately, museums couldn't hire an armored truck every time they wanted to borrow a painting.

Françoise Augier's shop, Dubois Gallery, sat between two antique stores near Robertson and Olympic. The decor of the shop was vaguely Victorian. Maroon Oriental carpets, dark wood tables topped with slabs of white marble, two cloisonné vases, and a coffee table with a collection of Sotheby catalogs. The walls were covered in masterpieces Reggie recognized: Picasso, Cézanne, Degas, van Gogh, da Vinci. It took him a moment to realize they all had to be forgeries.

Françoise Augier greeted Reggie warmly. Thin and brittle, in sensible shoes and a skirt that hung below her knees, she looked like a schoolmarm from the fifties. But she was the exact opposite of her appearance: warm and genuine, unlike other gallery owners on Melrose, where the general deportment was sarcastic elitism. Despite her age, which Reggie estimated to be near sixty, she had no wrinkles.

After Reggie explained what he needed, it took her under fifteen minutes to set up a camera rigged to intense lights and magnification lenses. She shot ten photos to make sure she got the entire inner circumference of the ring. She told Reggie she'd get the photos developed that evening and have them ready the next day.

Before he left, Reggie asked Françoise if she could find the gallery that handled the Belgian sculptor Jean Boulogne, or if she knew how to contact him in Europe. She said that would be simple. She'd let him know that afternoon.

As Reggie stepped out of the gallery, a tall man dressed head to foot in black leather walked past, banging hard against Reggie's shoulder. The man didn't even glance back.

Instinctively, Reggie put his hand in his pocket to see if the ring was still there. Of course it was, but as he made his way back to the car, he checked on it a half-dozen times. He knew his stomach wouldn't settle down until he returned the ring to Mike Morrison later that afternoon.

Whoever invented liquid soap must have been gay.

This was what Scott was thinking as he stood in the yellow-tiled shower at his gym, squirting handfuls of soap into his palm, then smearing it over his arms and thighs. He imagined a shower room of butt-naked men massaging their sperm over one another, then thought of the night when he was naked and got blood all over his arms and chest. He lifted his palm into the cascading water and imagined himself an Aztec priest standing high above a crowd, ripping out the heart of a young warrior whose spilled blood assured the fertility of the soil and swaying stalks of corn.

Someone opened the door to the men's locker room; cool air rushed in. Despite the sting of hot water shooting down Scott's back, a chill spread over his skin.

He'd done nothing to feel guilty about. He chastised himself for his attacks of panic. He'd done what needed to be done—a sacrifice that assured the continuity of life—his life.

He put his head under the spray and scrubbed his scalp vigorously. He should be celebrating—he'd closed his third sale this month, which made him Bay City's number one Realtor. He ought to call someone and go out for a nice dinner, but all he could think was that it wouldn't be any fun, not without

Laura. Then he realized: Today was the anniversary of when they first met. Funny he should remember it.

They'd met in the produce section at Gelson's. He saw her with a red plastic basket on her arm, looking at the stacks of avocados and tomatoes. It was the kind of grocery store where a clerk rearranged the fruit and vegetables as soon as you took one. Of course, you paid double for the privilege of seeing such perfect pyramids of produce, but no one seemed to mind. Laura stood there staring at the fruit. When she felt Scott watching her, she turned and looked at him. There was a kind of panic in her eyes, then interest; she held his gaze until he felt he had to say something.

"You can touch them, you know."

She smiled. "They're beautiful," she said.

Scott was fascinated. Was she crazy? She didn't look it. She was gorgeous. What kind of woman got mesmerized looking at fruit and vegetables? He had to find out.

"You want an avocado?" he asked.

She nodded.

He put his fingers around a dark green fruit in the middle of the stack. He glanced over at her, daring her to dare him. Her eyes—God, they were beautiful, cobalt blue—got big, and one corner of her mouth lifted. Slowly, he pulled out the avocado, holding out his other hand, like a magician casting a spell, to keep the pile from collapsing. He offered it to her and bowed.

Then she laughed. It was like wind chimes—no, more beautiful than that: like the wind blowing through a cave, playing crystal stalactites.

He glanced doubtfully at the avocados. "We better get out of here." As he took her by the elbow and led her down the aisle, she picked the vegetables she needed. By the time they reached the checkout, she'd invited him to dinner.

He probably should've wondered about her—a girl in L.A. inviting a man she'd just met into her home. But it didn't feel weird at all. It felt magical.

She'd made him pasta with red chard, mushrooms, sausage, and pine nuts, something he'd never tasted before. She said she'd learned the dish in Tuscany. After that, she often made dinner for him. Sometimes, as he drove up to her house, he'd watch her through the kitchen window as she moved from sink to stove. He'd seen his mother cook, her head bobbing up and down from a recipe, talking nervously to herself like someone trying to read a tech manual and hook up a stereo system at the same time. But Laura looked like she was dancing. She looked like she was thinking about something completely different, her hands moving on their own, a small frown on her lips. When she plucked and cleaned the vegetables, it was as if she were touching his body; it sent shivers through him. He'd stand there watching her until he couldn't take it anymore, then run up the stairs—his body shaking with excitement—and pound on her door.

God, he missed her.

Scott wanted to celebrate with Laura, so that was what he'd do. He toweled off quickly, dressed, and left the gym. On his drive to the beach, he stopped for a six-pack of beer, then shot down the peninsula and parked in the alley.

Laura's window was dark. It was around ten-thirty P.M. He wondered if anyone had moved in yet; he hoped not. He didn't think he could bear seeing someone else there. He snapped open the top on a can of beer, then rolled down the car windows. A light breeze blew in off the ocean. He heard the bougainvillea scratching against her window as it rocked in the wind. A crescent moon reflected in the glass. He could almost see her.

She had been so beautiful that night, so vulnerable. He would've done anything for her.

After the night he almost tried to rape her, something changed in Scott. He'd seen the beast in himself. Staring at that ax in the moonlight, his body shaking, holding on to the post at the bottom of her stairs like a sailor to the mast during a storm, he'd nearly collapsed at the thought of what he might do, the video in his brain flash-cutting: the ax, her neck, her blood, splattered walls. He could feel her there on the other side of the apartment door, listening for the sounds of his leaving, his footsteps, the car door, the engine. The rage stopped suddenly, as if he'd been tumbled among rapids, then swept into a shallow pool of water. He felt the cool mist on his face and heard the plaintive foghorn. It was so quiet. He felt his breath calming, his heartbeat slowing. His brain felt light, his thoughts clear.

He'd gone home. This wasn't the way to love Laura. The next day he'd called when he knew she wasn't home and left an apology on her message machine; he was willing to wait, weeks, months, if he had to. And if she didn't call, he would learn from his mistakes and go on. There was only one Laura in this world, but there were other women who were interesting and beautiful and needed love.

But he didn't have to wait months. She phoned him the following Friday night. Her voice was distressed, and it sounded like she'd been crying. She begged him to come down to the marina. He hesitated—astonished, really, at her sudden reversal—and besides, he had plans to get together with a woman he'd met at . . . But her voice—pleading and desperate. Well, sure. He'd be right there. Was something wrong? "Just come, please, Scott. I need you."

He didn't even change his shirt. He jumped in his car and raced to the beach. It was around eleven o'clock. There wasn't any parking close by, so he had to walk several blocks to her apartment.

She heard him come up the stairs and swung open the door. She was barefoot, wearing gym shorts and a T-shirt. The porch light was off; she grabbed his hand and pulled him inside. The lights were dark. "What's going on?" he asked as she dragged him into the living room, thinking he should take off his shoes, like he usually did, but Laura pulled hard.

Tears, catching the moonlight, glistened on her cheeks.

His heart filled with love for her. As he put his arms around her, Laura clung to him. He'd always wanted this from her, this total surrender, this need, this vulnerability. It completed him, as if somehow giving him permission to go into the world and make it his own. He was empowered. He would do anything for her. You waited all your life to be needed like this, a crisis that transforms you. He was her savior, her knight in shining armor, her superhero.

He pushed her hair out of her eyes, behind her ears, then kissed the side of her cheek; it was damp and salty. Yes, this was love.

This was how he wanted to remember her, needing him and only him. All the rest of it didn't make any difference—the body, the blood, the fear. All he needed was that moment, when he knew what love was. Even if he never felt it again, it was all worth it for that moment.

Before he'd even finished his second beer, Scott leaned back in his car seat and fell asleep with Laura in his arms.

If you walk down any street in Los Angeles and look into the parked cars, you'll see all these people just sitting behind the steering wheel. Sometimes I count. Every block always has at least two. Sometimes every car has someone in it. How come? What's so great about sitting in a car? Are they listening to the end of a song? Or maybe they're early for an appointment. Maybe they just had a bad experience and they're trying to put their head together before they face the freeway. Or is it the only place they can get any privacy? Sometimes in the winter, I sit in my truck because it's the only place to get warm. Maybe they're just cold.

It's funny. People don't expect you to see them in their cars, like they think they're invisible, and if they catch you, they give you this dirty look, like you're being rude. They act like they've been caught picking their nose.

Anyhow, I was walking to the marina jetty to go fish—around five A.M., like usual—and I saw a car parked in the alley with a guy sleeping inside. I recognized him. He was the guy who used to show up in her kitchen for morning coffee. I figured he must know by now she wasn't there, and if he knew she wasn't there, why was he hanging out? It was still dark. His face caught the streetlight. His blond hair was flopped over his forehead, and he had a sweet smile, like an angel. He looked harmless. But like Abuelita—my grandma—used to say: *Hasta el diablo fue un ángel en sus comienzos.* Even the devil was an angel when he began.

I got a funny feeling about him, so I decided to keep an eye on him.

Velma sat in front of Reggie's desk, going over her notes for the Venice Gang Task Force, in particular the San Juan murders.

"The FBI traced a number of calls from Li'l Richie's brother's house in Houston to Los Angeles. The dumb shit has been calling his girlfriend. They were ready to take him when he disappeared. They alerted security at the airports and bus stations in case he tries to get out of town."

"Has anyone actually seen him yet?"

"No. But they're sending a surveillance tape from the Houston airport. They think they might have a picture of him picking up someone."

"You'd think he'd know better than to hang out at airports."

"We're not talking master criminal here. He's a nineteen-year-old gangbanger."

"I'd like to take a look at the tape."

"I'll give it to you when it comes in."

The telephone rang. "Detective Brooks," Reggie answered.

"Hello. This is Françoise Augier at Dubois Gallery."

"Hi. I was just looking at the photos you sent over. Hold on a sec." As Reggie scrambled to unearth the infrared photos from his piles, Velma motioned that she'd be back and slipped out.

"I hope they help you," Françoise said. "The platinum on the inside of the ring was so worn that I was afraid we wouldn't find anything, but you can clearly make out the jeweler's stamp in the photos."

Reggie studied the image. It was a design of a crown with *BC* at the bottom and *578* on the top. "Do you know what the number and letters mean?"

"I can't help you there. Jewelry is a specialized field. I don't know much about it."

"What about the crown? And the squiggly thing above it?"

"Could be a logo. Maybe he was a royal jeweler. Your guess is as good as mine." Françoise continued. "I made a few inquiries about your sculptor Jean Boulogne. Capri Gallery on Melrose handles his business for the West Coast. I've met the owner several times, and he was willing to give me the number in Arles where Boulogne's spending the summer."

"Thanks. That's great." Reggie scribbled down the number. "Do you know anyone who might be able to trace the seal back to the original jeweler?"

She paused. "You might try Isaac Brovsky. He's here in L.A. He traces stolen art back to the original owners. He might be your best bet."

Reggie took the number and thanked Françoise. He'd make an appointment to visit Brovsky later that afternoon.

Scott checked his messages with the receptionist on his way into Bay City Realty. A Mr. and Mrs. Crofton wanted to see his listings in Santa Monica. He'd already told them they couldn't afford the area, but they were insistent. He figured he'd start out showing them dumps for half a million, to shake them up a bit, then take them to visit a pocket in Culver City that was just turning around. He had a modest three-bedroom on a large plot of land, not exactly charming, but clean. He wouldn't tell them about the gang wars two blocks away on Centinela.

He glanced at the rest of his messages. Mr. Gray, turning down the offer on the Wainwright place. Asshole. Even with the sizzling market, he'd have to wait weeks for a better offer on that dump. Connie Philips asking him to call back. Peter Flynn. That was one he wouldn't bother to return.

As he read his messages, he shuffled slowly down the hallway toward his desk, scuffing his shoes on the new carpet. Then he froze midstep.

"There he is! The divine Mr. Goodsell." Even before he turned the corner and looked into his boss's office, her voice rushed at him like a bomb blast. Her tall, voluptuous body was poised in a chair before Harrison's desk in a way that suggested an aggressive businesswoman as well as a seductress. With her oversize teeth and curly black hair, she looked even more predatory than he had remembered.

"Hey, Scott," called Harrison, his eyes startled as if jolted from a magic spell. "Come in for a moment, would you?"

Scott hesitated but, seeing no escape, braced himself for unpleasantness. He entered Harrison's office. For show, he shook Vivian's hand, then retreated several steps. He felt his face tighten, stretched in multifarious mutating masks before settling on a wide, eager smile.

Scott could see Vivian was in performance mode: her two-thousand-dollar suit and Rolex watch, her lips and nails painted bright red. He recognized her perfume, Amarige de Givenchy, cloying as overripe apricots.

"I take it you know each other?" Harrison, apparently taken in by Vivian's Fifth Avenue act, frowned slightly, imagining, perhaps, a fading opportunity for a fling with a New York sophisticate.

"Yes, indeed," said Vivian, "we're *oooold* friends," implying any number of things—illicit trysts, scandals narrowly averted, partners in crime. The effect was to make Harrison's eyebrows rise halfway up his balding pate.

As Vivian stood, Harrison jumped to his feet and went to her side. She looped her arm through his and sashayed toward Scott, teetering on heels the likes of which were seldom seen in California.

"Well, Scott"—Harrison was nearly stammering—"it should be a pleasure, then, for you to show Ms. Costanza around today." Scott couldn't think of many things less pleasurable. Harrison continued. "She tells me she's moving from New York and needs to buy a place relatively quickly. Since she doesn't know the area well, I thought you might show her around different neighborhoods, on the Westside, of course. Give her a sense of prices she can expect to pay in various areas, freeway access. That sort of thing." He turned to Vivian. "Do you have children, Ms. Costanza?"

"No."

Her answer seemed to please Harrison. "Well then, you don't have to restrict her to areas with good schools, although that's always good for resale."

"Oh, I won't be selling for a while," said Vivian.

"Perhaps someone else could take her around," said Scott, trying to keep the desperation out of his voice. "I have an appointment today with Mr. and Mrs. Crofton."

"Oh, the Croftons." Harrison sighed dismissively. "I'll have Melissa handle the Croftons. Don't worry about them."

Scott realized there was no point in arguing. He didn't really care about missing a commission from the Croftons. They were bargain hunters and, in this market, more trouble than they were worth. But the idea of spending the day with Vivian was not appealing.

Harrison clapped Scott on the shoulder like he was doing him a favor. "You two make a day of it. Have lunch on Bay City Realty. Enjoy yourselves."

Vivian gave Scott a reptilian smile. He thought it best to get her out of the office as soon as possible.

"Why don't we get started, then," Scott said. "We'll take my car."

"Excellent," said Harrison. He handed Vivian a notepad with the office's turquoise and pink logo across the top. "You'll probably want to take notes. L.A. is a big, confusing town."

Scott pulled Vivian by the elbow out the door and to his car. Where to go? The idea of driving into the desert and dumping her flashed across his mind.

"I think I'd like to see the Marina Peninsula first," she said as she got into the car. She crossed her legs and pulled up her skirt to just above her knees. "I hear they have a low crime rate."

He turned down Washington Boulevard to Lincoln, then south, thinking vaguely about the Ballona Wetlands near the airport and how he could hide a body there. "How long do you plan to keep up this act?" he asked.

"What act?"

"Pretending you want to buy a house in L.A.?"

"I'm not pretending. I think it's time to open a West Coast branch of the gallery. Besides, I'm going to stay here until I find out what you did to Laura."

"What does Laura have to do with anything?"

"No need to be coy, Scotty. I've been doing some checking around. Seems you're the only person Laura talked to before she left town. Not her landlord, not her boss, not her maid, not her friends at work. Poof. She's gone. Disappeared."

"She told me she sent a letter to her boss."

"Did she? I wonder who signed that letter." As she spoke, Vivian's voice rose operatically; she rolled her eyes and gestured like a magician setting up a trick in a vaudeville act.

"Laura did. What do you mean?"

Her eyes bored into Scott. "Well, I talked with her boss. He said she had to go visit her sick mother." Vivian suddenly smiled. "We both know her mother is dead."

Scott thought fast. "Obviously, she wanted a simple excuse. She told me Johnson was a lech, so I understand her not wanting to mention anything too personal or complicated."

"And you respect her privacy, so you've been telling everyone she left to care for her mother." Vivian's sarcasm flitted like a butterfly, just out of reach.

"That's what she asked me to do," said Scott, turning a corner sharply and throwing Vivian against the door. "You know how secretive Laura has always been."

"You are so full of shit. I think you killed her, Scotty. What'd you do with her? Pour acid over her body in the bathtub and flush her down the L.A. sewers? Or maybe you dumped her corpse in the Angeles Crest Forest."

"Oh, stop it. I didn't do anything with her. And as far as stalking her, I never threatened her. I only wanted to talk to her."

"Save your denials for the police. I'm not buying it."

Scott's chest tightened, but he managed to keep his voice light. "The police? Why would you want to annoy them?"

"I plan to file a missing-persons report."

"But Laura's not missing." Scott chuckled. "I just received a letter from her from Paris."

"I don't believe you. Laura would never go back to Europe without telling me."

"Well, there you have it. Laura is growing and changing. Maybe she didn't want to have to ask you along."

"Were you born charming, or is this a recent development?"

"You bring out the gallant in me."

"Fuck you. What's she doing in Paris? And why would she write to you? She hates you."

Scott knew that wasn't true. Laura had never hated him. "You make a lot of presumptions, Vivian. It's easy to speculate about what goes on between a couple, but you can never really know how they feel about each other. Not even you, Viv. Laura and I love each other. We have some issues, but we're working on them. Laura wrote me that she needed a break from L.A. and wanted some time to think about us." To Scott it felt real, the heartache and longing of a couple estranged but in love.

"People don't give up their jobs and apartments simply because they need a break."

"Maybe people don't, but Laura did. She's spontaneous. She gets these moods. You know how she is."

Scott was alluding to a trip Laura and Vivian had taken to Mexico, spur of the moment, after Laura had already accepted a job at a bank. When she lived in New York with Vivian, she often slipped out of the city to Vermont or Martha's

Vineyard without telling anyone, returning days later without explanation.

Vivian had no instant rejoinder. She looked out the window. They were passing sailboats, then wetlands. Scott assumed she didn't know exactly where the marina was. It probably wouldn't occur to her that he'd take her someplace else.

He turned right on Jefferson Boulevard to Playa del Rey. Expensive condos quickly gave way to desolate marsh.

Scott parked beside the road near Dockweiler State Beach, an isolated stretch of sand under LAX flight patterns. It was less benign than it looked: South Central gangs often used the beach as their battlefield. It was where the L.A. River dumped into the ocean, where debris met the sea, where the city flushed out its crap like a big asshole. Planes crashed, kids got stabbed, bodies washed up. Bad things happened at Dockweiler Beach.

Vivian seemed impatient to get out of the car. After Scott got out and opened her door, she slipped off her heels and walked barefoot toward the water, kicking up the sand like an actress waiting for a music cue. Scott found it irritating.

A cyclist sped by on the curvy bike path. A dozen crows, feasting on the eggs of least terns, cawed raucously. Miles of empty beach lay before them.

Vivian slipped off her soft suit jacket and folded it over her arm. Underneath, she wore a sleeveless shell; Scott noticed that her upper arms were beginning to go soft. "I know Laura would not disappear without telling me," she said.

"She's done it before."

"Not like this."

"No? Isn't that what she did when she came out to L.A.?"

"She called me once she got here."

"Well, she'll probably call you from Paris. She's probably called already but didn't want to leave a message." Scott recalled how it used to irritate him that Laura never left messages.

"I don't believe you," Vivian said softly. But Scott felt her begin to doubt herself. It was exhilarating, like reeling in a fish.

"Didn't she tell you how bored she was at work?" he asked.

"Yes. But she said she was excited about some classes she was taking."

"That's probably what inspired her to go to Paris."

Vivian looked at him, then shook her head. "You're weaving quite a pretty tale. I wonder if it will fool the police."

A couple walking hand in hand on the beach headed past, back to their car. Scott and Vivian were alone now. He led her to an area of tall grasses and sand dunes, part of the Ballona bird sanctuary. He turned to look at her. She seemed nervous now.

Scott kept his expression amiable. "I know we've never really liked each other much, Viv. I always figured it was the way things were between the best friend and the boyfriend, some kind of anti-incest instinct at work. The fact is, I'm glad Laura has such a good friend."

Vivian looked derisively at him. "You are such a bullshit artist. I bet you take that as a compliment."

"I'm being as truthful as I can. I'm sorry you don't believe me, Viv. I can't help it if you don't like me. You seem bent on making trouble for me, but there's no need for it. Laura's just fine. She'll call or write you when she's ready. That's her way. You know that."

Vivian seemed to deflate. He'd found her soft spot—her own timidity in claiming Laura's friendship. There *was* a coolness about Laura, a way she showed affection without ever really letting you know where you stood. An independence that eschewed emotional neediness. Scott didn't think it was a conscious thing Laura did, but it had manipulated him, and now he saw how it manipulated Vivian.

For a moment Scott was pleased with himself, but then Vivian turned and glared at him. "You think you have it all figured out, don't you? But I know you killed her, and I intend to prove it."

Scott was silenced by her intensity. He picked up a broken shell and ran his thumb over its sharp edge. He moistened his lips and glanced out toward the surf. "I would never harm Laura. She was a goddess to me."

"If she'd been a goddess, you wouldn't have been able to kill her."

"I *didn't* kill her! I haven't seen Laura in months. I wish only the best for her. I wish you'd believe me."

"You're such a liar, I bet you don't even know what's true."

He didn't respond, just gazed at her, relaxing his face of any expression. She looked away, then around at the sand dunes, fear in her eyes as if only now realizing how isolated they were. He enjoyed observing as her mind raced through different scenarios. Slowly, she stepped away from him. "I'd like to go back to my hotel," she said.

"Sure, Viv, whatever you want."

Isaac Brovsky lived in an older hacienda-style duplex off of La Brea Avenue, an area inhabited mostly by older Orthodox Jews and young Hispanic families. Reggie couldn't find street parking, so he pulled into the driveway and walked up to the second-floor apartment.

Brovsky greeted Reggie at the door. He was five feet four, spry, with thick glasses. He was around eighty, and his pants hung off him as if he'd lost weight. In the palm of his left hand was a growth the size of a kumquat. He smelled faintly of pee.

"Excellent," shouted Brovsky. "She has the original authentication certificate . . . Insurance records, too?" At first Reggie thought Brovsky was talking to someone inside, then saw that under his nest of white hair was a headset. "You make it too easy. I'll get ahold of the Frick this afternoon. What's her number?" Brovsky whipped out a Palm Pilot, input the number, then grinned at Reggie as he let him in. "I love these gadgets. Every time they come out with something new, I'm first in line."

"I'm sorry to interrupt your call," said Reggie.

"No, no. It's fine. A lady in Pennsylvania found proof that the Nazis stole a family painting by the French painter Théodore Géricault. It's hanging at the Frick in New York. They'll hate to do it, but they'll return it."

"You're still placing stolen art from World War Two?"

"Oh my, yes. Just today I got a lead on a Giovanni Bellini *Madonna and Child.* There's lots of work to do. Swiss banks are returning bank accounts. And then there are insurance claims. But I'm being rude. Please, come in."

The rooms were stacked floor to ceiling with books and paper. Brovsky led Reggie on a narrow path between the towers of paper, through the kitchen, where someone was cooking a huge pot of soup, to his office in back. The office was also piled high with stacks of paper but looked more organized. Two computers sat on opposite sides of the room. Behind one was a dark-haired young man in a yarmulke, typing madly. He ignored Reggie and Brovsky.

"Oh, I remember now. You're the cop with a ring. Let me see what you have."

Reggie handed him the infrared photo. Brovsky looked at it for a second, then disappeared behind a stack of books. "Nope," he said, shuffling into the dining room. The chairs and table were buried beneath books. He dove under the table and came back with a five-inch-thick leather-bound book. It easily weighed twenty pounds. Reggie helped with it as Brovsky motioned him to set it down on the dining room table.

"This book contains all the stamps for jewelers, goldsmiths, and silversmiths from the fifteenth century through the late twentieth century. Let me take a look at that photo again." Brovsky stabbed at it with a yellow fingernail. "Look here, that mark above the crown is an urn with a salamander in it. That's the personal emblem of the French king François I, who reigned between 1515 and 1547. That tells me this jeweler was highly favored by the king, probably working at the royal château at Fontainebleau. That's just south of Paris. The initials *BC* will give us the name of the jeweler." Brovsky opened the book to the middle.

"Are these pages vellum?" asked Reggie.

"Yes." Brovsky laughed. "European jewelers take themselves rather seriously. There are only five books in the world with such comprehensive information, all five hand-copied in 1970 by a monk in Athos. It's the only place in the world where monks still copy illuminated manuscripts. The books were commissioned by a Russian aristocrat exiled to Israel. He personally gave me one for my work. I've had it scanned into the computer for others' use, but I prefer the book."

Brovsky found the seal quickly. "I was right. The jeweler descends from the workshop of Benevenuto Cellini, an Italian sculptor commissioned by King François I. Evidently, he made jewelry, too. He was granted use of the king's emblem and established his own shop in Italy in 1554, under the patronage of Catherine de' Medici. In the middle of the nineteenth century, the family of jewelers moved to Sainte-Croix, Switzerland, where they now have a shop called Cellini. That's on the French border."

"The family's been in business for four hundred and fifty years?"

"That's not uncommon among European artisans." Brovsky led Reggie back to his office. "From here on, books are no good.

You have no idea how much the Internet has helped my work. Before, it could take over a year to connect a possible heir to a treasure. Now we can do it in days." Brovsky sank behind the second computer, adjusting a worn velvet pillow beneath him. He logged on to the website of a European trade organization for jewelers and gem dealers. Cellini was listed as a member. "Too bad Cellini doesn't have a website. But they have an e-mail address. Let's scan this in and send a message." Brovsky laid the photo on the glass bed, scanned in the image, then attached the file to an e-mail asking if the seal was Cellini's and whether they had records of sale. "If they're Swiss, they'll have records," Brovsky said confidently. "I've been doing this since 1950. Millions of dollars' worth of jewelry was stolen from the Jews. Most of it was melted down, but the better pieces continue to show up. Jewelry is harder to track down than art, because people tend to hold on to it rather than sell it to museums. We'll find out who it belongs to. It's my obsession. But I guess I don't have to tell you that."

Brovsky turned and started talking rapidly. "What? You're saying the Getty is questioning the documentation? Don't worry about it." Reggie realized he was on the phone again. "They've got enough problems with stolen art without stealing from holocaust victims. Give me his number." As Brovsky whipped out his Palm Pilot, he walked Reggie to the door. "I'll call you when I get a response. Should be in the next day or two." Reggie assumed Brovsky was talking to him; he handed him his card and left.

Scott stepped into his apartment, closed the door, and locked it, too tired to even turn on the lights. He preferred the darkness. His quadriceps were shaking, like after a long workout; his mouth was dry. He stumbled across the living room and turned on the TV. He felt better almost immediately—the familiar droning faces—although he was too whipped to even follow what the newscasters were saying. He pushed aside a pizza box and sank onto the couch.

When he shut his eyes, the image returned of the Mexican stepping out of the reeds at Ballona creek, whizzing like a dog. Disgusting! Where'd he come from? Peeing right in front of them, grinning like a crazy pervert. Jesus! Vivian had practically run back to the car. What an animal! Yet in a way, Scott was glad the Mexican had shown up. Scott had almost done something horrible. The thoughts that went through his head . . . He had come so close.

He recalled how clearly it had come to him, in an instant, cool as mercury, like a well-practiced military exercise: his plan to drive to the Ballona Wetlands, to lure her near the swamp where no one would see them, to fall on her and strangle her, holding her face under the putrid, tea-stained water, then to strip her clothes, leaving her naked, to be found in a week or a month, an unidentified body. He imagined telling Harrison that she was a looky-loo, a pushy New Yorker checking out the L.A. market, a would-be speculator, not a serious buyer, and if the body was ever identified and he was questioned, he'd calmly tell them that he'd driven her around a few neighborhoods, dropped her off at her hotel, then went back to the office, never to see her again.

He thought of how calm he'd be under interrogation, even with that black cop glaring at him like a cannibal. He'd play a man concerned but not overwrought, a man trying to help out with what little he knew.

He wasn't a murderer, he told himself. He did only what needed to be done, and it had turned out he hadn't needed to kill Vivian. They had talked on the way back to Venice, and it seemed to him that Vivian finally believed him and would go back to New York and leave him in peace.

But he'd do it if he had to. He knew he could.

He'd proved himself before, that last night with Laura. He'd been calm and methodical. He hadn't felt anything when he saw the body lying near the marble foyer. It was an empty casing, disposable flesh, a mess to be cleaned up. He'd felt a confidence take over, someone else stepping in like a maestro, competent and cool, pushing aside a clumsy pupil to do things properly.

It disturbed him now to think of how efficiently he'd taken care of things, as if he'd done it a hundred times before.

Was he finally splitting in two? He'd worried about it all through college. Hadn't it happened to Uncle Fritz, and also to a cousin on his mother's side? Didn't his mother struggle with depression? When he was younger, he thought schizophrenia was kind of a cool disease to have; it meant you were brilliant and artistic. You could claim Nijinsky and van Gogh as brethren. Was it happening to him now? Had Laura sent him over the edge?

He began to drift, imagining Laura's face as it was that night, vulnerable, pleading, her fate in his hands. Her most lovely.

He shook himself awake. Before he let himself completely fade, he needed to make a final call. He poured himself a Scotch, conscious that he'd been drinking a little more lately, but not overly concerned. Things would calm down soon. He sank down on the sofa again and picked up the phone.

Scott hated to involve Patricia, but he knew his youngest sister would do anything for him. As kids, they'd been close. He protected her from their other sisters and their mother. He was pretty sure he could trust her. He rang her number in Paris and asked her to FedEx him a map of the city. When he received it, he'd replace the map with a letter he'd typed and signed with Laura's name. By now he was confident that his forgery could pass professional scrutiny. He'd keep the letter in case Vivian carried out her threats about the police. He also asked Pat to send him a blank postcard every week. He would fill in the backs, copying from postcards Laura had sent him in the past. Tomorrow he would overnight one of Laura's credit cards to Pat, asking his sister to charge up a few hundred dollars. When the bill came to his mailbox, he'd pay it with a money order. He didn't yet dare forge Laura's name on checks.

He was oddly proud of his fabrication. It would be difficult to prove that Laura was not in France. The funny thing was, when Vivian was grilling him, the claim that Laura was in Paris had simply popped out of his mouth. And now it seemed true.

He imagined Laura strolling through the cafés on the Left Bank, or sitting for hours in the Rodin sculpture garden, watching pensively as if a drama were being played out before her. He often marveled at how she could sit so still, watching, and wished he could see the world through her eyes. He imagined her floating through the Louvre dressed in white chiffon, or past the booksellers along the Seine wearing black pants, a red and white sailor's jersey, and a beret. He imagined French and Algerian men chasing after her and her blinking at them, tilting her head, then turning away as if she didn't even see them.

He imagined receiving postcards from her, rough sketches of the view from her room, the Eiffel Tower, Notre Dame. He felt a lonely anticipation fluttering in his stomach; he was anxious for her return. When thoughts entered his mind that there was no possible way she could, he chased them off; he preferred his fantasy.

It was just as easy to believe something that wasn't true as something that was. All it took was repetition, investing the story with emotion, giving the lie a time and place, filling in the background canvas. If he believed it, it wasn't a lie, was it?

Later that evening, as Scott lay in bed watching television, he glanced at the bottom drawer of his bureau. He didn't normally let his girlfriends keep things at his place. Next thing, they'd be moving in. But with Laura, it had been different. Even though she seldom stayed over, he'd given her a drawer where she kept a few T-shirts, a change of underwear, stockings, and a set of workout clothes. He got out of bed, walked over to the bureau, and pulled open the drawer.

It smelled of Laura, cinnamon with a hint of blackberries. He ran his fingers over the garments. The T-shirts had the soft texture of expensive cotton, and her underwear was so silky that his barbell calluses snagged on the fabric.

He took off his clothes and slipped on her underwear. The deflated bra cups looked ridiculous until he stuffed a sock in each side. He admired himself in a full-length mirror, imagining what it was like to be her. He thought of shaving his legs and around that panty line, wondering if his skin would feel soft and smooth, like Laura's.

He imagined walking with her along the beach on a hot tropical island, her head on his shoulder, her sarong flapping in the wind, her long hair blowing over his face, catching on his lips.

He missed her. Ached for her. Why did Laura have to ruin it all? They could have been so happy together.

He'd been ripped up inside when she refused to marry him. Taking care of things for her made them one, united forever. He was getting hard just thinking about it: Laura's face that night, so childlike, so helpless, so trusting, as if he were the only one in the world who could save her.

In the mirror, he saw his erection peeking out of her panties. He put his hand around it and groaned, stepping toward the mirror, his breath moist against the cool glass, pressing her body against the cold marble floor, coming, blood on his fingers, blood coming on his reflection.

Embarrassed, he tore off her underwear and slipped on a pair of gym shorts. He wished he had a fireplace to burn the stuff. He'd have to get rid of it all tomorrow. He'd need to be careful, though. In this town, there were so many bums and trash pickers, you could never be sure about throwing something away.

It might pop up later.

PART FIVE

NONE

All morning and nothing but dead ends.

As soon as Reggie walked into the station, he got a call from his Mexican friend. Apparently, Scott Goodsell was stalking Laura's apartment, even though she wasn't there. Was he revisiting the crime scene? Suffering a guilty conscience and forcing himself to relive his horrible crime? Then there was that business of him threatening a woman in the Ballona Wetlands. That is, if the Mexican could be believed.

Reggie was getting ahead of himself, he knew. There was no body, no reported missing person, no crime, no suspect. But while he waited to hear about the ring, he felt he should proceed as if Scott were a suspect.

Reggie's first stop was at the harbormaster's, to see if Scott Goodsell owned a boat. No Goodsells owned boats. He checked under Bay City Realty, thinking maybe Scott's company had a boat. No dice. Second on the agenda were the boat clubs, to see if Scott was a member; at many of them, members could lease club boats. There were four main clubs: South Bay Yacht Racing Club; Santa Monica Windjammers Yacht Club (where Reggie and Audrey belonged); South Coast Corinthian Yacht Club; and Del Rey Yacht Club. Scott didn't belong to any of them.

There were two other places that rented out boats unsupervised. Reggie checked to see if Scott had rented a boat in April. No dice. Reggie asked the Coast Guard if Scott was even certified to operate a boat. He wasn't, which meant he couldn't rent. It was possible that Scott had an accomplice who had rented the boat. Reggie took down the names and numbers of everyone who had rented a boat from April 12 through April 15. It was a long shot, but when he had time, he'd check out all the people with L.A. addresses.

Late morning, Reggie found his friend Paul Axelrod in the Windjammers clubhouse, mending a spinnaker. Paul didn't actually work for the club, but he was always there, eager to help out. He had sold yachts in the eighties before the recession hit and no one wanted to buy a boat. Then he cashed out and retired. Paul was one of the last guys in the marina who knew how to mend a sail. He sat in a corner, red hair and beard, sewing the rainbow-colored spinnaker; he looked like a peasant in a Rembrandt painting.

Reggie told Paul the story of the arms, then showed him the map of ocean currents, the shoreline marked with two *X*'s. "I suspect the body was dumped around April 13. Twenty-one days later, the left arm washes up here on Venice Beach. Twenty-three days later, the other one shows up in Malibu."

Paul nimbly folded the sail like a pastry chef working phyllo dough. He set it aside and put on his bifocals to look at Reggie's map. "That time of year, the main current turns north about five knots an hour. It comes off the coast of Catalina, then east where two deep currents meet, one cold, one warm. The water outside this current moves real slow. The body could hang out there till it rotted away. On the other hand, a warm current moves swiftly up along the coast."

"What if he took a sailboat? Where do you think he'd dump it?"

"I don't think he'd take a sailboat. He'd want to get rid of the body fast. He'd take a motorboat and go straight out until he lost sight of land. As soon as he thought he was pretty safe, he'd dump the body."

Reggie tried to remember the last time he'd been in a motorboat but couldn't. "How long does it take to motor out before you lose sight of land?"

"Depends on the smog, but I'd say about forty-five minutes."

"Where would that put you?"

"Somewhere on this side of Catalina. Ten or twelve miles out. Of course, that's if we don't have much smog. Smog's not usually bad in April."

"How long would it take for a body to wash up from there?"

"Well, that puts you in that area of still water I talked about. Eventually, it would drift into the currents. Then it would probably take about a week to wash up."

It occurred to Reggie that Scott could have rented a boat south of the marina. "What if he took a boat from Long Beach, motored out till he couldn't see the shore, then dumped the body? How long would it take to reach Venice?"

Paul walked over to a wall map. He measured with a compass and punched in numbers on a calculator. "If it got caught up in the fast northerly current . . . I would say a week or so."

"I guess you're saying there's no real way to tell where the body was dumped, right?"

"I'm not helping much, am I?"

"You're helping a lot."

Paul scratched his beard. "You know, a guy who's shittin' his pants 'cause he's just killed his girlfriend and is trying to dump the body before anyone sees him isn't gonna be too careful about it. He's gonna get a boat, motor out a mile or two, then dump it."

"But wouldn't the arms have shown up earlier?"

"Guess the guy was lucky."

"No. If he was lucky, they wouldn't have shown up at all."

It was Tuesday, trash day in Scott's neighborhood. He got up early, divided Laura's clothes into three small trash bags, then took a stroll. He supposed he should probably drive to a different part of Los Angeles, but on the other hand, he didn't know the trash schedules for other neighborhoods and figured it was safer for stuff to be picked up immediately in his own neighborhood rather than sit around for a few days in another.

As Scott walked home, he remembered the box of Laura's financial papers in his closet. He figured he'd better get rid of that, too—at least not keep it in his apartment.

He made himself a cup of coffee, then pulled the box out from under piles of shoes and racquets. He felt he should at least go through it. He dragged it over to the couch and sat down, then took off the corrugated cover and began to finger through the files.

She was so organized it was a little scary. The manila files had typed labels, each in a Pendaflex hanging file with its own typed label: *Charles Schwab, Mutual Funds, Taxes, Insurance, Credit Cards, Bank, Pension Fund, Auto* (she actually kept all those auto-repair receipts), *Warranties* (she filed those, too). Then Scott found a file marked *Will.* Curious, he pulled the will and the stock files, then took them over to the couch. He put his feet up on the glass coffee table, which was covered with dust and coffee rings, and relaxed back into the sagging cushions.

He read the will first. Since she had no family, she had divided everything among a half-dozen environmental groups such as California Land Conservancy and the Sierra Club. Something about the will's language struck Scott as curious; it referred to separate trusts going to each beneficiary. Laura had been an accountant, but what was all this about? Something to avoid taxes?

He took out the last Schwab statement for March. Slowly, he pulled his feet off the coffee table. His heart began to flutter. She was practically a day trader. He imagined her sitting at work in her gray cubicle, docile as a mouse, model employee, sneaking on to the Internet to trade stocks. It looked like she made a couple of trades every day. On her lunch hour? How'd she get away with it? Then he reached the report summary at the end.

His mouth dropped open. She had assets of $298,462.35. He realized that was simply one Schwab account. He flipped through the others, then the bank accounts and the trust accounts. Shit! She was worth millions. At least one million, anyhow. He was astonished.

She had never once mentioned money. She never complained about it, like everyone else he knew, but then she never complained about anything. He'd known she was doing okay. She always carried a couple hundred on her, but that wasn't so unusual. Maybe he should've guessed. She lived in Marina del Rey, for chrissake. That wasn't cheap. But her car, a Toyota Camry, was a few years old, and he didn't think her wardrobe was anything special, although he did notice once how all her clothes were soft and never seemed to wrinkle. She wore no jewelry except the pearl necklace Scott had given her. She took weekend vacations on impulse, like to Vancouver or Cuernavaca, but he'd never thought about it much. But if she'd been so fucking rich, why did she work at that accounting job? He knew she didn't like it. Who would?

It appeared she handled all her accounts from her computer, and in these files were all her PIN numbers and passwords. Of course she had to write them down—there were too many to remember. Shit. Could he use the PIN numbers and transfer money to his account? Could he set up a dummy trust that wouldn't be traced back to him? Or could he transfer it to an unnumbered Swiss account?

It was way beyond him. He needed help. Peter Flynn was the only person he knew who might understand such things. But Peter was hopelessly honest. Plus, Scott hadn't been returning his phone calls; or rather, he'd called Peter's machine when he knew he wasn't home. Even Peter would be pissed off at him by now.

Could he get Peter to set up a Swiss bank account? Did he need a big chunk of money first? Dare he borrow a hundred thousand from an escrow account, make the transfers from Laura's accounts, then replace the escrow before anyone found out? It was too damn complicated.

The thought, however, was irresistible. He would be set for life. Half the money was rightfully his, anyhow. They were married, after all, or should've been.

How did she get so rich? It annoyed him that she'd kept this information from him. Didn't she trust him?

He decided he had to take a little, just to see if it could be done. He deserved that, at least. He'd taken care of her affairs. He couldn't have done better if he'd been executor to her will. Too bad he couldn't forge a new will and make everything over to himself, then declare her dead.

He picked up the phone and called Peter.

"Hello," answered Peter sleepily.

"Hey, Pete. It's Scott. How you doing?"

"Oh, hi, Scott." Peter sounded cool.

"Did I wake you up?"

"No. Just crunching some numbers. What can I do for you?"

What can I do for you? Scott realized Peter must be pretty mad at him to say that, as if Scott were an annoying client, no chitchat, just get to the point. "I'm sorry we've been playing phone tag. I've been super busy."

"Yeah. Me, too." Peter's voice remained flat.

"I miss racquetball."

Peter's silence resonated with hurt. He inhaled sharply, as if there were little room in his lungs for air, then spoke. "I can't play for a while. I twisted my knee."

"That's terrible. What happened?"

"I was running in Palisades Park, and my sneaker caught under a sprinkler head. I heard a crunch in my knee and went flying."

Scott could hear Peter softening up. He never stayed mad long. "Hey, I got some hockey tickets for Staples Center. Kings and the Red Wings. Wanna come?"

"You're kidding. When?"

"Friday night."

"Absolutely. God, that's great. Want me to drive?"

"Sure. I have parking passes and everything." Scott sure hoped he could round up some tickets. He'd have to pay through the nose, but he saw it as an investment. During the game, he'd find a way to ask about the Swiss account.

They arranged to meet at Peter's office early Friday evening.

After he hung up, Scott began to doze as he imagined how he would spend the money. He'd lived abroad, someplace where they spoke English, a large city like Sydney or Amsterdam. Maybe he'd have a couple of places. He'd like new clothes, one of those Jaguar XK8 sports coupes in silver, and he'd probably want to start a business of some sort, maybe import/export. He had started to slip into a haze, envisioning a gorgeous woman massaging his shoulders as he soaked in a rumbling Jacuzzi, tropical plants all around, looking down over the bustling harbor in Hong Kong, when he bolted straight up.

He got it. He would open a joint account at Schwab with five thousand dollars of his own money. He'd forge Laura's signature on the new account papers. He didn't figure they'd check the signature against her other accounts—not when she was depositing money—anyhow, he thought his forgery would pass even close scrutiny. He'd transfer money from her other accounts into the joint account, which he could do over the Internet with her PIN numbers. He could then withdraw whatever he wanted from the joint account. It would all be done over the Internet or the telephone.

If anyone asked, Scott would say he and Laura were engaged and had established a wedding account. Lots of people did that. He'd transfer a little at a time until he got the Swiss account set up. Then he'd move it all.

He might have to leave the country, his friends and family. Could he do that? Scott laughed out loud, a laugh he barely recognized, rough and wild. He tasted freedom. They caused him nothing but grief. Good riddance to them all.

Would it work?

He didn't know, but he felt extremely pleased with himself. He was wide awake now. He slipped on his loafers and a light jacket. He thought he'd go for a drive. Maybe he'd drop in on Connie.

Isaac Brovsky called Reggie and asked him to drop by. He appeared extremely excited when Reggie got there.

"We got an e-mail back from Cellini in Sainte-Croix. It's their seal, all right. They sold the ring to a Jacob Steinacker in 1939. Since the ring showed up here, I assumed that he immigrated to Los Angeles, which was very common before World War Two. I also assumed he didn't change his name to Stein or Steiner, which is a pretty big assumption. I checked through a database for synagogue members in Los Angeles, and I didn't come up with any Steinackers. A lot of Jewish newcomers worked for the studios, so I called the Motion Picture Pension Fund and asked them to check for Steinackers on the payroll from the forties and fifties. Well, we got a Jacob Steinacker who was a film cutter. He died in 1978. His beneficiaries were his wife, Ruth, and daughter, Beatrice."

"You think it's the same Jacob Steinacker?"

"Sometimes you can know only by checking oral histories with the descendants. I tried to track down Ruth Steinacker but got nowhere, so I figure she must've remarried. Your best bet is to go to the Hall of Records and look up the birth certificate for the daughter."

His entire life, Scott had felt like if he held out long enough, if he talked to enough people, made enough contacts, and managed to be in the right place at the right time, he could be somebody. All he needed was a lucky break.

That lucky break was Laura.

Setting up a joint account at Schwab was easy. He transferred twenty grand of Laura's stock portfolio (piece of cake), and Peter was looking into getting him a numbered Swiss account. And now he'd found street parking right in front of the California Jewelry Mart. With time on the meter! What were the odds of that?

He entered Dornbirn Jewelry to pick up his ring. Between the setting and the diamond, he was in about five grand—all because he had to get sentimental about Laura. Oh well. He'd show up at his mother's with Connie wearing the new ring, get Sammy off his back, dump Connie, then sell the ring and tell his mother that he'd let Connie keep the ring because she was so broken up about it. No, that wouldn't fly. He'd have to say it got lost, like he fucking should've said in the first place.

He held the ring between his fingers under a small fluorescent lamp. He thought it looked pretty good, as close to the original as he could remember. The white gold looked like platinum; he doubted if his sister and mother even knew if the other ring was platinum. He'd saved a grand there. The jeweler had burnished the inside and the edges so it looked well worn, then dunked it in something to age it a little. Scott looked at the diamond through the microscope and saw the same inclusions as the one he'd brought in. The jeweler hadn't switched it with glass. Scott was pleased.

Mrs. Dornbirn started to put it in a blue velvet box, but Scott pulled out the cracked leather one. She insisted on cleaning it, brushing out the dust and rubbing it down with alcohol. Scott placed the ring in the old box and stuck it in his pocket. He paid in cash and drove home.

He was proud of himself, and he wanted to show off the ring. He decided to call Connie and take her out to dinner at Gladstone's. She knew they were only pretending to be engaged, but he figured she'd get a real kick out of being presented with a ring in a restaurant. He'd let her wear it a few days, then they'd go to his mother's and get that over with. Connie deserved a couple of good meals for playing along. He rang her number and arranged to pick her up on Thursday night.

He felt enormously satisfied. He went to the kitchen, pulled a pint carton of Häagen-Dazs from the freezer, grabbed a chocolate-chip cookie and a spoon, then headed into the living room.

As soon as he'd settled down in front of the TV to watch some professional golf, Samantha called. "I want that ring, Scott."

The problem with family was you couldn't hang up on them. "You're a little late, Sammy. I gave it to my fiancée. That's who engagement rings are for—people who are engaged."

"Connie is no more your fiancée than I'm your fairy godmother."

"You're misinformed. Your brother has found true love at last."

"Bullshit. I want the ring. If you don't give it to me, I'm gonna tell Mom about Laura."

Oddly, for a second he didn't know who she was talking about. "What about Laura?"

"I know all about it. You know Mom's not the sort to cover up for you, either."

"What are you talking about?"

"Pat called me last night. She told me about the blank postcards she's been sending you. You'd better tell her what Laura's credit limit is, 'cause she's off to the Champs-Élysées to do some serious shopping. You know, I was suspicious when you stopped talking about Laura all of a sudden. So what'd you do, kill her?"

"Of course not." *Damn Pat!* He'd never trust her again.

"Maybe I should tell Mother about your schemes. I bet you never told her about the restraining order, did you?"

He wondered how Samantha had heard about that. "I've got to go, Sammy. I'll call you later." He hung up, furious. What in the hell was her problem? What was so important about that goddamn ring? She was obsessed with it. He'd give her the one he'd just made, but he knew she'd immediately run to a jeweler. He'd have to figure out another way to get her off his back. Give her a ticket to Paris to visit Patricia? No, that wouldn't be enough for her. She'd been blackmailing him since they were kids, threatening to tell Mom about broken plates, school detentions, fights, pranks. He was always buying her off, and he was sick of it.

The phone rang again. Goddammit! Why wouldn't they leave him alone! Scott thought of letting the machine get it, then, on a sudden impulse, changed his mind and grabbed the phone.

"It's your best friend, Scotty," the voice sang.

"Vivian, I'm working. Could you call back next year sometime?"

"Working, you? You can't tell me what you do is called work."

Realtors got no respect. "What do you want, Vivian?"

"I thought I'd do you the courtesy of telling you that I've filed a missing-persons report."

"For whom?" he said disingenuously.

"Don't ask stupid questions."

"For Laura? I thought you'd given up on that one, Viv. You know you're wasting your time. I just got another postcard from Laura today, as well as her credit-card bill. She seems to be having a great time in Europe without you."

"Whatever. You better start working on your story for the police."

"Police?"

"Sure. Everyone knows about you and her. So expect a call."

"Vivian, if you hate me so much, why are you warning me?"

"Because if you get nervous, you might make a mistake. You might get all sweaty and confess and cry in Mr. Detective's lap."

"Good night, Vivian." He waited a moment, heard nothing, then hung up. He could hardly breathe. Why were all the women turning into such bitches? Always manipulating you, like when they call and say "I love you," expecting you to say "I love you, too," when you don't feel it, not right then, anyhow, with them making you say it, and it pisses you off. As soon as you think you get one handled, another one takes a bite out of your butt. Even Laura, sweet, lovely Laura. Maybe they all have penis envy. Damned if he was going to let them bother him.

Vivian, he realized, was definitely becoming a problem. A problem he'd have to take care of soon.

* * *

Reggie had just returned from that miserable dungeon, the Hall of Records, still shaking out the visions of rowboat-size rats, dancing skeletons, and hooded executioners, when he got a call from Ronda Wiley. A Vivian Costanza had filled a missing-persons report for Laura Finnegan in Los Angeles. Reported missing as of April 20, nearly a week after Reggie figured Laura had disappeared.

"On the form, did Ms. Costanza fill in the blood type?" asked Reggie.

"Hold on. Let me look."

Reggie could feel his heart thumping as he waited.

"She put down A positive. Does that help?"

Yes. Yes. Yes. Reggie scribbled down Vivian's number and left a message at her hotel, the Loews in Santa Monica.

He whistled a few bars from "Yankee Doodle." He was on a roll.

At the Hall of Records, he'd brandished his badge and managed to avoid waiting an hour for the surly clerks to find the right microfiche. He'd threaded up one microfiche machine before he realized it was broken, then threaded a new machine—with the image upside down. Finally, he got it working, but he found no birth certificate for Beatrice Steinacker. He looked up Ruth Steinacker, who had divorced in 1956, then remarried Samuel Cohen. He also found a marriage license for a Beatrice Cohen, married to Anthony Goodsell in 1971, her birth name listed as Steinacker.

Bingo.

Scott was now connected to the ring. Still, there was no body, and all the evidence was circumstantial. Certainly not enough for the district attorney. But it might be enough for Captain McBride to authorize a DNA test on Laura's hair.

The next morning Reggie cornered McBride before the day shift arrived. What luck! McBride appeared to be in a good mood.

"Would you sit down, Reggie!" snapped McBride. "You're making me irritable."

"Yes, sir." Reggie was wrong about McBride's mood.

"Don't 'sir' me, for chrissake! How many years have we known each other? The rookies we get don't even 'sir' me except if they're in trouble."

Reggie slumped in front of McBride's desk like a repentant choirboy. It had been a lot of years, but he still didn't feel comfortable in front of the captain. Nobody did.

McBride was well respected, if not particularly well liked. He was fair and tolerated no jokes—no racial jokes, no lady-cop jokes, not even the harmless pranks his officers needed to keep sane. He was proud of the fact that his department had the fewest lawsuits against it in the city. He understood the political machine downtown and tempered his decisions accordingly. He was not, however, what you'd call easygoing.

Reggie knew it was time to get some muscle behind the investigation. He'd spent the previous evening putting all of his notes in a file. First there was the missing-persons report. Second, the ring on the arm had been bought by a man named Steinacker, the birth name of Scott's mother. Third, the restraining order. Fourth, Laura's blood type was A positive—same as the arms. In addition, there were the odd circumstances of her disappearance—how Scott had handled everything, paid her bills, put her belongings in storage.

But the longer Reggie sat watching McBride read his summary, the more his confidence began to fade.

"This fellow Scott Goodsell"—McBride peered over the file at Reggie, his bushy eyebrows angled sharply, like two diving pelicans—"how would you describe him?"

Reggie thought for a moment. "He's around six feet, one-seventy-five, blond, good-looking. He's never had to work very hard to get what he's wanted, but then he hasn't been all that ambitious. He's smart enough to be easily bored, but lacks the character and drive to do anything constructive. A surfer dude turned to real estate. That kind of says it all."

"You think he's the type to commit murder, then orchestrate an elaborate cover-up?"

"He likes games. Likes watching them, likes playing them—racquetball, tennis, basketball. Murder might be another game to him."

"The type who wants to perform the perfect murder?"

Reggie thought again. "I don't think it started out that way, but now I'll bet he takes a certain pride in it."

"Do you think he'll kill again?"

"I think he's come to see murder as a solution to his problems."

"If he has another problem, he'll murder again?"

"Yes."

McBride pressed his fingertips together in a tepee and rested his index fingers against his lower lip. Then he dropped his hands. "Do you know anything about Scott's family, Reggie?"

Reggie kicked himself. Why did he always jump into things before he was ready? "Apart from tracing the ring back to the Steinackers, no. I haven't gotten that far."

"Well, I *do* know something about his family." McBride closed the file and pushed back in his chair. "His mother, Bunny Goodsell, has been married three times. Do you know who her second husband was?"

"No."

"Richard Wyman."

"The lawyer? The guy running for office?"

"That *guy* is doing great in the polls and could easily be our next mayor. Chief Bollinger hates his guts."

Reggie caught his breath. Richard Wyman was a civil rights attorney who specialized in cases against law enforcement. Fancying himself an advocate for oppressed minorities, he took just about any complaint from any punk involved in a high-speed pursuit or petty crime, then sued the police for racial profiling and use of excessive force. Twenty percent of the cases had merit, the rest didn't. Wyman picked juries who hated cops, so he always won. His client might win only a dollar, but under the provisions of U.S. civil rights codes, Wyman got his full fee from the city. He wasn't in it for the clients. Richard Wyman made life hell for the LAPD. Every division in the city had at least one cop being sued by him. Reggie knew of one who'd named Wyman in his suicide note.

McBride continued, "Wyman is running on police reform. He wants to fire the top brass and restructure the whole department. Chief Bollinger denounced him in the *L.A. Times*—said if Wyman was our next mayor, he'd throw the city into chaos. Without naming names, he blamed him for the Compton riots."

Reggie ran his hand over his face. "We don't know if Beatrice Goodsell still speaks to her ex-husband. Just because Wyman was once married to her doesn't mean—"

"Don't even question it, Reggie. We're not going there."

"So we let Wyman's stepson get away with murder?"

"No, of course not. The chief would love a scandal against Wyman, but we have to be a thousand percent sure that the allegations stick. Otherwise it'll backfire against us. This might be a great opportunity to knock Wyman out of the mayoral race."

So McBride was with him, but McBride wanted war. "Will you let me get a warrant to search Scott's car and apartment?"

"No. I'm not sure we have enough evidence to convince a

judge yet. And the second a judge gets involved, Wyman will be all over the case."

"Will you authorize a DNA test?"

"No, not yet. I want you to work on the arms case with Mike Morrison. Turn up more evidence, and I'll get you DNA tests and search warrants. All you want, you betcha. Who knows, Reggie, if you handle this case right, it might break things open for you. We're talking at least a promotion. You interested in working RHD at Parker Center?"

The robbery-homicide division, the crème de la crème of the LAPD. Reggie felt a stab in his chest. It was all wrong. It seemed every time you tried to do something right in this town, things got all twisted. Make a career move on apprehending a murderer—in essence, profiting from Laura's death? Richard Wyman might be a weasel, but destroy him because of his stepson? No, that was not right at all.

"By waiting to open the case, aren't we taking a risk Scott will kill again? If I'm working on it alone, there's no way I can keep track of him twenty-four hours a day."

"You'll have to do the best you can. By the way, I do not want the sheriff's department to know you have a suspect."

"If he kills?"

"Goddammit, Reggie! Of course I don't want to put anyone at risk, but there's a lot at stake here. We might get Wyman."

Reggie was surprised by McBride's vehemence but thought he understood. McBride had known Wyman since his first civil rights case in the eighties. He had witnessed Wyman twisting public opinion, stirring up hate, rending apart the city like an earthquake breaking up freeways. Until Wyman was defeated, the city would never heal.

Reggie had to pursue Laura's killer despite his captain's ulterior motives. But it made him feel dirty and compromised.

* * *

As Reggie parked his unmarked cruiser by Grand Canal, ducks skittered across the muddy water. It always surprised him that wildlife managed to live in the city—birds and possum in the marina, bobcat and deer in the Santa Monica Mountains, coyote and raccoon in the Hollywood Hills. It made him happy to see Mother Nature taking back what was rightfully hers.

He walked up Washington Boulevard, toward Venice Pier, and stopped in front of Bay City Realty. The company had taken over a failed French Provençal restaurant, so the office had a homey look, with shutters and shingled siding. Reggie wondered if they'd found a use for the courtyard; when he looked around the side of the building, he saw they'd paved over the brick to make a parking lot.

Reggie planned to interview Scott at work to make him nervous. He wanted Scott's coworkers to look at him with suspicion, to start the wheels of speculation; then, when Reggie got around to interviewing them later, they might have already thought of something they'd noticed that was odd about Scott, a lie they'd caught him in, an appointment he missed, a confrontation in which he behaved irrationally. Also, it would be difficult for Scott to refuse to speak with a policeman in front of his colleagues.

When Reggie showed his badge to the receptionist, he got the saucer eyes he was looking for and was pretty sure that there would be some fresh gossip during the next coffee break.

The receptionist glanced at the large wall clock. "Scott has a staff meeting right now. Can you wait five minutes?"

Of course he could, but it might make a nice impression to pull Scott from a meeting. "I would like to, but it's very important. Would you see if he could step out for a moment?"

She looked hesitant, caught between authorities, then said, "Okay. I'll go ask." She disappeared down the hallway.

Scott came stumbling into the reception area, blinking like a mole at midday. Reggie thought he looked thinner.

When he spotted Reggie, Scott straightened up and swaggered toward him. "Good morning, Officer Brooks. Do you want to look at properties on the Westside this morning?" Apparently, Scott was saying this for the receptionist's benefit.

"Good morning, Mr. Goodsell. Do you have a moment? I'd like to ask you a few questions."

"Of course. I'd be most happy to answer your questions. The conference room is busy, so why don't we use an office here." Scott led Reggie into Harrison's office. He closed the door, hesitated, then took the chair behind his boss's desk. Reggie stood. Scott looked relieved to have the desk between them.

"The department has received a missing-persons report for Laura Finnegan. Since it's an official investigation now, I need to ask you a few more questions."

"As I told you, she's not missing, but go ahead. Shoot."

"Where were you from Friday, April 12, through Sunday, April 14? That's the weekend after Laura's last day at work."

"I don't have any idea." Scott laughed uncomfortably. "That was months ago."

"Do you have an appointment book? Maybe it would jog your memory."

"Well, yes."

"Do you have it here?"

"Yes," Scott said grudgingly. "Let me go get it." He left the room and came back with a blue leather-bound appointment book with the Bay City Realty logo on it. He sat back down behind the desk and flipped to the right page. "I had appointments all day on April 13 and 14. We're busiest on the weekends."

"Do you recall what you did in the evenings?"

"No. I probably stayed home."

"Do you have a roommate or anyone who could corroborate that?"

"No. I probably made telephone calls you could check."

Reggie had checked. On the night of April 12, Scott's phone had been uncharacteristically silent. "I talked with Laura's landlord, Jean Boulogne. He stores a variety of tools on his property, and he mentioned he's missing an ax. Would you know anything about that?"

"An ax? No."

"We've also had a chance to call all the registered nursing homes in upstate New York. There was no one named Mrs. Finnegan admitted in the last month."

It took a moment for Scott to remember what he'd told Reggie. Then he guffawed. "I'm sorry to break it to you, Officer, but you're wasting your time. Laura called me from France. She said her mother's illness was a ruse. She's been in Europe all this time."

Reggie was surprised. "You've heard from her?"

"Oh, yes. I've gotten postcards from her and everything."

"Really? So the story about her mother wasn't true?"

"Obviously not. She told me she used that story because she wanted an easy excuse to get out of town fast."

"Why'd she need an excuse at all?"

"I think she didn't know exactly where to go or what she wanted to do. It was easier to say she had a sick mother."

"Did you tell her I wanted to talk to her?"

"Sorry. It slipped my mind. I was kind of shocked to hear from her."

"It's essential that she call us. We have personnel actively looking for her."

"I understand."

Reggie looked at Scott severely. "Did you ever give Laura an engagement ring?"

"Well, I think you know I asked her to marry me. She turned me down."

"Did she keep the ring?"

"Of course not. Why would she?"

"Do you know where the ring is now?"

"I happen to have it with me."

"Really?"

Scott reached into his pocket and pulled out the cracked-leather jewel box. He smiled at Reggie.

Reggie opened the box and picked up the ring. "You know," said Reggie as he watched Scott closely, "this ring looks a lot like one on a hand that washed up on Venice Beach."

"It's just a ring," said Scott, shrugging.

"The one we found on the arm wasn't just a ring."

"What do you mean?"

"We got it appraised. Twice, in fact. It's worth close to half a million dollars." Scott's eyes seemed to darken, but otherwise, he didn't react. "We were surprised, too. It looked so simple."

Scott said coolly, "That's a lot of money for a ring."

"Sure is," said Reggie. "Do you own a boat, by the way?"

"You mean in the marina?"

"Yes. Or anywhere, for that matter."

"No. I'm afraid of water."

"Do you know how to sail?"

"God, no. You couldn't get me on a boat if you paid me."

"Is your mother Jewish?"

"What?" Scott jolted back defensively.

"It's not a crime, being Jewish," said Reggie, smiling.

"Yeah, I suppose you'd call her Jewish. But she doesn't practice or anything. She took us to all sorts of different churches when we were young."

"You have other siblings?"

"Yeah. Three sisters. One older, two younger."

"Where do they live?"

"Martha lives in North Carolina, Samantha lives in Los Angeles, and Patricia goes to school at UCLA."

"Is Patricia in L.A. during the summer break?"

"No, she's in Europe."

"France?"

Scott, apparently realizing his mistake, blushed, but he didn't miss a beat. "No, I don't think so. Greece, I think."

Reggie marveled at Scott's skills as a liar. "Is your mother's family from Europe?"

"Aren't most American Jews?"

"I suppose. Do you know a Vivian Costanza?"

Scott didn't react at all. "No. Why?"

"She's the one who filed the missing-persons report."

"Never heard of her. She related to Laura?"

Reggie smiled at the false insouciance. "Not as far as I know. You will be in town for the next few days?"

"Yes."

"Good. We may have more questions for you. Will you get a number from Laura if she calls again? And make sure to tell her to call me."

"I'd be glad to." Scott's tone was perfect—an earnest citizen wanting to help. Reggie couldn't hear even the slightest insincerity.

Reggie walked toward the door, then turned. "By the way, what's your mother's birth name?"

"Really, Sergeant Brooks, I hardly see how any of these questions will help you locate Laura."

"Funny thing—you know that ring I was telling you about? The one that showed up on the dismembered arm? We traced it back to a jeweler in Sainte-Croix, Switzerland. Those Swiss keep excellent records, you know. Turns out it was sold to a man named Steinacker. That name mean anything to you?"

Scott lost all expression, as if his face were slipping off. He said, "Isn't that interesting," and walked Reggie to the door.

As Reggie left Bay City Realty, excitement pulsed through his muscles; he knew he had the fox on the run. Yet he was confused by the ring. If Scott had given Laura the engagement ring, what was the ring in his pocket?

Later, Reggie ran another credit check on Laura. It appeared that charges were being made on her card in France. Reggie assumed someone else was using her card. He suspected Scott's sister Patricia.

After Scott picked up Connie in Malibu, he was hit with a sudden inspiration: Why not drinks at Toppers on the eighteenth floor of the Huntley Hotel in Santa Monica? They could watch the sun fade into the haze as the city lighted up. There was always a party up there, lots of foreign tourists who jumped around between tables, lots of embracing and cheek kissing. Why not have fun with this?

He drove down Pacific Coast Highway and up West Channel Road. The cop's interview kept edging in on his good mood, gnawing at him like a rat, a big black rat. Grandmother's ring on the arm? Impossible. The cop was trying to shake him up. And that stuff about Steinacker? And Sainte-Croix? That didn't even make sense. His grandparents had bought the ring in Grenoble. That's what Oma always said. And worth a fortune? Bullshit. He'd had it appraised: It was worth a couple of mortgage payments. The cop was yanking his chain.

As the evening air blew past his face, he glanced over at the passenger seat, nearly surprised to find Connie there. That's right—it was time to party. Instantly, he dismissed the annoying thoughts.

When they got to Toppers, it was packed. Scott figured the bar had been written up in some tourist guide; despite its having one of the best views in Los Angeles, there were hardly ever any Americans there. Tonight it was Greeks, joking, pouring drinks, and getting everyone's names, while the Germans, after a few glasses of retsina, bought the entire bar a round and started singing. Japanese tourists sat with their noses to the windows, pointing at the sun as it sank below the purple Santa Monica Mountains; the Australian men huddled by the bar, flirting with the female bartender.

When the Greeks spotted Scott giving Connie the ring, what was already a boisterous party exploded into a celebration. They hoisted Scott and Connie up in their chairs and carried them around the room, then back to the table, where they ordered champagne for the couple. All the men—and most of the tourists were men—wanted to practice their English on Connie. When the Greeks started dancing, Scott figured it was time to leave.

Around nine P.M., they finally made it to Gladstone's. They'd lost their reserved table, so they waited at the bar. Neither one of them wanted to drink any more, so they ordered club sodas. The maître d' said they'd probably have a ten-minute wait.

Thirty minutes and a margarita later, Scott thought maybe he was beginning to like Connie, that maybe it wouldn't be such a bad idea to be engaged to her for a while. She was so wholesome and strong, the kind of woman you'd imagine driving a prairie wagon through Montana. He had to admit, it made him feel kind of grown up to be engaged, like he could smoke a pipe and wear a pocket watch and people wouldn't laugh at him. Like he was a man. Maybe he'd stay engaged for a while—that is, until she started to take it seriously.

Finally, the maître d' showed them to their table, by a window overlooking the ocean. They ordered right away. The food was slow in coming, so they each had another drink.

As Scott stared out over the dark waves, his mind drifted; he imagined sitting at a café on an island in Greece, watching the local girls glance at him, then lower their eyes and hurry on. Connie was talking about something he didn't care about, and as he drifted off, her chatter turned into the banter of Greek fishermen hauling their nets onto the dock. Then she said a name that brought him back with a crash.

"Your sister was telling me about your last girlfriend. Laura was her name, wasn't it?" she said. "It made me a little curious."

Scott felt a sharp pain slice between his scalp and skull. He bumped the table and nearly upset the water glasses. "Since when are you talking to my sister?"

"Last week," she said lightly. "After dinner at your mom's house, Sammy said she'd like to see my line of sports clothing, so I gave her a card. She called me up, and we had lunch. I like her. We had a good time."

"Don't let her play you for a fool. Sammy is always plotting something. I can guarantee you she wants something from you."

"I didn't get that feeling at all. I thought she was nice."

Scott hoped his silence would steer Connie on to a different topic. Dense as a post, she rattled on.

"Whatever happened to Laura?"

"Do you mind? I'd rather not talk about her."

"Sammy said she left town kind of mysteriously." Connie ran her finger around the edge of her margarita glass, knocking off excess salt.

"Did Sammy ask you to grill me about her?"

"No, of course not."

Connie had begun to irritate him intensely, but Scott realized he would have to say something. He attempted nonchalance. "After we broke up, she went to Europe. She's touring France right now. I just got a postcard from Rouen. She loves Chartres."

"Sammy said you wanted to marry Laura?"

"Christ, Connie! Do we have to talk about her?" he said, a little too harshly. Thankfully, the waiter brought their food, which had the effect of clearing the air briefly: swordfish for him, mahimahi for her. The plates were too hot to touch.

"Sammy said that when Laura broke up with you, you became obsessed with her and started to stalk her. She warned me—said I should be careful with you." Connie said this simply, without smiling, as if weighing its merits.

"Sammy's a bitch. She can't keep a relationship, so she tries to ruin mine."

"She told me she was a lesbian."

"Sammy? No way."

"That's what she said."

Connie was probing for something, Scott knew, but he didn't know what. "Why are you so concerned about Laura? Are you afraid I'll become obsessed with you?" He lifted one side of his mouth, teasing.

"Oh, no," she said. "I don't suppose I'm the type of girl men get obsessed about."

True, but he knew better than to agree with something like that. "Why all the questions, then?"

Connie stabbed a morsel of fish and held it in the air, looking at it; its oily flesh glistened in the candlelight. She seemed close to tears. Scott scowled—it figured she was the kind of girl to get all weepy after a drink or two. She pressed her lips together, rested her fork on her plate, then took a breath. "I guess I'm always going out with guys who are still in love with someone else. It makes me wonder if something's wrong with me."

Scott nearly laughed. So she wasn't on to anything, simply preoccupied with herself, like everyone else in this town. He knew he was supposed to say something reassuring here, but he couldn't make the words come out. The alcohol was wearing off, and he was getting that raw, rutted feeling of sobering up while still conscious.

A rage swept over him like a cold ocean current. He felt something grabbing his ankles, pulling him beneath the water—the tentacles of female manipulation. He clenched his teeth and tried not to speak. Finally, he blurted, "I think you'd be better off not talking with my sister anymore." He heard himself, his authoritarian tone, like a father telling a daughter she couldn't see her beau.

Connie blushed deeply, and she didn't say much for the rest of the evening. He was glad of it. He ate his food quickly and, as soon as he was done, motioned to the waiter for the check.

Afterward, he took Connie home. She invited him in, so it took a little more time than he'd expected; it wasn't bad, but not like Laura. No one was like Laura.

Damn, all this talk about Laura—he wished he could just forget about her. He stopped by a liquor store for a six-pack, then headed home to watch tennis.

The evening had started out fun, Connie thought, then, besotted with alcohol, had collapsed like a mud slide. Connie almost never drank, and it seemed to make Scott irritable and mean. In the time between Gladstone's and her house, Scott didn't say a word to her. It was obvious he couldn't wait to get rid of her. She felt vaguely frightened of him, knowing she had displeased him. At the same time, she was angry at herself for caring that she'd displeased him.

She was surprised when he walked her to her door. The moon was full, their shadows bright against the house. She thanked him and said good night, quickly letting herself in and shutting the door. She slipped off her shoes and felt enormous relief, the kind you feel when, after dashing madly to catch a plane, you can sink into your seat. She slid open the sliding glass doors to the deck, then went to the bedroom to change out of her cocktail dress, slipping on a green silk robe.

She went into the kitchen for a glass of water. When she turned, Scott had appeared on the deck, propped on his elbows against the railing, looking at her through the open door. He propelled himself off the railing and walked toward her, pausing at the threshold. He leaned against the doorjamb and crossed his arms.

They stood there looking at each other, not speaking. A breeze off the ocean was teasing and cool. She knew what he wanted, and she felt drawn toward him; not him, exactly, but something beyond him, something sultry and anonymous. She was a little frightened, yet felt bewitched. Slowly, she walked toward him, letting her robe fall open. As he pulled her to him, pressing his mouth on hers, she felt herself sucked down beneath the waves, deep into the black ocean water.

He didn't say a word, backing her up into the bedroom, pushing her down on the bed, tearing off his clothes, lowering his weight on top of her, his hands squeezing her buttocks, his forehead pressed against her sternum; he'd plunged inside her, urgent thrusts, like a rutting Neptune, screaming as he came.

He collapsed for a few moments, then dressed and left, leaving the sliding glass door open behind him.

When Reggie arrived at the station that morning, McBride actually smiled. He handed Reggie a search warrant for Laura's employee records. Reggie closed the door to his office and dialed Brian Johnson's number.

"FBI Special Agent Clarence Whitefield speaking. How may I help you?"

Reggie yanked the receiver away from his face and looked at it, his brain spinning and coming up with nothing.

"Hello?" the receiver squawked.

Reggie suddenly felt a coffee burn in his stomach. "Yes . . . this is Detective Reggie Brooks, LAPD. I was trying to reach Brian Johnson."

There was a pause on the other end. "Could I ask what this is in regard to?" The voice was cautious.

"I have some questions about one of his company's former employees, Laura Finnegan."

Another short pause, then some mumbling, as if Whitefield had his hand over the receiver and was talking with someone else in the room. "Is this in regard to the commission of a crime?"

"Possibly."

More muffled mumbling. "Johnson is currently in FBI custody."

"What?"

"I'd rather not discuss it over the phone. If you'll meet me at FBI headquarters, I can probably clear it so you can talk to Johnson."

"In Westwood?"

"Correct."

"I'll be there in twenty minutes." Reggie hopped in a slick-back, shot north on Centinela to Wilshire, then east to Westwood. His thoughts were racing, trying to make sense of it all, but something felt jammed in the gears of his brain.

After going through security, Reggie was escorted into a small, dimly lit room with a dozen chairs in two rows, facing a one-way window. A large conference table was pushed over by the wall. Through the one-way window, Reggie saw Johnson sitting in a small lounge that looked like a stage set furnished from a seventies sitcom: Johnson was sweating through his white shirt, face red, hands in his lap.

A woman in a blue suit stood and approached Reggie, extending her hand. "Agent Cooper. Agent Whitefield said you were coming. You can talk with Johnson whenever you want." Over the sound system, they could clearly hear the echoing silence of the interview room, as well as Johnson's labored breathing and scratching. "It looks like he could use a friend."

When Reggie walked in, Johnson looked almost happy to see him. Then his face fell. "I thought you were my lawyer. I called him three hours ago, and he still hasn't showed."

"What's going on?" asked Reggie.

Johnson sighed heavily, then wiped his palms down his thighs. Reggie noticed that his socks didn't match. "I don't know. Last time you came to our offices, you saw we were in the middle of an audit. Just like every spring at the end of our fiscal year. Today I come in, and the doors are locked . . . I mean, our security cards don't work. The whole fucking place is crawling with FBI agents. I look through the reception window, and they've got these wagons, and they're loading up hard drives and files. There was an FBI agent in the lobby with an employee list. He checked off people's names and sent most of them home. But six of us got pulled aside for questioning. Then they brought me down here."

"Have you been charged with anything?" asked Reggie.

"No."

"You said you called your lawyer?"

"Three hours ago! He works right up the street!"

"Did they say why they're holding you?"

Johnson dropped his face in his hands, then sat back up. "There's a problem with the audit. They say it shows that twenty million dollars has been skimmed off from the accounts of our major clients over the last year. It was all done in small amounts, through bogus expenses and fake investments. They say it was all done from my computer, with my passwords; that the money was diverted to an account in my name. But I don't know anything about it!"

"Where's the money now?"

"I don't know! There's nothing in the account. It's been routed to offshore banks." Sweat poured off Johnson's face. "I don't know anything. They say they can't trace it, and they keep asking me where it is. Over and over. How would I know?"

"Could one of the other employees have used your computer and password?"

"That's what I keep telling them, but they don't believe me. Honestly, I don't know how someone would do it. My office is locked at night. No one knows my passwords. Besides, we have to change them every two weeks. I swear I've never taken money from clients. I know I'm not smart enough to get away with it."

"I'm sure they'll clear you if you're innocent."

Johnson made a ragged bleating sound. "That's not all." His collar was completely soaked. "It gets worse. They're looking at every website I ever logged on to."

"Let me guess. Pornography."

"I didn't do it during company hours. I didn't download anything, except once."

"You're more worried about that than getting caught stealing twenty million dollars?"

"But I didn't steal anything!"

Whitefield entered the interrogation room. "If you didn't, someone tried very hard to make it look like you did."

"Where's my lawyer?" demanded Johnson.

There was obviously no love lost between Johnson and Whitefield.

"If you tell us where the money is, I'm sure we can convince the DA to cut you some slack." Whitefield smirked.

"I'm not dealing without my lawyer present. I need to go to the restroom."

Whitefield nodded at Reggie, and they left. Outside, Whitefield instructed Agent Cooper to escort Johnson down the hall to the restroom. "See if he wants a soda. We don't want him dehydrated."

When they were alone, Reggie asked, "Have you run a polygraph on him?"

"Yeah. Three times. He passed once. The other two times were inconclusive."

"I don't think he did it," said Reggie.

"Sure he did. He left his electronic fingerprints all over the place. We have tech heads going over everyone's hard drive in the whole company. If someone else is involved, we'll find out."

"Where do you think the twenty million is now?"

"Who knows?"

"Can cash like that just disappear?"

"He sure knew what he was doing, I'll say that. Dummy corporations, moving money constantly. We're not even sure how he did it. You mentioned a former employee you wanted to question Johnson about?"

"Laura Finnegan."

Whitefield looked in a file and ran his finger down a list of names. "Yeah, she's here. Her hard drive was completely stripped in April. Sometimes, if you keep on crashing, that's all you can do. What did you want to ask about her?"

For a moment Reggie couldn't remember. "What was the date of the last transaction involving the stolen funds?" he asked.

"April twelfth. On the same day, one of Johnson's accounts was emptied except for a thousand dollars. He denies even knowing anything about the account, of course."

A cold wind ice-skated up Reggie's spine. Laura had disappeared between April 12 and 15. "Are you going to charge him?"

"Probably. We have a deputy DA en route. What did you

want to ask about Laura Finnegan?" Whitefield was clearly not a man to get sidetracked.

Reggie felt a strong urge to keep the FBI from taking a close look at Laura. At least until he knew more. "Well, you know about Johnson's record?"

"First thing we looked at. Sexual harassment. She have problems with him?"

"Yes."

"Why would a homicide detective who's head of an antigang task force be involved in that?"

So he'd been checked out. Reggie felt simultaneous dislike for this man and sympathy for the suffering Johnson. "A family favor," he said.

Whitefield looked at him blankly; it was obvious he didn't buy it. "Well," he said, "I don't think you're going to get anything more out of him now. He's clammed up till his lawyer shows. But he's not going anywhere. I don't think you'll have to worry about him feeling up the help."

Reggie left with his head spinning, wondering how Laura's disappearance figured into everything. All he could think of was how Laura had looked that day when she'd said to him at the juice bar after class, "Gentlemen such as Johnson generally get what they deserve," with a smile on her face that could melt butter.

Reggie began to feel a dry itch in his eyes and a pain between his shoulder blades. He sensed the hairy lips of doubt.

It had happened so fast. But Scott was proud of himself. He didn't hesitate, he didn't doubt himself, he didn't panic. When the time for action came, he was ready.

Scott knew he had to get rid of Laura's box of financial papers. He didn't want to destroy them, but he had to get the box out of his apartment. He decided to move it to his mother's for the time being, until he figured out someplace better. He sure hoped Peter got him that Swiss account soon. He might have to leave the country abruptly.

His mother's house had a three-car garage attached to the house and a two-car garage under the guesthouse. Over the years, the guesthouse garage had turned into a storage locker for Scott's sisters: all their junk from kindergarten to college, broken toys, posters for movies you couldn't find even on video anymore, old diaries, schoolbooks from classes in which they had crushes on their teachers, boxes of term papers, tattered valentines from second grade. Why had they kept all that shit? Like they'd ever need it again? Maybe they thought they'd be famous someday and were saving it for their biographers. They must think their own bowel movements are works of art. But that's sisters for you.

Scott opened the side door to the garage. One of his sisters had made an aisle through the mountains of boxes. Their mother was always scolding them to clean up their crap, and it looked like one of them had started and given up. The room smelled of dust, mildew, and a sharp, sweet odor he recognized as mice. He knew he should probably tell his mother about the water leak and the rodents, but he didn't want to listen to her rant, and his sisters would be royally pissed at him because then their mother would threaten to dump the shit unless they cleaned it out.

He shuffled to the back, banging his shins on a rusty old Schwinn, and crammed Laura's box under a stack of books. He covered the pile with a filthy blanket that created a dust cloud. He sneezed and felt his sinuses filling up. The place was a death trap. He could probably get tetanus from breathing the air. He went back into the house to wash his hands.

His mother's car wasn't in the driveway, so he figured she

was out. As he washed his hands in the kitchen, he was surprised to hear voices coming from the living room. Just his luck. He would've avoided the house if he'd known she was here. The last thing he wanted was to have a conversation with his mother, but at this point, he didn't see any way around it.

He braced himself, then scuffed his heels against the Saltillo tiles to make noise. "Hello? Anyone home?"

The far end of the living room had been turned into a solarium, with jungle plants, brocade furniture, and cheetah-print pillows. It reminded him of a sultan's boudoir. There, his mother lounged, her back to the window, facing him as he entered.

"Oh, Scott, darling. I'm so glad you're here. An old friend of yours dropped by."

Vivian sat across from her, dressed in black, sipping a drink. She smiled.

There was something slightly threatening in his mother's tone, like when she set him up to tell a lie. Was there sarcasm in the way she said *old friend*? What had Vivian told her?

His mother was wearing white satin lounging pajamas. She pushed herself back against the arm of the couch. Yet under her affected indolence, he perceived nervousness.

His mother continued, "Vivian says she was in town on business and wanted to look you up but had only my address for you. Isn't it fortunate you came by?"

"Hi, Vivian," he said, trying for friendly but not friendly enough to make her feel the least bit welcome.

"Vivian tells me she owns an art gallery in New York. Did you know she handles Wendy Sharpe? I've been coveting one of those works for years, but I wanted to wait until the girls left home." Mrs. Goodsell smirked at Vivian. "I didn't want the neighbors to say I was creating a poor environment."

Vivian smiled indulgently.

Scott glared at his mother's lounging pajamas and martini. It was only three in the afternoon. "A poor environment? Since when has that stopped you, Mother?"

Ignoring Scott's comment, she continued, "Well, anyhow, Vivian was telling me that she's planning a show out here for Wendy, and she's invited us. Isn't that exciting?"

Scott knew Vivian was here to pump his mother, to use her to manipulate him in some way. He watched her get up and cross the room to the fireplace. She picked up a glass bowl displayed on the mantel.

"Isn't this a lovely piece," she said to Bunny, glancing over at Scott.

"Oh, thank you, dear," Bunny gushed. "Scott gave that to me for my birthday. I don't know what got into him. It must've been terribly expensive. He's so extravagant sometimes."

"The colors and marbling are beautiful," said Vivian. "I would say it's early-sixteenth-century Venetian, from the school of Orazio Cozzi. Free-blown chalcedony glass, meant to imitate a Roman stone-cut vessel. Cozzi developed the technique, and no one was able to duplicate it. That makes his work extremely valuable."

"My goodness! You know so much about it," exclaimed Bunny.

"I've seen something like it before." Vivian glared at Scott. "You should be very proud, Mrs. Goodsell. It's museum quality. Not the kind of piece you'd ever want to part with."

Scott almost laughed. It was too absurd, Vivian threatening to expose him, stabbing at him with her double entendres. Like he cared.

"Oh, I know," said Bunny. "Scott can be so thoughtful."

Vivian smiled broadly. "Oh yes, I know."

Bunny shifted in her seat, her hand darting to her collar, closing the top button to hide her wrinkled, liver-spotted neck;

it was slated for surgery next month, and she was self-conscious about it. "Scott, darling. Vivian has told me something that's a little disturbing."

He became aware of a bitter coating on his tongue, as if he'd had too many espressos. "Oh yes? What's that?"

"Well, I take it Vivian is friends with Laura, and she tells me that Laura filed a restraining order on you. Why didn't you ever tell me about this?"

So word was out. What else had Vivian told? "I saw no reason to bother you, Mother. It was between Laura and me. A misunderstanding, really."

"But a restraining order!" she gasped. "That's awfully serious. She must've felt threatened. What did you do to her?"

"Nothing, Mother. When I broke up with her, I guess she felt bitter about it and wanted to get back at me." Scott smiled at Vivian, baiting her to contradict him. This was a little fun, messing with his mother. He was beginning to feel glad Vivian had dropped by.

"And she told me that Laura has disappeared. Her apartment is empty. Is that right?"

"Really? It's the first I've heard of it," said Scott.

"You didn't scare her so much that she left town, did you?"

"Who could be scared of me? Have I ever scared my sisters? Or you?" He slung his arm around his mother's neck in a mock headlock.

She giggled uncomfortably. "Well, I guess not."

"In fact, I would say I had more reason to be scared of you ladies." He kissed the top of her head and released her. Vivian's face looked like she might be sick.

"Don't you think you should find out where she is?" Bunny asked. "After all, you were practically engaged."

"The truth is, Mother, Laura is in France. We're still very close, but she needed time to herself. It makes me feel a little sad, of course, that she wants to be away from me. I try not to think about her." That last bit was true.

"You must be lonely," said Vivian, sarcasm exploding from her lips like a burst balloon.

Bunny didn't seem to notice. "Have you heard from her?"

"A postcard or two. I don't know when she plans to return."

"My poor dear. Well, I'm glad you're not pining away and have started dating again. Vivian, did you know Scott's engaged?"

Vivian looked at him with real surprise. "No, I didn't. Congratulations."

"A very nice girl. She was on the Olympic swim team."

"Kayaking team, Mother," Scott corrected, then wondered why he'd bothered.

Vivian looked at him, unbelieving. "Have you met her?" she asked Bunny.

"Oh, yes. Very nice girl, if a little chunky."

"She's muscular, Mother."

"Well, she looks chunky in clothes. It's how you look in a cocktail dress, is what I say."

Vivian looked confused, and Scott knew she was trying to put the pieces together. He figured he'd better get her out of there fast. She was a pest, and he saw only one solution. It might even be fun.

"Vivian," he said, "you probably want to get back to your hotel before rush hour. Do you need a ride?"

Vivian looked hesitant. "I'll take a taxi."

"Don't be absurd, honey. Scott would be glad to take you," said his mother, giving him a hug. "No one can say I didn't raise my boy to be a gentleman." Her drink was getting to her.

"I can drop you off on my way to work," said Scott. Vivian seemed to be trying to find a way out, but he hustled her out of the house before she could come up with anything.

Once he got her in the car, he drove to Sunset Boulevard. It was late afternoon. Where to go? He needed at least an hour with her, someplace quiet. This was all complicated by the fact that he had to show a house in Venice at five o'clock. Out of the corner of his eye, he noticed that she was talking to him; he turned to the passenger seat. Her face was stretching and contorting like a Halloween hologram; she was furious.

"I can't believe you took Laura's Venetian glass and gave it to your mother," she said.

"I didn't take it. Laura gave it to me."

She snorted in disbelief. "Laura would never part with it. It was special to her. We found it together at a flea market in Verona. The peasant who sold it to us had no idea of its value."

"Laura's afraid of earthquakes. She wanted me to take care of it."

"So you gave it to your mother? I don't believe you. Not for a second."

Scott shrugged. "I don't know why you pretend you're such a good friend of Laura's."

"What do you mean?"

"Are you forgetting the Waldorf-Astoria?"

Vivian pulled together her cardigan over her breasts. "As far as I'm concerned, that never happened. Anyhow, it let me know how evil you are."

"So you slept with me for Laura's sake?"

"That may sound odd to you, but yes, I did. It was a mistake, I admit."

"Why don't you just get off my case, Vivian? I have nothing against you. I'm living my life, minding my own business. Why don't you just go back to New York?"

She was shaking with anger. "Because you're a killer and a pervert."

"Pervert? You're the one selling Wendy Sharpe, making a

fortune from pictures of genitalia and blood. Next to you, I'm a saint."

"You know what makes you worse than a simple murderer? I don't think you killed her because you loved her. That would be too romantic. I think you killed her because you didn't like being denied. You're a spoiled brat. Laura said no to you, so you killed her."

He had to try to convince her. They passed UCLA and the San Diego Freeway, winding west on Sunset toward the Santa Monica Mountains and Will Rogers Park.

"Is that too much wind on you?" he asked politely. "Let me roll up the top."

"That's not necessary. I'm fine."

He ignored her. At the next traffic signal, he pressed the button. As the convertible top inched forward, the roof eclipsed the sun. When it clicked against the windshield, he reached up and locked it. "It gets chilly as we get closer to the ocean." He figured she wouldn't know they were still several miles from the water.

He swerved up a road that led to the hiking trails. This would be a good spot. Late afternoon, bound to be a few mountain bikers and hikers, but not many on a weekday.

"Where are we going?" Vivian demanded anxiously.

Scott didn't answer. He felt his face getting hot, his breath ragged. There were no houses now, only dry, dusty ridges of chaparral, wild laurel, and California oak. Certainly not deep woods, but it would have to do.

"Scott, slow down! Where the fuck are we?" Vivian turned to Scott, her eyes round, panicking. "You really did kill her, didn't you?"

"Fuck, no!" Scott slammed on the brakes. Her head smashed against the windshield as the car's back wheels spun sideways in the dirt. Her body slumped, her face was dazed. A piece of skin stuck to the windshield.

Scott's arms shook with adrenaline; his knuckles were white on the steering wheel. Thank God he hadn't been going fast enough for her to break the glass. Thank God he didn't have airbags.

The screech of tires echoed in the hills. The cloud of dust slowly dissipated. No one appeared, but someone must have heard. The area wasn't that isolated.

He looked over at Vivian. He knew she was only stunned. Now what? He straightened the car, drove a few hundred feet, then pulled up a dirt road that climbed a steep hill. He drove midway up the hill, around a curve, and pulled off to the side. One side dropped into a deep ravine; the other side was steep orange cliffs. A rattlesnake streaked across the road. A falcon coasted on air thermals rising from the canyon floor. Scott listened. A helicopter in the distance. A barking dog, probably from one of the houses on the ridge at the other side of the canyon.

Vivian slumped against the door. He wished he could find a more secluded spot. She groaned, waking. He yanked her arm, and she flopped against the seat. Slowly, she brought her hand to her face and groaned again. Scott handed her a water bottle. She took a sip.

"What happened?" she said, still groggy.

"I'm sorry, Vivian. I needed to make you listen, so relax. I have to tell you the truth." She wasn't saying anything, but Scott could tell she was listening. "Laura called me up—about six weeks ago—and asked me to come over. She sounded completely wigged out, not like Laura at all. I get over there, and she's a basket case. She'd done something really terrible, Vivian. She needed to leave the country fast. I told her I'd take care of everything. And that's what I did."

Vivian waited a moment before speaking. "What did she do?" Her voice was low, subdued.

"I can't tell you. I told her I wouldn't tell anyone. If she's caught, she'll spend the rest of her life in prison."

"Where is she now?"

"I don't know. We plan to meet in six months in Amsterdam. I don't know where she is now."

Suddenly, Vivian flung her fists at Scott's head, yelling, "I don't believe you! I don't believe you!" Scott grabbed her wrists, and she started kicking him, wriggling like an alligator in a snare.

He locked her legs between his, leveraging his body weight against her thighs. "Vivian, stop it! Please, you've got to listen to me. It's the truth." She bit his shoulder, and when he shook her off, she started to scream. He grabbed her around her neck and squeezed.

Spit bubbled at her lips. Her arms thrashed, her chest convulsed for air, her mouth sputtered, her throat gagged. She fought hard. He couldn't believe her strength. Her left arm lashed out and smashed his jaw. He leaned back, pulling her into his lap, and squeezed harder. Finally, her body relaxed. Scott looked at her skirt hiked over her knees, her breasts against his thighs, the mousy-brown roots of her dyed hair clearly visible; she revolted him.

Above, charging down in a cloud of dust, was a mountain biker, spandexed and helmeted, hips high in the air. Scott shoved Vivian's body as low as he could, praying the biker didn't stop and ask if they needed help. Before the biker could see him, Scott ducked down. Better the biker think he'd seen an empty car; that is, if he had time to think at all. A streak of fluorescent pink and green streaked by; the biker slapped his palm against the car roof, then whooped as he vaulted over a rock. He didn't stop, oblivious to anything but his adrenaline orgasm.

Scott listened as the biker crashed down the hill. He waited for a moment, then peeked over the dashboard. Bikers usually came in pairs. When no one came, he climbed out of the car and stood.

Goddammit! Why hadn't she believed him? What now? Could he dump the body here? Not in broad daylight. He began to feel dizzy. He remembered his five o'clock appointment; he had to get going.

He grabbed Vivian by the armpits and dragged her to the trunk. She would fit, he decided, and stuffed her in. When he got back in the driver's seat, he spotted her purse. He picked it up, got out, and shoved it in with her body, then closed the trunk. Now what?

He would go to his appointment, then wait until dark. He'd figure out something, he was sure.

As he started the car and slowly backed down the dirt road, panic spun his brain like a blender. When they found her body, would the police question him? Had she told anyone she was going to visit his mother? Would his mother tell the police that Vivian had left with Scott? He didn't think so.

What if her body didn't show up? The hotel would discover her disappearance in a day or two. Would they call the police? Or would they keep on charging her credit card until it was obvious she wasn't coming back?

He pulled back onto Sunset. He had just enough time to get the car washed before his showing. He'd get a second one with a complete wipe-down of the interior after he dumped the body.

Keep your mind on the details, he told himself. The rest will be easy.

PART SIX

VESPERS

He got a new girlfriend. She lived up the coast in Malibu.

Her house jutted out over the ocean, and at high tide, waves rolled up to the pilings beneath her balcony. I bet she had problems with mildew and rot, and during big storms, she must've gotten water in her living room. You'd think if someone wanted to live that close to the water, they'd live on a boat instead of having to worry about their home washing into the ocean. But that's not what people do. Not in Malibu, anyhow.

One evening I followed his Beemer there, then came back the next morning to fish. I wanted to see if he spent the night. I didn't figure he would. He was the kind of guy who thinks spending the night is giving in to a girl, like it means they have a relationship or something. From what I saw, I didn't think they were like that. Not like a couple or anything. More like they were in it for the sex.

His car was gone, but I saw the girl taking out her kayak. The water was flat with almost no waves, and when she climbed in, she hardly got wet. She let the kayak drift for a few moments, dragging her hands in the water, the swells gently rocking her. She was staring off into the distance, but it was more like she was staring into herself.

She sat up, adjusted her seat, and got ready to paddle. A shadow passed over her like there was a cloud above, but the sky was clear. She was frightened of something, but I knew it wasn't the water or sharks or nothing like that.

She started paddling like mad.

They say the Gabrieleno Indians who used to live here took their canoes to the islands, and when I saw her, I believed it. I'd need a motorboat to keep up.

She went out at dawn every day, so I started fishing in the mornings around Malibu. It was perfect, 'cause I'd just got a monthlong remodeling job on a kitchen in Encino. I fished a bit, then took the scenic route up the coast and over the mountains on Mulholland into the Valley.

Someone needed to watch out for her. I figured it might as well be me.

When Velma strode into Reggie's office and shut the door without a sound, he knew he was in for a tongue-lashing, the kind that flays your skin and makes your knees weak, the kind that doesn't care about chain of command, the kind that sends you back to the first time you broke a window.

"Reggie! You're pissing me off! I got the most respect for you, but this shit's gotta stop." Velma paced back and forth in front of his desk. "I'm sorry about Audrey leaving and everything, I'm sorry your life is fucked up. Whose isn't? I know you're off doing somethin' on the side. I don't give a damn if you got a woman. I don't give a damn if you're scamming. I just want you to do your fucking job!"

Reggie noticed her breasts straining against her blouse, making a gap between the buttons, and he remembered how at the July Fourth police picnic last year, Audrey had dubbed her Perky Perkins. What made him think of that now?

"I got my own job to do," Velma ranted. "I don't need yours, too. You're never around when we need you. Like a jerk, I've been covering for you, figuring you'd snap out of it. Newcomb comes looking for you, and I tell him you're taking a hands-on approach to the Oakwood situation. I say you're making a point to get to know everyone in the neighborhood by name."

"That's a great idea," he said.

"Fuck, Reggie! This is a fucking hard job. We're out there pulling twenty-four-hour shifts, and you aren't giving us shit! We all got fucking problems, Reggie. I'd like to see my own kid once in a while."

Reggie let her run out of steam, let the silence sit there like a cold dumpling. "You're right. I appreciate your calling me on it."

Velma sank down in the chair beside his desk. Her rage spent, she looked tired, like the job was getting to her, too.

Reggie noticed a videotape in her hand. "What's that?"

She tossed it on his desk. "It just came in from the Houston FBI—the surveillance tape from George Bush Intercontinental Airport. The one with Li'l Richie."

"You take a look at it?"

She flared up again, like a brush fire in a gust of wind. "I don't fucking have time for everything, Reggie!"

Reggie picked up the tape and leaned back in his chair. He let her stew in silence for a minute, then said quietly, "I need another week, Velma. Can you give me that?"

She glared at him hard, like a woman looking at her man who says he's given up drinking. Then she shrugged.

Reggie continued, "Sometimes you have to disappoint people you care about to do what you gotta do. It's not okay. I know that. You have to live with yourself, knowing you're letting everyone down. But sometimes you don't have a choice."

"That's some righteous bullshit," she said.

"You're right, but you have me under the gun. It's the best I could come up with."

She almost smiled, her shoulders relaxing.

"Bring me up to date on the San Juan case," Reggie said. "I'll take a look at the tape later."

It almost made Scott laugh.

He was trembling, it was so funny. Mr. Yuppie had asked if he was all right. Scott said he was fine but had forgotten to take his medicine that morning. That shut him up.

What amused Scott was Mr. Yuppie running his hands over the side of his BMW, saying he almost bought one just like it instead of his new Ford Explorer, caressing the rear fender, sliding his hand over the trunk with Vivian stuffed inside.

Then Scott said—he couldn't help himself, it popped out like a hiccup—"You wouldn't believe the trunk space in this baby," and he giggled, and Mr. Yuppie smiled pleasantly (though you could tell he was thinking about the medicine), and Scott felt almost disappointed that he didn't ask to see the trunk. The look on his face would have almost made it worthwhile.

When did bodies begin to smell? he wondered. Didn't their bowels release at death? Maybe good ol' Viv was too constipated to let go. He hadn't wanted to kill her. It was an accident, really. All these stupid women with their stupid questions, asking *Why this? Why that?* like the world was supposed to make sense, pretending they cared, but really only wanting to control you.

The world was a better place without Vivian Costanza, he decided. He'd done the universe a favor.

After poking around the house like two amateur detectives, Mr. and Mrs. Yuppie decided $625,000 was too much to pay for a two-bedroom shack on the edge of Oakwood. They had to see the place to figure that out? Scott offered to show them more modestly priced homes in Mar Vista, with better neighborhoods, lower crime, and bigger yards, but they were exhausted from the shock of it all. He knew the type: They'd wait until prices went even higher, then, in a panic, they'd buy at the top of the market. He watched them get into the shiny green Ford Explorer, brand-new. They probably paid top dollar for that, too, so worried about being left behind that they didn't foresee rising oil prices and the bottom falling out of the SUV market. Suckers, he thought. He was glad when they drove off. He couldn't stand dealing with people anymore.

Fear caught her in bursts of panic when she glanced at the calendar, or when she was driving on the freeways between client appointments, when she let her mind wander and worry. Connie tried to rationalize it away: She was only a week late, and she was accustomed to skipping periods during training or when dieting. But a second week passed, and she had to admit that she wasn't in training, she was eating well, and she was having sex.

Connie called her sister, Marge.

"Did you take a test?"

"I don't need to. I know."

"What are you going to do?"

Connie was silent for a moment. She hadn't thought that far ahead yet, the anxious waiting for blood making her irritable, overriding her personality like a persistent migraine. She'd had a couple of abortions in her early twenties, and it dawned on her that she was close to thirty, and if she ever wanted children, she'd better start thinking about it. It also occurred to her that she shouldn't wait until she found a man to marry, a man who wanted children. That might never happen. She was suspicious of single women who had children out of loneliness or desperation, blaming some fictitious biological clock. Yet somehow, she felt the child inside her wanted to be born.

"Are you still there, Connie?"

"Yeah, sorry. I don't know what I'm going to do."

"Have you told Scott?"

Another flash of fear washed over her, only this was different, a fear that spread from deep inside her womb, a burning sensation that made her want to leap out of her skin.

"No," Connie said.

"How serious are you about him?"

Serious, not serious, *what strange words to use,* she thought. "He's great, and we have fun . . . but there's something I don't trust about him."

"Like what?"

Connie thought of their dinner at Gladstone's, how angry he'd become when she mentioned Laura. She was glad she hadn't asked about the restraining order. And the way he looked at her when he wanted her, as if she were something to eat. "I can't describe it. It's like I'm not always sure how he'll react to things."

Her sister sighed heavily, then breathed silently, listening so intently that Connie could almost feel her. "He hasn't hit you, has he?" Marge's voice was barely a whisper.

"No," Connie said carefully. She knew what Marge was thinking: that people with abusive parents seek out abusive relationships, and that even though they never saw their father hit their mother, he came as close to it as a speeding train to the walls of a mountain pass. After they left home, they wondered if, in his rages, he hit her when they weren't around.

"Well, follow your instincts, girlfriend. Don't even think of marrying him if you feel you can't trust him."

Marriage, Connie knew, wasn't an option. She didn't dare tell Marge that in a sense, they were engaged, or at least Scott's mother thought so. If Marge knew she had played along with such a ridiculous charade, she might figure her sister deserved what she got, which was sort of what Connie herself thought.

After Connie hung up, she made an appointment with her

gynecologist for later in the week. She then made herself a tuna sandwich with tomato and avocado. The food tasted unusually bright and good, and she wondered if it was due to the pregnancy.

It was late afternoon. She decided to take the kayak out, and paddled up the coast almost to Pepperdine University. Out here she could think, her fears fading with the rhythm of her arms as they pulled her through the water, swells lifting and dropping her like the chest of a breathing animal. Out here she felt safe. Nature protected her. She felt at home, daughter to mother ocean, sister to dolphin and pelican.

An image came to mind of the child floating in her womb, and of her floating on top of the waves. It felt perfectly natural, as it should be: a pregnant woman in a boat on the sea. As she propelled herself through the water, dipping her paddle in long, steady strokes, a power she never knew before diffused through her, her fear transforming into a protective maternal ferocity; she felt she could conquer anything.

Hours later, when she pulled the kayak onto the beach beside her house, she knew she would keep the baby.

Scott had several hours before it was dark. He cruised around Venice, up and down the canal bridges, then through the alleys. New construction was everywhere—like the unfinished sets of a Broadway musical—one of the by-products of the blazing real estate market. Plots hopelessly contaminated by oil rigs that had dotted the shore in the twenties were now being cleaned up and built on. Opportunities lay everywhere: for building contractors, Mexican laborers, Realtors, landscapers, home buyers. And murderers with bodies to dump.

Scott found several prospective spots where the ground was soft, where laborers had graded the sand for foundations, but he discarded them for one reason or another. One lot was too close to a house, another too visible from the street. He crossed a bridge to the other side of Dell Avenue, where they were rebuilding a damaged sidewalk along Carroll Canal. He watched the Mexican laborers pack up for the day, right in the middle of filling in a ditch. He could see that they planned to fill in the ditch, pack it, lay rebar on top, then pour cement.

The spot was perfect. He waited impatiently for the laborers to leave.

The sidewalk ran in front of a little park for the ducks, between a vacant house for sale and a house under construction. Scott looked around, hoping one of the laborers had left a shovel. No such luck, but in the duck park, propped up beside a trash can, he found an old spade used for cleaning up dog poop.

He planned to wait until after nine, when everyone was done walking their dogs, and inside for the night. The houses here might cost a million dollars, but it was still Venice, and people didn't wander around much after dark.

He parked on Venice Boulevard and thought of taking a walk, but worried about his car getting stolen with Vivian's body in the trunk. Wouldn't that surprise the guys at the chop shop?

So he sat there, fretting about what could go wrong, from his collapsing under Vivian's weight to a police cruiser catching him in its headlights just as he lifted her out of the trunk, scenes he imagined with such intensity that he began to shiver and hyperventilate. His thighs itched madly. He scratched so hard that he left white streaks in the fabric of his pants; the itching got worse.

He felt as if his body were contracting into itself, as if his head might explode straight up through the roof of his car, like a cartoon character eating hot chili. At twenty to nine, he couldn't wait any longer.

He drove around the block and parked in an alley behind an abandoned liquor store. He cursed the whiteness of his car and tried to hide it under an oleander bush. He stepped into the street to see if it was visible.

As a car crested the arch of the canal bridge, its headlights hit his Beemer, and his license number popped out like a sign for a bordello in a dark alley. Jesus!

He reparked his car on the other side of the store. There were no bushes to hide under, but at least it was hidden from the street.

He walked back to the trunk and unlocked it. He looked around and listened: ducks, traffic on Washington, a car alarm several blocks away. He opened the trunk.

She lay on her left side, knees bent. He slipped on the black driving gloves he'd jammed into his pocket. He grabbed Vivian by the wrist and yanked her arm; her flaccid body flopped toward him like a fish. As he pulled her out, he jumped back, horrified by her half-purple face, but then realized it must be her blood settling.

She seemed heavier than before, and so awkward. He sat back on the fender, grabbed her around the waist, and pulled her to a sitting position. Then he stood, flipped her left arm around his neck, grabbed her waist with his right arm, set his teeth, and leaned back. He staggered a few steps, hoisting most of her bulk on his right hip. God, she weighed a ton. No ballerina here.

When he reached up with his left hand to close the trunk, he saw one of her shoes caught in the carpeting. He thought of sticking it in his pocket but decided to leave it there with her purse. He'd take care of them later.

Suddenly, the ducks started squawking wildly. Scott heard someone coming. He looked over Vivian's shoulder and saw a small man with a Great Dane that was lunging at the ducks.

The man could barely control the animal, grappling with both hands, yanking the dog up over the bridge, angrily yelling, "Come!" ten times in a row, as if the dog might finally understand.

He was too busy with his dog to notice the man standing there with a dead body.

After the man and the dog disappeared, Scott staggered up the narrow street, Vivian's feet dragging beside him. Her head rolled onto his shoulder, her hair was in his mouth. The smell of her scalp sickened him. His right arm throbbed with pain.

Car lights floated up and over the canal bridge. He swung Vivian's body toward him and buried his head in her neck. He hoped the driver would think he saw a pair of young lovers overcome by the romance of the canals, the smell of jasmine in the air, the soporific lapping of the water against the rowboats. The lights passed over them, then continued down the grade to Venice Boulevard.

He nearly gagged on Vivian's perfume, her large breasts pressed against him. He almost dumped her right there, when, out of the corner of his eye, he saw a figure strolling away from him on the other side of the canal. It was enough to remind him why he was there, the consequences of being caught. *Get control of yourself! It's not much farther,* he told himself, trying to placate his panic. He shifted the body to his left side and recommenced his slow, bumpy shuffle.

He staggered past the duck park, nearly slipping on guano, then, gaining his balance, dragged her past the vacant house toward the new construction. He stopped where the sidewalk ended at an open ditch, the edge ragged with rebar. He stood with her in his arms and looked around. Lights from inside the houses reflected on the water like riverboats at night; the houses appeared to be moving. He heard the sounds of dishes being set out for dinner and faint classical guitar music.

Quickly, he heaved Vivian into the pit. A shiver tore through his body; he rubbed his triceps and waited to catch his breath. He walked back to the duck park, grabbed the shovel, and hurried back. The ducks scooted out of his way. He knelt beside Vivian and wiped off her neck with her blouse. Had he touched her on any other place without gloves? He didn't think so. He looked at her feet: Both shoes were now missing. Damn! He'd have to look for the other one on the way back.

He leaned on the spade; his arms had hardly any strength left. He gritted his teeth. Pushing from his lower back, he dug a shovelful of dirt. It made more noise than he expected, but no one seemed to notice. He tossed the dirt into the pit, as he'd seen the Mexicans doing that afternoon. He discovered a way to quietly slip the spade into the sand, guiding it with the sole of his shoe. He paused between shovelfuls, listening. Either they'd find the body tomorrow or they'd cover it with cement. At this point he hardly cared. He simply wanted to be done with it.

After five minutes, he'd covered her. He leveled out the sand to the height of the rebar. He wondered if the Mexicans would notice that their work had been done for them. He hoped they'd be too hungover to notice.

As he backed up from the construction area, he swept away his tracks with a T-shirt one of the laborers had left. He put the spade back in the duck park, then looked around for Vivian's shoe.

A woman approaching him on the road slowed and shortened the leash to her terrier. "You looking for something?" she asked, her voice polite, mildly alarmed.

Scott had been standing under the glow of a streetlamp. He stepped into the shadows, slowly, so as not to alarm her. "My little girl says she dropped her stuffed rabbit out here. She was in the duck park with her mother this afternoon. She won't go to bed without it."

"She in the terrible twos?" the woman asked, her voice softening.

"You got it."

"It'd bc easier to find in the morning. All this construction makes it dangerous to be poking around."

He could see better now; she was a woman in her sixties, wearing a knee-length trench coat. "I don't think I can face her without it."

"I know what you mean," she said, amused. "Good luck."

She walked away, her terrier sweeping from side to side like a metal detector. He hoped she hadn't gotten a good look at him, hunched there in the dark. But if she had, she'd remember a young daddy, stooped and tired, afraid of his daughter's temper tantrums.

He gave up on trying to find Vivian's shoe, wondering now if one of the dogs had taken it. When he got back to his car, he took her purse and the other shoe from the trunk. He drove behind Baja Cantina on Washington Boulevard. He took the cash from her wallet, $184; thought of keeping a credit card; then decided against it. He was about to toss her purse into the restaurant Dumpster when he saw a homeless man around the corner eyeing him suspiciously; Scott pulled back his arm and drove around the block.

He parked a block away, on Via Dolce, then took a walk. He emptied the wallet in a storm drain, then tossed the purse, wallet, and shoe in different residential trash cans along a four-block area.

There was only one loose end, he thought as he got back into his car: She was still registered at Loews Hotel in Santa Monica. In a day or two, the maid would notice she hadn't been back to her room. What would they do then? Contact the police? Would they pack up her stuff and store it until she came back? She'd probably prepaid with a credit card. That's what they cared about—getting paid. They couldn't possibly call the police every time someone left without checking out. He figured that had to happen quite often. Probably every day.

When Reggie called Loews Hotel a second time, the receptionist said there was no Vivian Costanza registered. He asked to speak to a manager. A Mr. Silva got on the line. When Reggie asked if Vivian had checked out, Silva said he couldn't give out that information on the phone. Reggie sighed. Police got no respect in this town.

Before he left for Loews, Reggie called Ronda Wiley and asked if they had come up with any new information on Laura.

"We have credit-card charges from Paris: clothes, books, art supplies, and a ticket to London."

"Doesn't it seem odd that there are no hotel charges?"

"She could be staying with friends, I suppose. I called the credit-card company for signature receipts. That always takes a while."

"Good. Anything else?" asked Reggie.

"We checked her data against all the Jane Does who've come in the last three months."

"No dice?"

"Nope."

"It looks like Vivian Costanza checked out of her hotel. Do you have another number for her?" As he said this, he remembered that he had Vivian's home number—from Laura's phone bill—in his car.

"She left?" asked Ronda, surprised. "She told me she'd call before she returned to New York. She gave me her gallery and home number in Manhattan. Just a sec." After some rustling of papers, Ronda gave Reggie the numbers.

Reggie first left a message on Vivian's home phone, then called the gallery. A lyrical voice with a Puerto Rican accent answered. "Helloooo. Galleria Costanza. This is Amaldo. How may I be of service to you this morning?" The voice zipped up and down several octaves, nearly breaking into song.

"This is Police Detective Reggie Brooks from Los Angeles. May I speak to Vivian Costanza?"

"Oh, my. Are you a real cop?"

Reggie hesitated. "Yes. LAPD."

"Ooooh. I'm getting chills. You're black, aren't you? I can tell by your voice. You went to college, though, am I right?"

Reggie sighed. "This is quite important. May I speak with Miss Costanza?"

"Has that girl gone and gotten herself into trouble? I warned her about Hollywood. All those loose willies."

Reggie was reduced to begging. "Please, may I speak with her?"

"Oh, Vivian's not here."

"Do you know if she's returned to New York?"

"Not as far as I know."

"Do you speak with her often?"

"Oh yes. Several times a day. She's been very anxious about sales on the last Wendy Sharpe exhibit. But she needn't worry. They're flying off the walls."

Reggie didn't know who Wendy Sharpe was and didn't ask. "When was the last time you spoke with her?"

"That would be . . . let's see . . . three days ago."

"Is it unusual for her to go so long without calling you?"

"Yes, come to think of it. I hope she's run off to Palm Springs with some Hollywood stud muffin. She needed some exercise, if you know what I mean."

Reggie gave Amaldo his number and asked him to call if he heard from Vivian, and if she did call, to have her phone Reggie immediately.

"How tall are you?" asked Amaldo.

Reggie hung up. He pulled on his sport coat and headed out of the station.

The Loews was one of a string of new luxury hotels built on the beach between Venice and Santa Monica. Despite its pink marble interiors and elegant landscape of palm trees and impatiens, it was the kind of cheap construction that would look shabby in a couple of years; its peach-white stucco exterior was already water-stained under the balconies. Rooms started at $249 a night.

Reggie parked his slickback in front. None of the half-dozen Hispanic valets offered to park it for him; they scattered in all directions like mice.

Reggie marched over the red carpet up to the front desk. He flashed his badge and asked to speak with Mr. Silva.

Mr. Silva was much more cooperative in person. Apparently, Vivian had not checked out, though the maid reported that she had not slept in her bed for two days, and she hadn't stopped for messages. Since the room had been reserved by another person for that night, the maid was now collecting Vivian's belongings to put in storage. "It happens all the time," Silva said. "People simply disappear. We don't want to run up their credit-card bills unnecessarily, and we need the room. So we store their stuff for six months. For a fee, of course. Some come back. Some don't."

Reggie asked to see the room. Silva looked like he might ask for a warrant, then didn't. He took a key and rode with Reggie to the fourth floor.

Thankfully, the maid had yet to get there. The room looked like Vivian had intended to return: a half-packed suitcase lay open; cosmetics were spread out in the bathroom; a silk peignoir with an ostrich-feather collar lay tossed over a chair.

There was no evidence of a struggle, no evidence of a second person's presence. Reggie would have liked to dust for fingerprints, but he had no authority here. He did ask the maid to wear gloves when she gathered Vivian's belongings into clear plastic bags. "We always wear gloves," the maid replied. "You know, because of AIDS and hepatitis and stuff." He'd dust for fingerprints later, if he found cause for a warrant.

Vivian had brought a lot of clothes from New York, business suits, mostly, one cocktail dress, seven pairs of shoes. She seemed to have a preference for black. He checked the pockets of her bags. There were cards for a number of art galleries and restaurants around town. Reggie found one for Bob Harrison at Bay City Realty; a number, probably his home phone, was on the back.

When Reggie didn't find Vivian's address book, he figured she carried it with her. He found a number scratched on a pad by the telephone; he called it.

"You have reached the residence of Beatrice Goodsell. Please leave a message." The beep was a three-tone gong. He hung up. Why did Vivian have the home number for Scott's mother?

Later, Reggie ran a credit check on Vivian. She hadn't used her cards in three days. He began to get a sick feeling in his stomach.

Two mornings in a row, Scott got up before seven, jogged down to Palisades Park, then up Montana to a Starbucks on Fourteenth Street, where he bought coffee and a paper. Still no body had been reported. He figured by now the sidewalk was finished, and after that, they might not find her body for years.

It was Saturday. Even though it was cloudy, he thought he'd take his bike down to Venice while it was early. He wanted to see what Carroll Canal looked like in daylight. The idea of revisiting the spot oddly excited him.

He put on black bike shorts, a gray T-shirt, and, although he hated to wear one and didn't think there was any particular reason to be cautious, a bike helmet to hide his hair. He took San Vicente Boulevard and Ocean Avenue to the Santa Monica Pier, then rode down to the bike path between the boardwalk and the beach. When he got to Venice Boulevard, he turned inland to the canals.

He walked his bike along Carroll Canal, on the side opposite the duck park and the construction site. He was astonished: It looked like no one had touched the site. He was grateful that his handiwork appeared undisturbed, but it made him uncomfortable that they hadn't gotten around to laying the rebar and pouring the cement. He was afraid there was a work stoppage of some sort. He'd seen sites lie abandoned like this for weeks, while the contractor waited on supplies or building permits or a city inspection. He began to worry. Maybe he should move the body. He hadn't buried it very deeply.

Two women walking by the construction site looked over at him, then at the site, wondering what he was staring at. He moved on. He'd wait another couple of days. If the workers hadn't started again by Monday, he'd consider moving the body. But that seemed extremely risky; he'd gotten away with it once, and it hardly seemed possible that he could go unnoticed a second time.

As he pushed his bike down the sidewalk, he ran into a gang of ducks led by two enormous geese. They quacked angrily at him, moving grudgingly out of his way, leaving a slippery mess of white and brown droppings that looked to Scott like rotting viscera. He was revolted. Disgusting lice-infested vermin! As if the canals weren't polluted enough without their stinky crap. The water was probably half urine. It sure smelled like it. He couldn't imagine how people found them charming. If he lived in the canals, they would drive him crazy. He gave a laggard mallard a swift kick in the butt, sending him squawking into the water.

The women across the canal looked at Scott with round mouths of indignation. Scott laughed. He got on his bike and rode off.

When he got home, he took a shower and got ready for his first showing of the day, a stucco box in a bad area of Culver City; it looked deceptively benign in the morning, which was the only time he'd show it. He was just about to leave when there was a knock on his door. Probably one of his irritating neighbors. He shouted that he was coming, slipped on his shoes, and stumbled to the door.

Connie stood at the top of the stairs, dressed in one of her candy-colored latex outfits, her bike shoes clacking against the cement like tap shoes. She leaned her bike against the railing. "May I come in?" she asked.

"Sure, I guess. I have to leave in a minute." Scott was surprised she'd known his address, but then he remembered their first date, almost a year ago, when they'd stopped by to pick up something or other—his cell phone, if he remembered right. He hated to invite her in. Then he figured it didn't really matter. "Come on in," he said at last.

She entered his apartment, looking around like she was afraid to touch anything. It made him mad; the place wasn't that messy. But the look on her face was repulsion. Or was he imagining it? He guessed it did smell kind of funny. What *was* that? Cumin? An Indian family had moved in next door, and the place always reeked of something he couldn't quite place: some kind of meat with curry, or rancid fat. What did he care? As soon as he got his Swiss account, he was gone.

He opened the windows. Connie was still standing by the door. "Well, what's up?" he asked.

"I left two messages on your machine, but you didn't call back," said Connie.

"When?" As Scott hunted for the things he needed to take with him—address book, property profile, cell phone, business cards—he barely listened.

"Wednesday. Also Thursday."

He honestly didn't remember. "I wish I could stay and chat, but I'm already late."

"I won't take much of your time. I came by to tell you I'm pregnant," she said matter-of-factly.

Scott was astonished. That hadn't happened in a while, so long ago, in fact, that he'd stopped worrying about contraception. He figured the women he dated were old enough to take care of themselves. He suddenly felt extremely annoyed, like when he came out of a store to find a meter maid writing him a parking ticket. "I suppose you think it's mine?"

"There's no doubt."

He snapped his briefcase closed and pulled on his jacket. "How much is an abortion these days?" he said. He tried to sound jocular, but it came out hostile. He didn't care. "Four hundred dollars? I guess RU-486 is about the same price. I'm good for half."

"I'm keeping it," she said.

His scalp itched like crazy. "Just like that? Don't I get a say here?"

"Not really. An unwed father has no legal rights regarding the fetus."

He was outraged. The injustice of it all. This woman with his baby. The thought made his mouth taste of vinegar.

"Don't worry, I'm not asking you for financial support or anything. You don't ever even need to see the baby. In fact, I'd rather you didn't."

"Then why in fuck did you come to tell me about it?"

She was near tears. "I thought you'd want to know, that's all."

"I fucking don't want to know." He couldn't wait to get out of the country. It was this thought—that soon he'd be away from this cesspool of a city—that kept him from exploding. How the fuck did he get into such a mess? That stupid ring and that fucking engagement farce for his mother. Damn it all!

Connie was looking scared. Scott tried to control his voice. "Look. I don't care about the baby. Do whatever you want with it. I appreciate your playing along with the engagement thing. I hope you didn't take it seriously."

"No, of course not. You were very clear about that." She sounded hurt.

He glanced at her hands, then looked for his keys and cell phone. "Good. I need the ring back, however."

"I gave it to your sister."

He spun around, furious. "You what?"

Connie backed up two steps. "I gave it to Samantha. She told me that her grandmother gave it to her and that it was really hers. So I let her have it."

"I can't believe you did that! It wasn't yours to give to anyone," he fumed.

"I felt uncomfortable keeping it. Besides, you didn't answer my calls. Samantha asked for it. What was I supposed to do?"

He wanted to hit her so badly that he could feel his fingernails digging into his palms. His thighs began to vibrate. "Get out!" he yelled. "Get out!"

She jumped like a frightened cat and ran out the door.

He listened gratefully as she set her bike down at the bottom of the stairs and spun off. Shaking overtook his body, and a sharp pain hit below his sternum. He clutched his chest and sank onto the sofa. He was too young for a heart attack. He slurped down some cold coffee left in a nearby cup. If he took shallow breaths, it didn't hurt too much. After a minute, the shaking stopped.

He couldn't believe the insane loathing he felt for that woman. How dare she take his sperm and make a baby, threaten to keep it, a copy of himself that would wonder about him even if he never saw it? Someday the little monster, like an avenging angel, would track him down and demand to know why he'd left, demand attention and feelings as if it had a right to them. How dare she use an umbilical cord to strangle the life out of him, cooking up from her mess of blood and tissue a little beast that would live to hate him just as he hated his father?

He wouldn't let her get away with it. How fucked were the laws to say a woman could keep a baby without the father's permission? Fucking women's rights. What about his rights?

It was time to put these women in their place.

The receptionist at Bay City Realty asked Reggie to wait for Bob Harrison to finish signing closing papers with a client. In a few moments, Harrison popped out of his office with a young couple who looked like they'd just agreed to donate a kidney. The husband was particularly pale. Harrison clapped a hand on each of their shoulders, laughing like a Texas rancher at a Sunday-afternoon barbecue. He made a great show of handing them the house keys, then walked them out to their car. When he came back, he wiped his forehead with a plaid handkerchief. "Phew, it's getting humid out there," he said.

"They say it's going to rain," said the receptionist.

"This time of year?"

"An early hurricane in the Pacific is coming up the coast along Baja. Hurricane Angelo."

"The rain will be good for my tomatoes." He turned and noticed Reggie.

Even though he wasn't wearing a uniform, Reggie saw *cop*

flash in bright lights behind Harrison's eyes. Reggie introduced himself and asked if he could have a word. Harrison told the receptionist to hold his calls, then ushered Reggie into his office.

"Have you ever met a woman by the name of Vivian Costanza?" Reggie asked.

Harrison blinked twice. "Yes, she came in last week. She told us she was planning a move from New York and wanted a residence on the Westside."

"Did you show her any properties?"

"I gave her to one of our finest Realtors, Scott Goodsell. He showed her a few places, but apparently, she wasn't that serious about buying yet."

"Did she seem to know Scott?"

"Now that you mention it, yes. I think she said they were casual acquaintances or something like that. No, *old friends* was what she said."

"Do you know if Scott saw her again?"

"No, I don't know. Can I ask what this is all about?"

"Miss Costanza left her hotel without checking out. We'd like to talk to her. Does Scott have any personal friends you know of?"

"His best friend is Peter Flynn. Works at Bank of America. A loan officer."

"Do you have his number?"

"No. But you could ask Amy, the receptionist. She has copies of all incoming messages on her message pad. He calls Scott all the time. Great guy."

"I found your card in her hotel room." Reggie handed him the card. "Is that your home phone on the back?"

Harrison laughed uncomfortably. "Yes." Fuchsia crept over his bald pate like a sunrise over the desert. "She's my type of woman. Quite a dish."

A dish? Did people really talk like that anymore? Did they ever? If Audrey heard him refer to any woman as a dish, he'd be sleeping in the tree house for a month. "Did you meet her outside of this office?"

Harrison frowned. "No. I never saw her again. I didn't have a chance, you know. Not with a girl like her. But you can't blame a guy for trying."

Reggie had to ask. "Where were you last Wednesday between the end of work and Thursday morning?"

Harrison's eyes got big and scared. "I worked until around eight, then went over to a friend's house for poker. I got home around two."

"Can anyone account for your getting home at two?"

Harrison turned red again. "Yeah, my mother. I live with my mother"—he said this as if he were admitting to a juvenile arrest record—"and my neighbor. I kicked over a trash can going up the stairs, and my neighbor yelled at me. Are you asking for an alibi?"

Reggie smiled. "I may need to call them, if you could write down their numbers."

"Well, sure," Harrison said, scribbling down the numbers on a Bay City Realty pad. His hands were shaking. He tore off the top sheet and handed it to Reggie.

Reggie got Peter Flynn's number from the receptionist, then left. As he got into his car, he felt the first drops of rain.

The next morning Mike Morrison called Reggie at ten minutes after nine. "You still interested in the arms case?"

"Absolutely."

"There's a guy here, a private investigator down from Portland. I think you might want to talk to him."

"I'll be right there." When Reggie told the desk sergeant he was stepping out for an hour, he saw Velma shoot him a dirty look.

As Reggie drove up Pacific Coast Highway to Malibu, it began to rain hard. The blacktop steamed, and the air smelled of hot wet dirt.

Traffic slowed, bumper to bumper. Reggie's mind began to wander. He thought of something Father John had said that morning. They met once a week now at the Rose Café in Venice. They took their coffee down to the beach and, as they chatted, walked on the hard sand toward the Santa Monica Pier.

"When I was a monk, we stopped work seven times during the day, to gather and pray, to center ourselves and reach out to divine love." Father John was looking out at the ocean. A school of dolphins swam north beyond the breakers. "Life should be a continual thanksgiving, Reggie. You don't have to be a monk to stop and pray."

As the traffic ground to a stop, Reggie smiled to himself. That's a cop's life, he thought, work and praying you don't get killed at work.

At the Malibu/Lost Hills station, Reggie ambled past the detective desks and saw Morrison standing in an interview room, stuffing down a muffin. Beside him sat a large man flipping through a blue murder book, rocking his head back and forth like a grizzly bear sniffing huckleberries.

"Hey, Reggie. This is Private Investigator Harry Gribble."

When Gribble stood, the table screeched across the floor, and the aluminum chair fell over. He was huge, his muscles wrapped in fat like a beaver-fur coat. He wore a red plaid flannel shirt, black sweatpants, and logging boots. He looked less like a private investigator than a North Woods hermit who'd just stepped from his log cabin to use the outhouse.

After straightening the table and righting the chair, Morrison rolled in another chair, and everyone sat down. Gribble told his story.

"I'm down from Portland looking for a young woman, a runaway, Stacy Savage, nineteen, white. She's been missing since last year. Her parents hired me to find her. Looks like she was into the rave scene—ecstasy, crack cocaine. She must've run into some trouble, 'cause she checked in at the Harley House in Hollywood. That's how I tracked her to Los Angeles." The Harley House, Reggie knew, was a refuge for runaways and child prostitutes. "She left a few months ago. One of the kids there said he'd heard she moved into a group house in Venice. I checked the café bulletin boards for rooms available, made some calls, and traced her to a group house on Brooks in Venice. Shc was off drugs and enrolled at Santa Monica College. Looked like she was trying to clean up her act. One of her housemates says she disappeared around the middle of April."

Reggie glanced sharply at Mike, who nodded and raised his eyebrows: *Keep listening.*

"Her housemate said last month they boxed up her stuff and rented the room again. He let me look at the box. Not much there, but it didn't look like she'd packed up and left, either. Her toothbrush, nail polish, cosmetics were all there. Her housemate says she was dating a guy named Kevin who works at a camera shop in Santa Monica. I talked to him. He seems pretty straight. Says he hasn't seen her since April. So I went downtown to see what you've got for Janc Does in April and May. I'd looked over a dozen or so when I came across the arms case. Then I came out to see Mike here."

"Apart from the time frame, what makes you think the arms might be hers?" asked Reggie.

Gribble flipped to an autopsy photo in a plastic sheath. "Same blood type, for one: A positive. And see this scar on her elbow? Her mother said she got a scar like that when she was ten years old, falling off her bike."

"You think her mother could identify the arms?"

"Nah. And I wouldn't put her through that until we're real sure."

"You got a fingerprint for Stacy?"

"Nothing on file. The police tried pulling latents from her room at home, but they didn't get a clear print."

"What about the ring she was wearing?"

"The mother didn't know about any ring. Neither did her boyfriend."

"Did Detective Morrison tell you how valuable the ring was?"

"Amazing, huh? She probably stole it. She was picked up several times for shoplifting in Portland. Never got charged, though. Too bad, 'cause then we'd have prints."

Reggie turned to Morrison. "You think it's enough to go for a DNA test?"

"Good enough for me."

"The family's already got a DNA test for Stacy," said Gribble. "Did one for a body dump in Washington that turned out not to be her. Her mother is overnighting a copy down to me."

"Can you guys get a rush on the DNA?" Reggie asked Morrison.

"I'll see what kind of favors I can pull in. I hear they're testing a new gadget down at Parker Center that's instant and ninety-nine percent accurate. I'll see if I can't sneak it through. Otherwise, well, you know . . ."

"Weeks?" asked Gribble.

"Weeks on a rush."

Satisfied that he wouldn't get immediate results, Gribble promised to drop off a copy of Stacy Savage's DNA test results before he returned to Portland.

After Gribble lumbered out, Morrison turned to Reggie. "So, what do you think?"

"Based on a blood type and a small scar—I'd say it's a stretch," Reggie said.

Morrison frowned. "I agree, but what else do we have to go on?"

"Nothing."

"Right. Nothing."

Reggie wasn't about to give up anything on Laura. He realized at some point, Morrison would learn that he'd held out on him. He felt bad, but there was nothing he could do about it now. McBride had been clear.

Reggie felt ambivalent about this turn of events. If the arms turned out not to be Laura's, that meant she could be alive. Surely there was no truth to Scott's ever-changing stories, but where was she? And what about the millions stolen from Thompson & Thompson, which had disappeared from Johnson's account the same day she did? And if the arms were Stacy Savage's, how and why did Stacy Savage have Scott's grandmother's ring?

Six-thirty A.M. Reggie was in his backyard practicing kendo in nothing but gym shorts, his body laboring, dripping with sweat, jabbing, kicking, pivoting. He swung the sword over his head, then down in a *Z*, slicing off the heads of his enemies.

He tried not to think about work, about Laura, but he found himself increasingly agitated, his balance off, his movements clumsy.

Frustrated, he jabbed the sword into the ground and caught his breath. The world spun around him. He imagined Laura in her kitchen, looking out over the bougainvillea, smiling. He sensed an achy tension in his shoulders, a building anger that felt like betrayal. After all this work, maybe she was still alive.

As he wiped his face with a towel, he thought of the pile of towels and other clothes overflowing the laundry basket, and knew he'd have to figure out how to run the washing machine pretty soon. He noticed the line of purple iris and snapdragons edging the lawn. After that big storm, at least he didn't have to water.

Damn, he missed his wife. She did so much around the house he'd never noticed before. As he looked around the yard—at the herbs she'd planted close to the kitchen door and the roses she'd trained to climb the back wall—something Father John had said came to him: *Whatever aspect of the soul we neglect will become the source of pain.* Reggie felt weak-kneed with regret and longing. He wanted his family.

He stomped into the house, poured himself a glass of orange juice, and picked up the phone.

Reggie had no idea what to expect. He was nervous about it, as if he were calling a girl for a first date.

The maid answered. Then Audrey got on the line. She sounded cheerful and rested. Reggie let her voice reverberate through his body; it tingled up his spine and made his pores constrict, as if chilled. "Hello?" she repeated.

"Hey," said Reggie.

"Hey." Her voice grew husky, as if her throat were coated in creamy hot chocolate.

"You get the hot sauces?"

"Yeah. Ring of Fire. You remembered."

"Sure . . . sure I remembered. I miss you."

She hesitated, the kind of hesitation where you hear someone doing an emotional inventory.

"How are the boys?" he asked.

"Fabulous. They adore sailing. They each have a Sunfish. They race every day. You wouldn't believe their tans. They're brown as Hershey Kisses."

"I don't suppose that pleases your parents much."

"They're not as bad as you think." She paused. "We're having fun, Reggie. The kids love it here."

She paused again, long enough for Reggie to wonder if she meant she planned to stay.

Then she broke the silence. "I think we make things harder than they need to be."

"Maybe."

"The kids adore their grandparents and the rest of the family. People are so nice here."

Was she baiting him? Wanting him to say it wasn't his fault she'd cut them off from her family, but her own protracted adolescent rebellion? He didn't want to argue. That was the last thing he wanted. "I wish you were next to me right now."

"Stop it, Reggie."

"What are you wearing?"

"Reggie!"

"When are you coming home?"

"You can't do this to me, Reggie. We've got to talk."

"We are talking."

"I'm talking. You've got your hand on your dick."

Reggie laughed. "I miss you, babe."

"I've got to go, Reggie. Mom's making us all play croquet out on the lawn."

"I'll call you later. I love you."

"Okay."

That was the best he was going to get? *Okay?* Well, at least she hadn't hung up on him.

Before heading to the station, Reggie noticed the FBI tape that he'd promised to view for Velma. He'd been too tired to watch it the night before. He popped it in the VCR while he finished eating his English muffin and drinking his coffee.

Of course, the FBI didn't say where on the tape they thought they'd seen Li'l Richie, so Reggie had to sit through nearly twenty minutes of people coming and going, dragging suitcases, arguing, making him dopey, wondering how in the world the people who watched these tapes for a living didn't go brain-dead.

Then he saw her.

He jumped from his chair, spilling coffee down his pants. He rewound ten seconds of tape, then punched the play button. It was her! Laura! Walking up to the Lufthansa ticket counter.

Reggie shrieked, punching the air with his fists. But wait. It couldn't be her, could it? No. Did this mean the arms belonged to Stacy Savage? Could Laura possibly be alive?

Excited, he made a copy of the tape on his dubbing deck while he changed his pants—a not so clean pair—then dashed to the station. He ordered the tape enhanced, then called Lufthansa to check the date and time for a ticket sold to a Laura Finnegan. They found no such sale. Had she used another name?

He played the tape on the VCR in his office, needing to see her again. Could it really be her?

His exhilaration soon fizzled. After the fourth and fifth viewings, he had doubts; after the sixth, he knew it wasn't her.

Goddammit! He was letting her make him crazy. Pretty soon he'd be following women down the street thinking they were Laura. Hadn't he already caught himself believing he'd seen her on the freeway, only to accelerate past a woman totally unlike her?

He had to get control of himself.

Scott woke with the thought of Samantha. He forgot the dream immediately; only her irritating, needling voice lingered. He jumped out of bed and pulled on a pair of running shorts and a T-shirt. He poured a glass of orange juice, then laced up his running shoes. Why should he worry about Sammy? He knew she'd go only so far. When they'd fought as kids, she always stopped before she left marks.

He went for a quick jog down Montana and bought a paper. He was almost disappointed not to find it on the front page; he had to dig all the way down to the Metro section. A small article without pictures. Construction workers had found an unidentified body in the Venice canals. Fucking ducks. How long would it take them to identify her? Weeks, he supposed, if no one reported her missing right away. But somebody would eventually.

Would the police come to him? No one knew he'd seen her that day except his mother. She wouldn't tell them. Besides, he had an alibi: He was showing a house in Venice.

Unworried, he moved through his routine of showering and shaving. He put in another call to Peter. Why wasn't his buddy answering his calls? It didn't take that long to find out how to open a Swiss bank account.

As he was dressing, the telephone rang, and he jumped for it. At this hour, it was either Peter or the police. "Hello?"

"Aren't you up early? Here I hoped to wake you up."

"What do you want, Sammy?" Scott did not want to talk to her.

"The ring is fake."

The fucking ring again. He'd almost forgotten about it. "I heard how you wheedled it out of Connie. That wasn't nice."

"Fake, fake, fake, fake," she sang as if counting out Monopoly money. "What'd you do with the real one?"

"It certainly is not fake. The diamond is real. The gold is real."

"It's not Grandmother's."

"What makes you so sure?"

"I'm not stupid, Scott."

"So I lost the ring. What in hell does it matter? You wanted a ring so people will think you're engaged. You got a ring."

"Oma's was worth a fortune."

Scott drew in a shallow, noiseless breath and held it. That was what the cop had said. "What makes you think that?" When he laughed, it sounded false even to him.

"She told me."

Scott remembered Oma's words: *You carry with you all the riches you'll ever need.* No. It wasn't true. It couldn't be. His grandmother loved him. "If it were worth a fortune, Oma would've told me. Besides, I had it appraised at a few thousand. To Oma, that probably *was* a fortune."

"I guess she didn't trust you not to run out and sell it. Imagine that. She told me they sold everything they had in Germany—three businesses, two houses, farmland, furniture, everything—and used that money to buy the ring in Switzerland. She wanted the ring passed down through the family, to remind us of what we suffered under the Nazis."

"Aren't you being a tad sentimental, Sammy? That's not like you. Anyhow, what does it matter? Our family isn't some kind of royal dynasty. It'd be better for the gene pool if we all died out."

"How can you say such a thing?"

"Admit it, Sammy. We all hate each other. Why should we pretend we're some kind of happy family? We ought to do the world a favor and terminate it. We have a good start. I'm not having kids, you're a dyke, Martha's been trying to get pregnant for ten years, and Mother made sure to get Pat on the pill at thirteen."

"What makes you so spiteful?"

"I'm not spiteful, I'm a realist. Why don't you just pretend the ring you've got has all that glorious history? It's just a thing. You can attribute any myth to it you want."

"You don't get it, do you?"

"Bye, Sammy."

"What happened to the real ring? I bet you sold it. Or gave it to Laura. And what happened to Laura, anyhow? You're getting yourself in deep shit, bro. Don't count on us to help get you out of it."

"I've never counted on you for anything." Scott slammed down the phone, shaking, shocked by the venom spewing out of him. Where did that come from? But now that he'd said it, it felt like the truth. What in hell did he need his family for? Family values, ha! Just a way for people to get off on controlling others. It was nothing more than slavery sanctioned by church and state. Just because he happened to share a similar gene map, he was obligated to feel something for them? Bullshit! He felt more empathy for a complete stranger or a dog, even. He wasn't buying in to this family shit. There was nothing in it for him; his mother had made it clear he'd get no family money until she died. She thought she could control him that way? Fuck her. Fuck her millions. Soon he'd have plenty of his own.

Later that day, when Scott got home from work, he checked Laura's answering service. There was a message from Capital One, her credit-card company. They had a few questions about some recent charges and were freezing her account until she called back. He'd been careful to pay her bills. What in hell was Pat charging up? Sisters! As soon as he got out of the country, he'd never have to deal with them again.

This thought cheered him. He flipped through a dozen or so travel brochures he'd picked up that afternoon. Every place looked good: New Zealand, Australia, Brazil. No, it was winter there. The brochure for Barbados looked fabulous—*Release your spirit, refresh your soul*—white beaches, turquoise water. No. He'd stick with his original plan and go to Amsterdam first. He picked up the phone and booked a reservation for the following week. That should give him time to tie up loose ends.

He called Schwab and had them cut him a check for half the money in the joint account. That gave him twenty thousand in cash. As soon as Peter got him the Swiss account, he'd move all of Laura's assets into the joint account, then wire that money to Switzerland. He could do this quickly. He was just waiting on Peter, who was acting like a flake all of a sudden. Scott picked up the phone and left another message on his machine.

As Scott imagined all of Laura's money in his name, and the sumptuous breakfast he'd have at a luxury hotel in Amsterdam, he poured himself a second cup of coffee and sat on the couch. He then discovered that Laura's latest statement, which he'd left on the coffee table, was missing.

When Reggie heard about the body dump in Venice—a tall dark-haired woman who matched the description of Vivian Costanza given by both Mr. Silva and Bob Harrison—he raced down to the canals.

Velma was already on the scene. Yellow tape stretched across the construction site, and police officers were taking statements.

The workmen said they'd been held up a few days because of that weird June rain. When they returned, they found that rainwater had eroded the packed sand. Velma pulled aside the Guatemalan laborer who'd found the body. "There was about a dozen ducks pecking away near the sidewalk," he told them,—"right over here—quack, quack, quack, making a fuss." The man gestured to the spot, acting out the story. "The geese were super aggressive, snapping and honking. Wouldn't let us get near the place. This one goose dove at my hand and yanked off my glove. Finally, we chased the birds away and started working. I pulled a rake over the sand to level it off, and it caught on something. I gave it a jerk, and up popped the head of a lady, eyes all bugged out, one side of her face all purple. It was like something out of a monster movie."

"Where's the body now?" Reggie asked Velma.

"SID's already been here, and the coroner's taken the body. It wasn't pretty."

"You have a Polaroid of her face?"

"Here"—Velma handed him a photo—"this one's not bad."

The face was black and blue, the skin bloated and cracked. "Would you get a copy of her prints to me as soon as you can?"

"Sure," said Velma. "You know who she is?"

Reggie didn't stop to answer. As soon as he got back to the station, he printed out a photo of Vivian from the Department of Motor Vehicles in New York. The photo was years old—she had short hair—but it was her.

PART SEVEN

COMPLINE

Scott wasn't terribly surprised to read that the police had finally identified Vivian's body. What surprised him was that the local television stations hadn't picked up the story. They still seemed preoccupied with the Westlake shootout, as if that were the only story in a city of six million. Dozens of L.A. residents were killed weekly, scientific wonders were discovered, companies went bankrupt, new environmental toxins were found, building developments were proposed, laws were passed, but the local stations covered the same story over and over. Why spend money on new stories when people would tune in to hear the old ones? Why hire reporters at all? They'd rather give airtime to the weatherman—as if one ever needed to hear about the weather in L.A.—and it occurred to Scott that the weather segment was getting longer every year. It now included fluff features on teacher of the week and local family fun. Perhaps people didn't want news but reassurance, and what was more reassuring than L.A. weather? Whatever. Scott figured the less news, the better for him.

He switched off the television. He felt fatigued; he lay down on his bed, still dressed, intending to get up and call Peter again. If it was impossible to get a Swiss account, maybe he could get one in the Canary Islands or Liechtenstein.

He tried to imagine living in Liechtenstein, carrying home his skis at dusk through the quaint, narrow streets, the golden sun slipping behind the mountains, a chill rising from the earth. He would eat dinner in a rustic inn, earlier than the Europeans, so he'd be alone in front of his rabbit stew with mushrooms and peppers. And maybe an heiress from Geneva whom he'd seen on the slopes would come in, exhausted and famished, content to eat at six P.M., and they would eat their stews on opposite sides of the restaurant until she raised a glass of wine and invited him over to her table, and after coffee and cognac, she would bend and whisper in his ear . . .

The image faded into the silver-orange water of the marina channel at dawn, the distant mountains sponged in misty blue, the yellow streetlights flickering out. Scott wandered into the alley, which grew darker and darker as it twisted, and then he was lost in the cramped back streets of Kyoto. He wandered up a path to a teahouse and slid open a rice-paper screen. Scott saw Laura smiling at him, dressed in a kimono, her face painted white like a geisha's, her hair piled on her head. Then her face became a white porcelain mask, frozen in a laugh. "I'm alive," she said. "I'm all right, Scott. I was saved by a Japanese fisherman." She led him to a futon and began to undress, but something was wrong with her arms. As the last of her undergarments fell to the ground, he realized her left arm was where her right arm should be and vice versa. "Make love to me, Scott," she said, walking toward him, reaching with her backward arms, now stretching like pulled taffy, becoming hideously long, grabbing for him. "Please make love to me, Scott." He backed away, repulsed, but his legs were stuck, as if in mud. Her mellifluous voice repeated his name: "Scott, Scott, make love to me, Scott."

He bolted awake, breathing hard, his eyes darting around the room, seeking Laura in the shadows, her arms like blind white eels reaching out to him. It was a dream. Of course it was a dream. As he sat up in bed, nauseated and clammy, his head wobbled, his muscles ached, and his legs tangled in the sheets like a fish in a net.

What was happening to him? Was he becoming one of those people driven crazy by their dreams? The next time the cops called, would he betray himself, burbling stupidly about Laura, the geisha, the arms? Would he stammer out a confession like a third-rate actor taking the stand on an hour-long courtroom drama? How could this happen to him? He, a murderer? His every word guarded, every action premeditated? That wasn't him. He was a surfer. Spontaneity was his middle name. Hadn't his buddies nicknamed him Sponto? He never planned beyond dinner, but now he was forced to script out his life like a film director.

How did this all begin, this nightmare that had become his life? It started with Laura's dream of murder. The irony finally hit him. He started laughing maniacally, ripping his lungs raw: She dreamed he would murder her. If not for that dream, none of this ever would have happened; he and Laura would be married by now, living in a starter home up in the Palisades; Vivian would be happy selling pictures of misogyny in New York; and Laura's money would be his. No cops to harass him, no pregnant girlfriends to threaten him, and Oma's ring on Laura's finger, where it fucking belonged.

Reggie parked his unmarked car on the street and walked up the serpentine path to Beatrice Goodsell's house. He felt conspicuous; his was the only car parked on the street. It was that kind of neighborhood.

After they had identified Vivian's body, McBride agreed to let Reggie interview Mrs. Goodsell and order DNA tests. Reggie was working on a search warrant for Scott's car and apartment. Things were about to get messy.

A middle-aged black woman answered the door. Reggie, astonished, couldn't find any words; her frilly white apron did him in.

She'd seen the look before. "Oh, for heaven's sake, I'm not a slave," she snapped. "Come in. Mrs. Goodsell is waiting for you in the solarium."

It was Reggie's first inkling of the kind of woman Mrs. Goodsell was: the kind of woman, formerly married to a white Jewish civil-rights attorney, who would hire a black maid. She probably had to pay triple the going rate, but to her it was worth it to see the look on her former husband's face when he came to visit the children.

Reggie found her sitting at a small writing desk, looking thoughtful. "Excuse me, Mrs. Goodsell?"

"Oh, it's you. What did you say your name was?" She was dressed in a white linen suit.

"Detective Reggie Brooks, Pacific Division. I would like to ask you a few questions."

"Oh, yes. I was just thinking, but I'm done now. Please have a seat."

Reggie perched on the edge of a pink-striped Louis XV chair. It creaked. He tried not to put his full weight on it. It occurred to him that she'd intended him to sit there, knowing it would make him uncomfortable. He began, "As I told you on the phone, we found the body of Vivian Costanza. We found your telephone number on the nightstand in her hotel room at Loews in Santa Monica."

"Oh really?"

"Did you know Miss Costanza?"

"Am I under suspicion?"

"No."

"I don't know how I could possibly help you."

By answering my questions, Reggie thought, but didn't say. "Did you ever speak with Miss Costanza?"

"I'm sure you've already checked numbers called from her hotel telephone room, so you know the answer to that question."

"She apparently did call your number. Did you talk with her?"

"I spoke with a woman who called herself Vivian Costanza."

Reggie couldn't believe it. Cagey as a lawyer. Of course; she had been married to Wyman. "Did you ever meet her?"

"A woman who called herself Vivian Costanza came to my house one afternoon."

"Do you remember what day that was?"

"Last Tuesday or Wednesday."

"Do you remember which?"

"No."

"Do you remember what you talked about?"

"She represents the artist Wendy Sharpe in New York. I'm very interested in her work."

Since his talk with Amaldo, Reggie had asked around. Françoise Augier had filled him in on the notorious photographer. "Did you talk about anything else?"

"That was so riveting, it's the only thing I recall."

"Does Miss Costanza know your son?"

"She may have mentioned something about him. I don't remember."

"Was your son here when you spoke with Miss Costanza?"

"Is Scott in some kind of trouble?"

"Please answer my question, Mrs. Goodsell. Was your son here when Miss Costanza visited?"

She looked at Reggie as if she were aiming a gun at him. "You don't know who my former husband is, do you?"

Reggie forced a smile. "You insist on answering my questions with questions. Yes, I do know Richard Wyman, and I know he's your former husband. Do you see your son often, Mrs. Goodsell?"

"As often as a grown son sees his mother."

"How often is that?"

"It varies. Not enough, of course."

Reggie pulled an evidence bag from his pocket and handed it to Mrs. Goodsell.

"What's this?" She looked repulsed until she saw what was in the bag; then she looked alarmed.

"Have you ever seen this ring before?" Earlier that day, Reggie had driven to Malibu and signed out the ring. Mike Morrison had gotten the appraisal Reggie had sent; the ring was now kept in a safe.

Mrs. Goodsell walked to an end table and took out a pair of glasses. She put them on as if she were deeply ashamed of them. "May I take it out of the bag?"

"Sure."

She looked at it for a long time, then directly at Reggie. "I don't recognize it. Was there a theft of some kind?"

Reggie admired how well she lied. As well as her son.

"It showed up on the hand of a body we believe to be Laura Finnegan's."

She pressed her lips together. "I think I'd better call my attorney."

"You're perfectly entitled to. We can continue this down at the station with your lawyer present."

"Are you threatening me?" She jerked her chin forward like a velociraptor.

"No, not at all. But unless your answers are self-incriminating, your lawyer will instruct you to answer our questions."

"Excuse me. I need to call Richard."

Reggie sighed. It was going to be a long day. This woman could make anyone homicidal.

The first thing Scott did when he woke up was grab the phone and dial Peter. A groggy voice answered.

"Why in hell haven't you been answering my calls?"

"I've been busy, Scott. Our department has been changing over to new accounting software. You wouldn't believe the problems it's causing."

"So what have you found out for me?"

Scott heard Peter grunt as he sat up in bed. A displaced cat yowled. It figured, that Peter slept with his cat.

"I made some calls for you," Peter said. "I found out that getting an unnumbered Swiss bank account is not so easy. You need a minimum deposit of two hundred thousand dollars. And you can't do it by mail. You have to go in person. You also need a personal recommendation from one of their clients, and they're really strict about where the money comes from. They want documentation. They want copies of your passport and will make inquiries about your occupation and address."

"Shit. What about offshore banking?"

"Well, for that, you need fifty grand to purchase an offshore bank charter and license it, like in Montserrat, in the Caribbean. Then you've got to commission a native resident as your part-time bank agent. You have to set up an office there. It gets complicated, but there are a lot of advantages—you can borrow money and pay yourself interest, there are no capital-gains taxes, and you can attract other depositors to your offshore bank—"

"That's way too much work."

"You can hire a financial management service to do the work, but that'll set you back twenty thousand, and they charge a one percent maintenance fee, plus two-fifty per hour in legal fees."

"Jesus! I just want to get my money out of the country."

"That can be done with a simple account, but you'll get less than one percent interest."

"Is it safe from the IRS, from the FBI?"

Peter hesitated. "Yes, so far . . . but the foreign countries are under pressure—"

"Why is it so fucking hard? Drug dealers set up accounts. Even terrorists set up accounts."

"Exactly. That's why they're making it more difficult. Not difficult enough to keep drug money out, but difficult enough so it at least looks like they're doing something to prevent money laundering."

"Well, let's do it. How soon can you get me an account?"

"I can't. I can recommend an experienced offshore adviser, but a good one won't work with you unless you have a few million."

"That's crazy! I just want a bank account."

"I'd like to help, but I don't know enough. And I'd be risking my job."

"Christ. What are you good for?"

"I did the best I could. I can get you an account in Belize."

"Oh, that sounds real safe."

"No reason to get sarcastic. What's the big deal, anyway?"

"The big deal is I asked you to do something for me, and you failed. That's all. Friends don't fail friends."

Peter's voice became petulant. "I resent being talked to like—"

"Are you recording this call?" Scott became aware of a faint clicking on the line.

"What? No, of course not. Why would I do something—"

"I've got to go." Scott slammed down the phone. They were all against him. He didn't need Peter. He didn't need anyone. He was charming, resourceful, and soon he'd be rich. He'd choose a tax haven and figure it out once he got there. He dialed his travel agent and changed his flight to Barbados. Once his account was set up, he'd fly to Amsterdam.

Now he had two days to take care of everything. Where to start? Nervously, Scott picked up a pile of unread mail and sifted through it. He pulled out a heavy ivory envelope with black script letterhead in the upper left-hand corner. ADLER & AARONSON, ATTORNEYS AT LAW. He ripped it open. What else could go wrong? He read out loud, mumbling the legalese—*representing client's interest . . . established paternity . . . misrepresentation of intent to marry . . . child support until the age of eighteen*—until he began to understand. He slammed his fist into the wall. "Fucking goddammit!"

Apparently, Connie had filed a paternity suit. She had the gall to use their engagement charade against him! It occurred to him that there were probably several dozen people who could testify that they were engaged: waiters at Gladstone's, shit, all those Greeks at Toppers, and what about his sister and mother? His mother's cook had even baked them an engagement cake. Would his family testify for him in court and say it was a farce? Probably not. He was fucked.

He didn't get it. Connie didn't need the money, and she'd told him he didn't need to be involved. So what was going on here?

He wouldn't let himself get dragged down like this. No way. He was going to do something about it.

Friends don't fail friends! Peter mimicked. What kind of bullshit thing was that to say? The phrase stabbed right down through the center of his body, like a gigantic icicle breaking off from the eaves of a barn and harpooning a snowbank.

Peter couldn't let the conversation go, not as he showered and got ready to go to work, not as he sat through an endless staff meeting, not as he endured the training session on the new accounting software. The more he thought about it, the angrier he got.

Where did Scott get off, being so superior? Fuck his rich family and good looks that made girls cream whenever he smiled at them. Scott had never had to struggle for a thing. He wasn't saddled with student loans or his mother's nursing care. Fuck his charm and his blond hair and the way everyone brightened when they recognized him. Fuck the way he always called, expecting Peter to be free for a game of pickup or racquetball or to see a Dodgers game or to have breakfast, like Peter should be grateful. Fuck his monologues about his sexual conquests—great gals, every one of them—dumped as soon as they started to have feelings for him, all of them letting him get away with it because he chatted them up and never let them say how they felt.

Fuck his sob story when Laura dumped him. He even had Peter feeling sorry for him. Fuck him!

Scott had always said to him, "You're the best friend a guy could have," so Peter had tried to be that guy, but then he overheard Scott say the same thing to the Mexican who washed his car. That was what friendship meant to him? Putting a little extra shine on his dashboard for a five-dollar tip? Fuck that!

Peter realized he'd stopped believing Scott's stories. Maybe Laura wasn't visiting her sick mother. Maybe Scott had done something to her, Laura, a goddess, who once came to Peter asking for financial advice, begging him not to tell Scott about her affairs, but needing, she said, his expertise. And this Swiss bank account Scott wanted, he was probably trying to steal from her now.

Peter had let Scott use him, and both of them knew it. Then Scott had the gall to tell Peter he'd failed him as a friend?

Peter couldn't let it rest. He hated this anxious, sullied feeling. He wasn't the type of guy to say *fuck you* and walk away. It might be the end of their friendship, but he had to talk to Scott. Maybe Scott never really was his friend, but Peter felt he owed it to them both to tell Scott how badly he treated people.

Peter decided after he met his last client for the day that he would drive to Scott's house and have it out with him.

When Reggie called Peter Flynn and said he was a cop, he heard a sharp intake of air and what sounded like a knee jerking against a pencil drawer.

"How can I help you, sir?" asked Peter carefully, like a cadet who'd pulled a caper and wasn't sure whether he had to own up.

Reggie asked Peter how well he knew Scott, if he knew Laura Finnegan, had he noticed a change in Scott since her disappearance, did he know a Vivian Costanza. Peter's answers were noncommittal, indicating he did know about the restraining order and Scott's apparent obsession. He said he'd found Scott slightly more irritable lately. He did not know a Vivian Costanza.

"Anything else you can tell me about him?"

Peter hesitated, then said, "Yes, there's one thing."

"What's that?"

"He asked me to get him a bank account in Switzerland, a numbered account."

"When was that?"

"I'd say about two weeks ago."

"Did you get him one?"

"No. I looked into it, but it's pretty complicated. It's more of a favor than I wanted to do for him. Not that it's illegal—not at all—but it could expose me to a certain amount of scrutiny if he were to come under financial investigation."

"You suspect he might?"

"No. Not in the least. Scott comes from a wealthy family. But I'd rather err on the side of caution."

Several things occurred to Reggie: that Scott was illegally coming in to a load of money; that Scott was planning to leave the country; and that both of these things had to do with the disappearances of Laura and Vivian. Then it occurred to him to ask, "Did you ever give Laura financial advice of any kind?"

There was a long pause on the other end. "Not that I remember."

Reggie knew Peter was lying. *Not that I remember* is not *no.* "Come on, Peter. You both worked in finance. You're telling me when the three of you got together, you never talked shop? Never talked investments?"

"I can't recall anything like that." Peter's voice tightened, rising in pitch.

Why was he lying? Maybe he was in on it with Laura? Maybe all three of them? Shit!

"I don't believe it. You're telling me that when the three of you went on sailing trips, you didn't share stock tips, talk about the NASDAQ, compare real estate prices?"

"Sailing? We never sailed. We did go flying together."

"Flying? Scott has an airplane?"

"No. No, of course not. He rents out of the Santa Monica airport."

Reggie nearly slammed down the phone. Why hadn't he thought of that before? *Shit!*

As Reggie turned from Sunset on to the San Diego Freeway, he checked his cell-phone messages. One from Detective Mike

Morrison. One from Velma Perkins. The freeway was at a complete standstill. He called Velma first.

"The FBI picked up Li'l Richie in Houston. They're holding him for us."

"Fantastic. Do the paperwork, and we'll send you and Sanchez down to pick him up."

"God, I could use the break. We'll interview his brother while we're down there."

"You've done a great job, Velma. You deserve a few days in the sun."

All of the cars in front of Reggie had their blinkers on to change lanes: No one was moving. He dialed Malibu/Lost Hills.

"I got DNA results back from the arms," said Morrison. "I took that and the test from Stacy Savage to an expert witness we use over at UCLA. He said he'd want to run it by a colleague, but he was positive both were from the same person."

Reggie felt flattened. The arms weren't Laura's. *But they had to be!* But they weren't. Did Scott kill this Stacy girl? Did he kill Vivian? Where was Laura?

The whole fucking case was unraveling.

The traffic crawled. *Fuck it!* Reggie put on his siren and used the shoulder. He headed west, exited on Bundy, then went south to the Santa Monica airport.

Connie supposed he was looking after her interests. That's what lawyers were paid to do, right? Still, she didn't feel good about it. She didn't feel good about stealing Laura Finnegan's Charles Schwab statement from Scott's apartment. She didn't want to get involved with the disappearance of a woman she'd never met, a woman whom everyone spoke of with such reverence. Connie imagined a woman of luminous beauty who never doubted herself, who passed serenely through life like a silk scarf on a wide, placid river. Even Scott's sister Samantha couldn't find anything bad to say about her.

But if Connie hadn't wanted to get involved, why did she swipe Laura's portfolio statement? She had to admit it was jealousy; she wanted to know about the woman who had such a hold on Scott, wanted to know her secrets, like a little girl rooting through a big sister's drawers. Such pettiness made her feel ashamed.

After she read the statement—noting Laura's considerable wealth; and the date, well after Laura's disappearance; and the address, Culver City, not Marina del Rey, where Laura had lived; and the joint account between Laura and Scott, which had increased by fifty thousand dollars in the last month, funds taken from Laura's other accounts—Connie knew she had to give it to the police.

First she called her lawyer, Marty Adler, for an appointment.

Adler was a petite balding fellow with a bit of a gut who rhapsodized to her about his bicycle rides to Topanga Canyon (a mere four miles on a flat bike path) as if this mildly athletic feat would somehow make him irresistible. He fawned over her and called her his Olympian, and whenever they had an appointment, his secretary and paralegal were always out to lunch and his partner was in court. He made her uncomfortable. Yet he'd guided her through the morass of commercial endorsements, interviews, and job offers that had followed the Olympics, and he was instrumental in building her successful business out of little more than modest celebrity. She had much to be grateful to him for, but she hated the way he squeezed her hand, as if something might flow from her into him, magically transforming him into a seven-foot basketball player.

Adler shared an office suite with his partner, Seth Aaronson, on the fourteenth floor of the Occidental Petroleum Building in Westwood. Aaronson had conventional mahogany-and-maroon-carpet taste, but Adler's office looked like the bedroom of an adolescent boy: posters of sports heroes, pendants, Plexiglas-encased baseballs, signed photos, and enormous two-toned jerseys. Those jerseys always made Connie take a step back, wondering why in the world anyone would want someone else's sweaty shirt hanging on the wall.

Sitting behind an enormous desk in front of a picture window that looked out on the Santa Monica Mountains, Adler resembled a child playing grown-up.

After their ritual of hand squeezing, Connie gave him the bank statements and told him some of the background. He seemed very interested in the joint account. When he asked Connie to define her relationship with Scott, he blushed. She then told him that she was pregnant.

"Connie, Connie, Connie. Do you know how expensive it is to rear a child nowadays?" he asked, tapping his index finger on the desk for emphasis. "Unless you plan to carry your infant around in a sling to visit your clients, you're going to need full-time child care. Do you have any idea how costly that is? Even if you pay for all the child's expenses and devote yourself completely, Scott will still have legal rights. Unless you get the court to terminate his parental rights, he can sue for custody at any time until the child is eighteen."

Connie hadn't thought about that.

"I don't have to tell you that rearing a child on your own is an enormous responsibility. It's too much for one person. Have you thought about the constraints on your personal life? Have you asked yourself whether it's fair to bring up a child without a father?"

Connie was suddenly furious. Why wasn't he being supportive? Why wasn't he happy for her? "Are you suggesting I get an abortion?"

Adler seemed to recognize that his emotions were getting the better of him; his face stiffened, and he took a deep breath. "That, of course, is your own decision."

"I'm keeping the baby," she said firmly.

He looked at her a long time, like he was running through the outcomes of several scenarios. It was then that he suggested she consider suing for paternity.

Later in the week, after he had researched Scott's family, Adler called Connie and insisted on the paternity suit; not only was Scott's family wealthy, he said, but Richard Wyman would no doubt negotiate a settlement to keep his own name out of the papers. If Connie was willing to sue for paternity, Adler said, he'd front the legal fees.

Why did she agree? It went against her better instincts. Because, she admitted, she had a weak character. She'd spent her life mindlessly obeying her mostly male coaches. Now she did what her lawyer and accountant told her to do.

Adler instructed her not to see Scott in any capacity. If Scott called, she was to say she couldn't speak to him and refer him to her lawyer. So why did she agree to see him at her house? He sounded calm and reasonable on the phone. Charming, as always. What harm could come of it?

She liked Scott. She couldn't bear his being angry with her. She knew it wasn't love, but what was it? He drew her to him, pulling her like a magnet. Behind his eyes, which locked in on her, behind his tanned chest and strong arms, there was a nebulous purple-black thing that summoned something out of her, like an oil well pumping black fluid up out of the ocean, something from another lifetime, secrets she didn't know she had. His call was irresistible. Was it her soul he summoned?

When his heavy muscular shoulders lay on top of her, she felt an urgent need to open and sacrifice herself, to let herself be absorbed into him.

It wasn't love, but she'd never felt this way before. Was it passion? She knew it was dangerous. Yet she wanted it. She thought that maybe if she saw him again, he would say something that would break the spell.

She had a few hours before he was expected. She pulled on a wetsuit top, brushed her hair back in a ponytail, and climbed down the rocks under her deck to where she stored her kayaks. She hoisted the yellow one onto her hip and carried it down to the water's edge. She hooked in her seat and slid together her paddle; she waited for a break between the waves and shoved off into the water.

She needed the water. It centered her, calmed her. This dark thing that had been unleashed in her connected her to the water in a new way, as if she could feel the ocean floor while she floated above it. She grew stronger as she paddled, the undulating power of the ocean flowing into her body.

Here in the water she was safe. Poseidon would let no harm come to his child. The water protected her.

Reggie parked by one of the old airport administration buildings, now rented to Santa Monica College for extension classes, and walked back to the hangars. A young man in a blue jumpsuit was working on the engine of a two-person Ultra Lite; he turned out to be an instructor at Justin Aviation, which also rented small aircraft. The flight instructor recognized the name Scott Goodsell. He led Reggie back to his office and pulled up the booking sheet on his computer.

"The last time he rented was on April thirteenth. He took out a single-engine Cessna 172N."

"What's the baggage allowance on that?"

"A hundred and twenty pounds."

Reggie inhaled sharply. Big enough for a body.

"Looks like he flew it for about two hours." The flight instructor tapped at his keyboard. "The airport manager can tell you exactly when he took off and landed. It says here he's reserved the plane again for tonight at eight."

Reggie jolted. Vivian was in the morgue. Was Scott leaving town? Or was he going to kill again? "Is the plane he last rented here?"

"Sure. It's right over there." The man led Reggie to a small white plane in the corner of the hangar.

"Could you open the cargo hold?" asked Reggie. He shined a flashlight over the carpeted interior. There was a long brown streak, sixteen inches long, two inches wide. "That looks like dried blood to me."

The flight instructor's eyes opened wide.

Reggie whipped out his cell phone and called SID, asking for someone who could give him an on-site blood type.

An hour later, after the SID technician confirmed that the smear was blood, which tested A positive, Reggie radioed for a patrol unit to Montana and Fourteenth to pick up Scott Goodsell.

Don't panic, Scott told himself. If the police had something on you, they would've arrested you rather than beating around the bush with innuendo.

He had just hung up from a conversation with his mother. She was in one of her wicked-stepmother moods. "Why do the police have Oma's ring? I want an answer now, and don't try to lie to me."

So what the cop said had been true. There was only one explanation, but it made Scott shaky and sick inside.

It's not too late, he thought. He'd take care of Connie, then fly out of here, down to Mexico. He'd take a commercial plane out of Cancún to Barbados, then to Amsterdam. There he'd wait for Laura. She'd clear it up for him. Then they'd be together forever.

She said she'd wait for him that night he'd become some kind of crazy butcher, her face all weepy as she pulled him inside her apartment.

A body, female, lay faceup on the floor, close to the sliding glass doors to the balcony, eyes open. Her neck was at an unnatural angle. Did he know her? No. She was a small woman, dark hair, young, not over twenty.

When Scott glanced at Laura, she broke down in tears. She hugged herself, pulling her knees together, her back slightly bent, her bare arms trembling. It was self-defense, she said through her sobs. The woman had been harassing Laura, demanding that she leave her boyfriend alone.

"What boyfriend?" Scott asked, blocking a flash of rage.

"I only dated him once. We didn't even sleep together."

"Calm down, Laura," he said, trying to calm himself, to silence the buzzing in his ears. "What are you talking about?"

"A friend from work set us up. I thought I should try dating again . . . because we weren't . . . It doesn't matter, Scott. His name is Kevin. We went out once. I wasn't going to see him again, but his girlfriend started calling me every night. She was hysterical. She screamed that I ruined her life, that Kevin broke it off with her, that they had planned to get married. I stopped answering the phone. Then she came over."

"This evening?"

"Yes. About ten o'clock. I let her in so she could talk it out, but she threw a glass at me. Then she started hitting me and coming at me with these long nails and scratching me. So I . . . I kicked her." Laura broke down again.

Scott had never seen Laura like this. It tore him apart.

"I did a chest kick, just to knock the wind out of her, like I learned in class, but she's so short that I hit her chin with my heel. There was this crack . . . *Oh, Scott* . . . It was horrible, and she fell just like that."

The irony struck him. She'd learned martial arts to defend herself against him, and now she needed his help to take care of someone she'd killed with a high kick.

Scott knelt beside the body. He placed his fingers on the base of the woman's neck. The body was warm, but there was no pulse.

"It was an accident. I can't believe anything like this could happen." Laura sank to the floor as if her legs could no longer hold her up; she pulled her shins to her chest and touched her head to her knees. The moon shined on the high arches of her feet; they seemed so perfect to Scott, so strong and graceful. Not deadly weapons. She looked up at Scott, her chin trembling, her eyes so lost, so helpless. "Scott, help me."

It was clear to the superhero what he had to do. He was Laura's defender, preserver of her terrible secret. Like a medieval dragon assigned to protect the Holy Grail, he would protect Laura. At any cost.

He didn't think of the dead woman as human but as an empty body. He took her by the wrists and dragged her to the bathroom. He guessed she weighed no more than 110 pounds. He leaned her against the tub, then flopped her inside.

He turned on the overhead light, which glared too brightly; it induced efficiency, thought and action, clear and orderly. The old-fashioned claw tub had a freestanding showerhead. Scott pulled the shower curtain out of the tub and to one side; it was still damp from Laura's last shower. He asked Laura to bring him heavy-duty garbage bags. As he unbuttoned and pulled off the woman's blouse, then her camisole, he noticed her acrid body odor, mixed with cheap jasmine perfume. He slid off her shoes and jeans. She wore no underwear and had a Brazilian bikini wax, her pubic hair a tiny domino strip around her vulva. Details assailed him, humanizing her: a mole on her shoulder, a fine gold necklace, long painted nails, a pierced belly button, a thick scar on her left elbow. He didn't even know her name. Paralyzed with fear, he gulped for breath; he felt his head detach from his body and float above her. Time stood still.

Man is spiritual, not material. Where were these words coming from? A childhood ecumenical field trip? If it was a dead body, an empty vessel, then it wasn't human.

He turned. Laura stood behind him, leaning against the doorjamb, a box of garbage bags in her hand. Her face looked attentive and trusting, like that of a child watching her father build a campfire. Scott's fear dissipated, and when he looked back into the tub, the body was again a body, refuse, empty of anything human.

He walked outside on the deck to clear his head. He took a deep breath; the cool mist woke him. The neighbors' condos were dark. He let his eyes wander around the dark rectangles, over the azalea bushes, around the yard. The sculptor's ax, wedged on a stump, cast a shadow like a sundial. He still felt dizzy but sensed an urgency to act. As he walked down the steps, he couldn't feel his body, watching as it seemed to move on its own. He yanked the ax by the handle and carried it back into Laura's apartment. He liked its weight, its worn oak handle; it felt like a friend.

He went back into the bathroom with a sense of mission. This other person took over, the cool, confident technician. He asked Laura if she had gym bags. She came back with two black canvas bags, each big enough for two queen-size pillows.

They looked new. All the better, he thought. Less of Laura's hair and sweat, or whatever else might be traced back to her.

He shook out two garbage bags and put one inside the other, then did the same with two more bags, so he had two sets of double bags. He was pleased with the heavy-duty plastic. He placed the woman's clothes in the tub at her feet, then removed his own clothes and took them out to the living room.

He covered the woman's face with her camisole and picked up the ax. Four cuts, he decided. The blade was razor-sharp. Three inches below her hip bone was a crease left by her tight jeans from her pubis to her outer thigh. He raised the ax over his head and aimed.

He was surprised. No spurting blood, merely a slow creeping spill that made him think of ketchup. He rocked the ax back and forth to sever the ball joint, then raised the leg to slice through the skin on her back. He wrapped her blouse over the stump and placed it in one of the garbage bags. He repeated the procedure for the other leg and each arm, careful not to get any blood on the outside of the garbage bags.

That left the torso and the head. The smell of blood, metallic and bitter, filled the room. He began to feel nauseated. He asked Laura to hand him another garbage bag and slipped it over her head and torso. Carefully, he rinsed his hands and the outside of the bag. Then he placed the bag in a second garbage bag. He tied off both bags with twist ties and put each in a gym bag.

He carried the bags to the front door. Laura seemed dazed. Must be shock, he thought. He seated her in a living room chair while he went back to the bathroom. He scrubbed the tub with cleanser, careful to dispose of the sponge in one of the gym bags. He poured bleach down the drain. Then he took a shower.

As the hot water soothed his body, his mind raced, planning the next step.

He dried off and dressed in the living room. They agreed that she would leave the next morning, heading out of the country. He gave her all the cash he had on hand, about three hundred dollars. Then he gave her the engagement ring to sell. It was worth a few thousand, he said. Once she left the country, she mustn't use her credit cards. She should take a bus to the border, then fly from Mexico. He would take care of her apartment; he'd tell everyone she had to leave unexpectedly. "I'll take care of everything, Laura. You disappear. Don't even tell me where. If I don't know, I can't tell. I won't let anything happen to you, Laura."

They agreed to meet in six months in Amsterdam. No communication before then.

Now he realized, as he left her apartment to bring around his car, that she must have slipped the engagement ring on the woman's hand. He imagined her opening the bag and digging around to find the dismembered hand and cramming the ring onto the limp finger. That must have been what she'd done. And come to think of it, when he put the bags in the cockpit, he did remember seeing a smear of blood on the bag that he hadn't noticed before. When he said his final good-byes to Laura, had she been wearing the ring? He couldn't remember.

Then the full force hit him: His knees wobbled, and he slid to the floor beside the telephone. Laura had set him up for her own murder.

Did she know Vivian would hunt her down, forcing a confrontation? Had she known he'd cover for her even if it meant killing someone? Had she planned it all?

He had to believe there was another explanation.

Would she be in Amsterdam in a few months? Would she be at the St. Nicolaas Hotel, as they'd planned? He'd make sure he was there in September, waiting in Vondelpark, watching the leaves fall. Then she'd clear it up.

But first he had to save his own skin.

* * *

Peter sat in his blue Volvo outside Scott's apartment. He was about to get out of his car when he saw Scott turn off the lights and leave his apartment with two suitcases and an empty duffel bag. Scott got into his BMW and turned west on Montana.

There was nothing to do but follow him.

As Peter tailed the white car down the California Incline, then north on Pacific Coast Highway, he remembered how Laura had once looked at him when the three of them were having breakfast together. Scott was talking a mile a minute about something, and Laura had looked across the table at Peter. The whole world slowed down, and it was just the two of them alone, and she was talking to him telepathically, or at least that was the way it seemed to him, as though she was saying, *It could be us, you and I. That would make me happy.*

Yeah, he admitted, she'd gotten to him, too.

Peter saw Scott slowing in the center lane with his turn signal on. Peter passed, then, at the next intersection, swung back.

The BMW was parked beside a brown bungalow that jutted out over the water. Peter stopped twenty yards farther up the highway.

The waves were calm, but a breeze was picking up, making the water a little choppy. Two surfers floated on their boards just beyond the breakers. A Mexican fisherman tossed a line from the rocks.

Slowly, it dawned on Peter that he might be implicated in whatever nefarious deeds Scott was involved in. That whole thing with the foreign account. And what about Laura's disappearance? Peter had talked to Laura just days before she disappeared. Now, Scott with two suitcases, looking like he was splitting town, leaving Peter to answer all the questions? No way. Peter admitted he could be a chump sometimes, but he wasn't stupid.

But could he rat on a friend? He didn't know for sure Scott had done anything illegal.

Peter felt the edge of the cop's business card in his pocket. He got a tight feeling in his chest that said he'd be spending the next few days in a linoleum and cinder-block room, telling the truth yet made to feel as if he were lying.

He watched Scott in the rearview mirror. When Scott pulled a knife out of his trunk, Peter picked up his cell phone.

Reggie was getting the shakes. The patrol unit he'd sent over to Santa Monica radioed in and said Scott wasn't home. He knew he couldn't wait for Scott to get picked up. Scott was spooked, a flight risk.

After Reggie assigned a unit to hang out at the Santa Monica airport, he got into his cruiser. He wasn't sure where to go. As he coasted down Centinela back to the station, he felt an awful dread that a murderer was going to slip through his fingers. Five blocks from the station, his cell phone rang. It was Velma.

Someone had called in an anonymous tip.

Reggie made a U-turn in the middle of an intersection and raced toward Malibu.

After Scott pulled off Pacific Coast Highway on the sandy shoulder above Connie's house, he sat. He was an hour early. He needed the time to plan, to gather his courage. He knew Connie seldom locked the sliding glass door to her deck. He thought he would try to catch her in the shower. That would take care of the blood. Then he'd do what he needed to get her into a duffel bag—purchased for the occasion—and to the airport.

But when he saw that her kayak was gone, he had a better idea.

Every few years the newspapers reported a shark attack on a

kayak in Malibu. Last year it was a UCLA college student and his girlfriend. The Coast Guard found the kayaks, then his mangled body, with a leg and an arm ripped off. They identified him first by his engraved Rolex watch and second by his fine Beverly Hills orthodontia. They never found the girl, but her kayak had been chomped in two and smeared with blood. A girl like Connie was tempting fate by kayaking every day, even in the winter, when sharks fed in the cool coastal waters. No one would be surprised that such an adventurous girl would die a dramatic death.

Scott congratulated himself on his brilliance. He wasn't some demented psychopath; no, he was a performance artist, creating, innovating from his environment. He wasn't, after all, a murderer by choice, but one forced into unpleasant methods by perfidious females. He was no more a murderer than a farm boy sent to war, killing honorably, heroically.

Scott opened his trunk and shook out a wetsuit. He also had scuba gear, fins, towels, and a deboning knife.

He thought his plan was shrewd in its simplicity. When she paddled back at dusk, he'd swim out to her. All anyone would see from shore—if anyone was looking—was her kayak flipping over, a brief disturbance in the water, obscured for a moment by a wave, then the empty tranquillity of the vast ocean. As the orange sun set over the glinting water, anyone who observed the scene might come to believe they'd imagined it.

Later, Scott would stop in at the surf shop in Malibu Village and at a few local bars to start a rumor about a shark sighting. By the time her body washed up, there'd be a great white alert—twenty feet long, head as big as a rowboat—and he'd be on his way to Barbados.

So like I said, I'd been going up to Malibu in the evenings to fish. That evening I was alone on the rocks. It was the middle of the week, and even though it was June, by late afternoon it was pretty cold. I saw two surfers give up on the waves and paddle to shore. Then I was the only one.

I saw him drive up in his white convertible. For the longest time, he stood watching her paddle. She wasn't out far, maybe half the length of the pier. There was something about the way he was watching her that scared me, like an egret stalking a fish in ankle-deep water, following it slowly until it predicts precisely the moment the fish will turn.

He walked back to his car, stripped off his clothes, and pulled on the wetsuit, like you see the surfers do up and down Pacific Coast Highway. Some use a towel around their waist; others don't care who sees them naked. They usually change between the rocks and their cars, so if you're driving fast, you can't see what they're doing. That was exactly how he changed. The only thing was, he didn't have a surfboard.

After he got on his wetsuit, he pulled a scuba mask and flippers from his trunk. He closed the trunk and tiptoed over the rocks to the water.

So I thought to myself, I've got to rescue her.

I needed a boat. I climbed down to the sand, hopping from rock to rock toward the row of houses that hangs out over the water. A lot of them have boats stored underneath their decks, and nobody locks them: kayaks, rowboats, dinghies, canoes. I'd never kayaked before, and I didn't think this was the time to try it out. I dragged an inflatable dinghy down to the water's edge. Under another house, I found a kayak paddle.

As soon as I saw him dive under the water, I pushed out the dinghy. I had a tough time getting over the waves; they kept on crashing on top of me and filling the bottom of the dinghy. My sneakers and jeans were soaking wet. When I got beyond the breakers, I spent a few minutes scooping out water with my hat. Then I paddled hard. It was slow going. The dinghy was too wide for the paddle, and if I used it on one side, like with a canoe, I ended up going in circles.

I finally got the hang of it and paddled out several hundred feet. My stomach was all queasy, so I closed my eyes and pretended I was in a hammock. That kind of worked.

The sun was resting on the edge of the sea. The girl was way out; all I could see was a speck of yellow and the sun shining on her paddle as it dipped back and forth. She looked like she was trying to paddle to the sun.

I began wondering where he was, where he planned to intercept her. I let my eyes sweep over the surface of the water, looking for his air pipe. I figured he had to surface every once in a while to see where he was going, but I didn't spot him.

The girl started back, her paddle smacking the water like the propeller of a plane. I knew I had to get as close to her as I could—to warn her. I couldn't move very fast, so I tried to get to where I thought she'd pass me.

She was working her shoulders like a jockey on a horse. When she got close, she looked up and yelled, "How's it going?" with a big smile on her face. I waved and shouted like crazy.

She didn't pause. Just kept paddling.

By now Connie's shoulders were warmed up—tingling and slightly achy. She was looking forward to a warm shower. She didn't have a watch and was a little worried she'd stayed out too long. She'd have to hurry to be ready for Scott. She didn't want to get caught half dressed. He seemed to like to surprise her, and it sapped her defenses.

A breeze was picking up. As her kayak plunged over the whitecaps, water splashed her hair. It wasn't dangerous, but she had to work to keep the kayak straight. Normally, the challenge would be fun, but now it irritated her; she simply wanted to get to shore.

She thought she saw something dark swimming under the water—a dolphin, maybe?—then glanced up at the sky and realized it was only the shadow from a small cloud. But for some reason, it made her uneasy.

As she paddled beneath the Malibu Pier, a swell lifted her and threatened to slam her against a massive cement piling. She pushed off with her paddle and let the next wave carry her through.

In the distance, she saw her house. Was that Scott's white BMW parked by the road? He must be early. Distracted as she felt, she knew she couldn't have been out that long.

A surge of energy pulsed through her, a panicky need to get to shore. She paddled hard, counting to herself, then singing in a toneless way a stupid song from Girl Scouts—why was she recalling it now?—grunting out a note with each stroke. Her strokes evened out.

Suddenly, something black lunged at the kayak like a huge serpent, tackling her around the waist. She screamed and fell into the water. The kayak tipped over. She grabbed for it, but her hands slipped off. A man in a scuba mask—*Scott?*—splashed toward her, grabbing at her arms. She held fast to her paddle and tried to beat him off, kicking hard with her legs to get to the kayak, but it kept sliding away. He dove and came up under her, snatching at her arms and her head.

She saw something glint in his hand.

She grabbed at the canvas seat, trying to pull herself back into the kayak. As he tackled her legs with his left arm, slashing at her with the knife, missing, scraping the side of the boat, she kicked loose and somersaulted over the top.

They were both trying to climb in the kayak, spinning it like a hot dog on a spit. She smacked him in the face with her paddle, then balanced it across the kayak and vaulted herself up like a gymnast on the parallel bars. She tried to get away, but he yanked the paddle out of her hands, throwing it fifteen feet away. He lunged and flipped the kayak again. She fell into the water, and they were back to spinning the kayak.

She managed to climb back on and straddle the overturned kayak, thrashing her arms in the water, trying to propel herself closer to the paddle. She grabbed it just as he pulled himself up on the nose of the kayak. She stood, struggling for balance, then lifted the paddle up and back like a baseball bat. He crouched, his knife in one hand, ready to leap.

They stared at each other.

It didn't surprise her that he was trying to kill her. She'd always felt it lurking, his appetite, his malevolence. What did surprise her was that she didn't passively accept death, as she had always feared she would. A thought—no, a ferocious instinct—zapped through her body like an electrical current: No one's going to hurt my baby!

She swung her paddle with everything she had, right at Scott's neck, then slid into the water. Scott fell back howling, spurting blood out of his eye like a harpooned tuna.

She reached out to the kayak, then twisted around, looking for Scott. She saw him sinking, his arms folding over his head like the petals of a rose at night.

The waves turned red with his blood.

I'm coming, Laura. It's Scott. Wait for me. I'm coming.

A blanket of red petals fluttered over him, softly warming him, embracing him. Here we go, he thought, hold on. Falling in a red hot-air balloon, falling, falling into the sea. He felt happy, so warm, the water reaching out to him, folding him to its heart, carrying him to Laura.

I did everything for you, Laura.
I love you, Laura.
I love you.
I love you.

By the time Reggie got to Malibu, Mike Morrison was already there. The Coast Guard had a boat out with searchlights, but it was dark, and fog was setting in.

Connie was wrapped in a pink and white Mexican blanket. On her head sat a sombrero. The Mexican fisherman was standing close by, pouring her coffee from a thermos like a Red Cross nurse. Morrison was taking her statement.

Peter Flynn sat in a patrol car, shell-shocked, crying. He'd witnessed the whole thing. He couldn't even talk, but he'd managed to show his license when Morrison asked for ID. As soon as he calmed down, Morrison would take him to the station and get his statement.

Neighbors stood around watching, asking questions. The traffic on Pacific Coast Highway had slowed to a dirge, even though there was nothing to see.

When Reggie reported that Scott was Richard Wyman's stepson, Morrison immediately ordered everyone off the beach except the police. Then he sent a forensics man out to the Coast Guard boat with instructions to follow strict procedures when they found Scott's body.

Reggie observed the two surfers who had called the police on their cell phone when they first saw the fight on the kayak. They stood at the edge of the road, determined to wait till the body was found, jumping from foot to foot, bobbing their heads like two agitated roosters.

There wasn't much for Reggie to do, but he hung around for a while. It was as if he didn't want it to be over, his connection with Laura now severed forever.

When the coroner's van took away Scott's body, Reggie climbed in his squad car and headed back to the station.

A week later, when Reggie was going through his mail, he came across a small package wrapped in brown paper, neatly addressed to him in a woman's script. The postmark was from Andorra. As he ripped off the paper, he recalled that Andorra was a tiny country between Spain and France known as a place where citizenship didn't require residence; a tax haven, a place of prosperous banks where it was impolite to ask personal questions, particularly about someone's finances. Inside was a gift-wrapped package the size of a Baby Ben alarm clock. Reggie tore away the paper and pulled open a cardboard box. Nested in tissue was a plastic action figure. Bruce Lee.

Where was she? Living off the millions she'd stolen, on some tropical island? Yet she wanted Reggie to know she was alive, posting a package to him from Andorra on her way to paradise. Why? To torture him? To tell him she cared? To invite him to search for her?

Even though Reggie now suspected that Laura had murdered a young woman and set up Scott, that she had intentionally destroyed the life of her boss, and that the millions she'd stolen would be paid for not by her wealthy clients, nor by her company, but through higher insurance premiums—by average taxpayers, the very people who trusted him to protect their city—he knew he wouldn't tell the FBI.

She had awakened his soul, released the tourniquet around his heart. For that he would always be grateful.

Part of him had a beautiful wife, two sons, and a job that needed to be done.

Part of him lived out there with her.

But he no longer felt torn between his loves. The thought

that Laura was somewhere in the world, at liberty and lawless, made him happy.

He picked up the phone and, while dancing Bruce Lee over a stack of unfinished homicide reports, made a reservation for Martha's Vineyard.

It's February. Many months have passed. I still walk past her apartment on the way to the jetty. It's now rented by a middle-aged woman who doesn't get up until after it's light and I'm on my way home with my fish. She doesn't have time to gaze out the window but runs around like she's late for work. She's not there much. Maybe she's an executive who travels, or maybe she's got a man friend.

The lady with the kayak is in the maternity ward at Daniel Freeman Marina Hospital. Around midnight I can't sleep, so I take the truck to the hospital. The cop is there in the waiting room. The two of us stay up all night. We wait for the child to be born.

Around four A.M. a nurse comes and tells us it's gonna be two or three more hours. We take a break. We get fresh coffee and head down to Marina Point. After we park my truck, I give him a spare fishing rod. I figure we might as well cast a line.

When we walk by the houses at the end of the peninsula, all the windows are dark. I feel a jolt of sadness when I look at her window. I see the cop look, too.

As we head down the jetty, we hear dolphins blowing air in the channel and see their bodies arc and dive in the moonlight. We climb out onto the rocks at the end. It's cold and damp and very dark. We are both hungry.

We cast our lines and talk. We talk about our wives and kids and wait for the sun to come up.

My grandma once told me that Maya priests believed that if

they didn't pray every day for the sun to rise it wouldn't. I wonder if it isn't the Maya in me that makes me come here, doing my part, praying for a new day. Waiting for the light makes me love it more. While the rest of the city sleeps, I keep vigil, in silence, waiting for the dawn to bring life, and when it comes, it fills me with joy.

The sun climbs up to the edge of the sea, and a lip of pink peeks over the horizon. For a moment I think I see Laura's smile. The cop sees it, too, but we don't say anything.

Slowly, the sun rises. Racing sculls row quietly on the channel. As the purple mist lifts, and the pink dawn reflects in the windows of the million-dollar homes, and the great blue herons stand poised on the rocks, one leg up, and the pelicans plunge into the surf like meteors, a fish tugs at my line, struggling to be free.

EPILOGUE

Lorenzo Berti wasn't going to let the argument he'd had with his brother this morning upset him. They had almost come to blows. Alfredo wanted to sell the family palazzo, which had been in the family since 1560, when Cosimo de' Medici I sold it to Umberto Berti. So what if it was going to cost them a billion lire to keep it from falling into the street. Sell the family history? Imagine!

It was too beautiful a day to worry about incipient family feuds. It was spring in Tuscany. Here Lorenzo was, sitting in a café in Piazza della Signora, sipping an afternoon espresso, the scent of almond blossoms drifting down from the hills of Fiesole. He breathed deeply, savoring the smells of his beloved Florence—roasted coffee, chestnuts, leather. The weather was slightly cool. Delightful.

In front of Palazzo Vecchio, he watched two Japanese youths feed bread to the pigeons between a copy of Michelangelo's *David* and the writhing *Hercules and Cacus*. Today even the tourists didn't bother him. He realized that even though he saw these sculptures every day, he hardly ever looked at them. He let his eyes drift under the arches of the Loggia dei Lanzi to Perseus holding up the dripping head of Medusa, Hercules battling with Nessus the centaur, Ajax supporting the corpse of

Patroclus, the rape of the Sabine women, Judith displaying the head of Holofernes. For the first time, he saw how violent these beautiful sculptures were. Three corpses, two without heads.

He dismissed the unpleasant thought, and it flew up and spiraled away from the piazza on the wings of a bird.

The café was beginning to fill with people trying to wake up from their midday meals. He sipped his espresso, closing his eyes as he let the bitter coffee slide down his tongue. He exhaled a satisfied sigh. Sometimes there was nothing better in the world than to be a young Florentine male without so very much to do.

When he opened his eyes, he noticed a woman taking a seat three tables away. He caught his breath. She was tall and slim, with long dark hair and blue eyes. She wore a white chiffon dress that moved gently in the breeze. She looked like she had just stepped out of a Botticelli painting. What a vision! He was enchanted by her every gesture, so graceful, so poignant. What a goddess!

Lorenzo's eyes kept drifting back to her. He quickly signaled the waiter over.

"Giancarlo, do you know who that woman is?"

The waiter clucked his tongue. "They call her La Contessa. She's American. She bought the old Bracassi villa on Viale Michelangelo."

"The one that looks over the city?"

"*Sí, certo.* She's very wealthy, they say. She teaches ballet to little girls in a studio over by Piazza Santa Croce. My niece studies with her."

"What's her real name?"

"They only call her Signora Laura or La Contessa."

"She's married, then?" Lorenzo said, disappointed.

Giancarlo laughed. "No, no. She's not married, but I don't think she has much need for men."

"*Che cos'è?* What do you mean?"

The waiter shrugged.

Lorenzo glanced over at her once more. "Such a beautiful woman shouldn't have to sit alone."

"You'd better come up with a better line than that if you go over there."

"You think I have a shot?"

"No. But you'll try. Good luck, Signor."

Lorenzo imagined it in a flash, their life together, she dressed in white chiffon, standing with their children, a boy and a girl, waving from the balcony of Villa Bracassi over a garden of topiary and potted lemon trees, smiling at him as if he made the sun rise. She was the woman of his dreams.

She's Venus. I would do anything for a woman like her.

And with that thought, Lorenzo Berti tucked in his shirt and, like many a brave man before him, boldly walked toward his fate.